Praise for *Love Reconsidered*

"Grief, loss, and second chances are illuminated in *Love Reconsidered*, and its surprising and heartwarming twists offer insights into the true meaning of love."

—Kris Radish,
best-selling author of *The Year of Necessary Lies*

"*Love Reconsidered* takes us deep into the country of loss and grief, where no one wants to go, but all will enter. Phyllis Piano crafts the tale of two families as they move towards acceptance, with sensitivity and expert twists and turns."

—Linda Dahl, award-winning author,
including of *The Bad Dream Notebook*

—

Past Praise for Phyllis Piano's *Hostile Takeover: A Love Story*

"What goes best with professional affairs? A lover who cons you. Fans of the *The Catch* will simply consume this entertaining cocktail of first love and business acquisitions which will put our heroine in the ultimate conundrum: should she follow her heart and risk losing everything or choose the safety net of her career? Gorgeously entertaining, expertly crafted and wildly addictive, readers of *Hostile Takeover* will be left with a stomach full of butterflies and a new favorite soul-warming love story on their bookshelf."

—*Redbook Magazine*
"15 Fall Books You Should Read Based On
Your Favorite TV Shows and Movies"

"A brilliant ode to the bravery it takes to follow your heart and mind in sync, *Hostile Takeover* is like warm literary caramel for every soul this fall."

—*Working Mother Magazine*,
"21 New Books to Fall for This Autumn"

"...A warm and cozy love story set in the corporate world, *Hostile Takeover* will make your Sunday morning spent in bed fly by."

—BuzzFeed
"8 Cozy Fall Romance Reads"

"Piano has done a great job of marrying the corporate world with the complicated world of the heart. Love and business collide in this novel where the intricate dealings of business intersect with one woman's past and change everything about her future. Fun and entertaining, *Hostile Takeover* will definitely make you a believer in true love."

—Kris Radish,
best-selling author of *The Year of Necessary Lies*

"*Hostile Takeover* is touching story about love lost and found. Piano's heroine, Molly Parr, is unsinkable as she navigates stormy romances and the murky waters of the corporate world. Smart and sassy, Molly rides the waves of life, living by her motto, 'you have to love with your head and your heart.'"

—Judith Hennessey, author of *First Rodeo*
and co-owner of White Raven Productions

———

2017 Benjamin Franklin IBPA Award: Gold Medal
2017 Independent Press Awards : Romance, Winner

Love
Reconsidered

Love
Reconsidered

A NOVEL

Phyllis J. Piano

SparkPress, a BookSparks imprint
A Division of SparkPoint Studio, LLC

Published by SparkPress, a BookSparks imprint,
A division of SparkPoint Studio, LLC
Tempe, Arizona, USA, 85281
www.gosparkpress.com

Published 2017

Printed in the United States of America

ISBN: 978-1-943006-20-5 (pbk)
ISBN: 978-1-943006-22-9 (e-bk)
Library of Congress Control Number: 2017936149

Cover design © Julie Metz, Ltd./metzdesign.com
Formatting by Katherine Lloyd/theDESKonline.com

*This book is dedicated to those who
tragically lost a loved one but have found
the strength to enjoy life once again.*

chapter one

Aleen

Driving past the picturesque California countryside near her home, Aleen Riddick turned left on the boulevard and immediately tensed up when she saw the flowers pinned to the tree, full-bodied red roses, literally weeping petals to the ground. So beautiful, so sad.

The flowers were a reminder of when everything changed. One day, she was a forty-something working woman with a committed, successful husband and a bright, wonderful daughter, but the next night, the lives of those she loved were altered forever.

While she was concerned about her own mental well-being, her thoughts always turned to her beautiful eighteen-year-old daughter, Sunny. She had been like a breath of fresh air, so full of life, funny, thoughtful. . . . How many teenagers could you say that about?

Durk and Aleen couldn't have been prouder of Sunny. They'd heard the outrageous stories about the antics of their friends' teenagers, and they would stay quiet, as their daughter was something else. If she did anything that would worry her parents, she hid it really well.

But just over three months ago, everything changed for her

lovely daughter. These days, her disposition was not sunny at all. No, melancholy filled her now. When Aleen looked into her eyes, all she saw was this dark depth of despair, and her mother felt powerless against it.

She shook her head to snap out of it and focus on finding a place to park. *All Sunny needs right now is her mom in a car accident,* Aleen thought to herself, shuddering.

It was a beautiful morning, the majestic mountains in the background, the flowering bushes growing alongside the road, and the occasional orange tree sprouting fruit. But Aleen wasn't in the mood to enjoy the scenery. The beautiful roses had evoked the scene of the worst night of her life. She had to stop.

Pulling over, Aleen parked her sturdy SUV, with nearly 106,000 miles on the odometer, and walked over to the flowers. While there were many bouquets and arrangements on the ground around the tree, she went to her knees to touch the weeping roses, gathering the fallen petals in her hands.

As the soft, vibrant red petals cascaded through her fingers onto the grass, sadness enveloped Aleen, and she started to cry, softly at first, and then the silent sobs racked her body. She rocked back and forth, covering her eyes with her hands.

Suddenly, she felt a tickling and then something stroking her face. Aleen looked up to see two corgi dogs licking her, and she couldn't help but laugh through her tears.

"Hey," she said to the dogs, petting them as they jumped on her.

"Sorry about that." Ted Hammand left the leash loose so the dogs could continue to lick Aleen and jump on her playfully as she sat on the ground. Ted was about Aleen's age and just under six feet, with a kind face, wispy brown hair, and wire-rimmed glasses. He wore khakis and a polo shirt, looking the part of the suburban dad.

"Oh, Ted," Aleen said. "I didn't see you there at first, or your friends." She sat upright and petted the dogs. Trying to make herself presentable, she took a handkerchief from her pocket to dab at her deep-blue eyes, which were now rimmed red, and smooth her light-brown hair as it blew in the wind. "When did you get them?"

"Well, you may have heard I just moved into a townhouse right here," Ted said, pointing at the condo development behind them, "and I decided to get the dogs. Gerrie would never allow pets, even though Stu and I always wanted one. . . ." His voice faltered at the mention of his son's name.

"Anyway, this is Hope, and this is Cash." Ted continued. "They're brother and sister. The breeder wanted to keep them as a pair because they were raised together as pups, so I took them both. They're five years old, and I have to say they provide pretty good company and entertainment."

The dogs wrestled on the ground and nipped at each other playfully.

"They have wonderful personalities, and I'm sure they're a help to you . . . a comfort," Aleen said. "I'd heard about the condo. I hope it's working out for you," she offered quietly. "It's just so close to where Stu . . ."

"Yes. It is what it is," Ted said quietly. "I haven't adjusted to it yet, but I'm sure you understand. On the bright side, the dogs have made it feel more like home and lifted my spirits, actually.

"But I'm more concerned about you right now. Is it one of those days?" Ted sat in the grass next to Aleen.

"'Fraid so, Ted. I saw the flowers, the weeping petals, and I had to stop. The roses are so beautiful but so sad. Sunny and I bring flowers here, too. It's emotional every time. I guess I assumed Gerrie put the flowers out."

"No," Ted said firmly. "I did. I check on them almost every

day and refresh them when they wilt. Being so close now, I come by here several times a day as I walk the dogs.

"You probably noticed the authorities don't let us put the candles at the base of the tree anymore. It's a hazard they said, but they overlooked it right after the accident."

"I did notice. I try not to look over and upset myself, but most days, I can't help but glance over when I drive by. And sorry I thought it was Gerrie who brought the flowers," Aleen added. "I should have known it was you. I'm also sorry I'm here, crying in the grass, making a fool of myself and upsetting you, too."

Ted shook his head dismissively. "Don't worry about that. You and Sunny have brought flowers to this spot many times, which means a lot to me. Our lives have been drastically changed, and it just hasn't been that long since . . ." His voice faded once more.

"Well, I'm glad I ran into you," he said, regaining his composure and changing the subject. "Did you know Sunny was coming over today?"

"I had no idea. We used to share everything, but she's very different since the accident."

"We all are, Aleen. We all are." Ted stared down at the grass for a moment. "I invited her over for the Packers game. She used to come over to watch the games with Stu and me. It's the beginning of the season. Why don't you come over, too? We were just going to order some pizzas."

"How nice of you," Aleen said with a look of surprise. "I guess I never really paid attention to your Sunday game days before. I'm on the way to the grocery store, so why don't I pick up some pizzas at the store and bring them over?"

"That sounds good. I'm sure Sunny will be glad you're there," he replied.

"I'm not so sure about that . . ." A look of concern pinched Aleen's face.

"She enjoyed the games in the past, so maybe it'll lift her mood," Ted said. "You may not remember, but I'm originally from Wisconsin. Being a Packers fan is in the blood. My dad, my grandfather, and all my uncles were rabid fans. My mom, too! I passed along my passion to Stu, and he was a huge supporter as well, even though he never lived in Wisconsin.

"Sunny used to come by and watch the games with us many Sundays, so she's a big Packers fan, too. I just think it's important to carry on the tradition now that Stu . . ." Ted's face clouded over, as it was difficult to finish the sentence.

"I understand, Ted, and I would be honored to be part of your football ritual. I may not make it to the condo until well after halftime. I have to do the grocery shopping for the week and a few errands, but I'll be there."

"Excellent." Ted gathered up the leashes and stood from the grass, Hope and Cash at his heels. "I plan to give Sunny Stu's favorite Packers T-shirt to wear during the game," he said softly.

"Oh, Ted . . ."

"I hope she likes it," he said, brushing dirt and grass from his pants.

"I'm sure she'll treasure it," Aleen replied confidently.

"You have a wonderful daughter, you know? It's clear she hasn't been the same lately. She's suffering," Ted told Aleen, his voice wavering. "I really believe she tries to be her best for me, to help me."

"Well, I'm glad, and I'm sure you're helping her as well. Both of you loved Stu so much. It gives me hope she may find her way back to being herself again someday soon." Aleen touched his arm.

"I'm glad we had a few minutes to chat," Ted said, pulling himself together. "It helps to talk about Stu, and it's so much easier with you because you understand everything."

"True. Bottling things up doesn't work. Sunny and I tried counseling, but frankly, it wasn't helpful because we didn't like the counselor. I heard you had a similar experience," Aleen said.

"Yes, same deal. Maybe it was the just the wrong person. It's hard to talk to friends, too. When I see someone I know and they have that glaze of pity in their eyes, I just freeze up, and the conversations never take off."

"I hate that, too." The look in Aleen's eyes told Ted she understood all too well.

"I saw how upset you were when I first walked over with the dogs," Ted commented, turning the attention back to his friend.

"Will we ever be okay, Ted?" she asked, tears forming in her eyes.

"It sure doesn't feel like it right now," he replied, his face a mask of sadness.

chapter two

Sunny

Sunny Abigail Riddick sat on her bed, fiddling with her long blond hair and trying to study before she went over to Stu's dad's new condo for the game. She'd just started engineering school at UCLA. Sunny always loved tinkering and finding out how things worked. Somehow, she had always known she wanted to be an engineer like her father.

Her dad used his experience and expertise to capture a big job managing a team of engineers at the huge company based just fifteen minutes from their house. Her mom worked there, too, as an executive assistant.

Sunny had idolized her father, but after the split from her mother, she had no time for him. Thinking about her dad made her frustrated and angry; she threw her textbook across the bed, and it hit the ground with a thud.

They'd all agreed Sunny would start school as planned, that everything should go on as normal. "As normal," she mocked aloud to herself.

"As if anything is normal. . . ." She spat the words and splayed herself across the bed.

She closed her eyes and thought of Stu Hammand. Sunny

smiled dreamily and remembered the afternoon about three months ago at his house. It was how she could make it through . . . to remember the wonderful times with him.

Sunny thought of him when her mind wandered in class, in the car driving to school, when she locked herself in her room, which was most of the time lately . . . just about all the time she could, really.

Stu and Sunny met at their local high school when she was sixteen and he was almost seventeen. They'd been inseparable from the moment they saw each other. Both sets of parents nagged them about getting serious so young, but neither listened. Their souls were connected, and they couldn't wait to see each other at school and whenever they could sneak away together. They texted and messaged each other constantly when they were apart.

She looked out her bedroom window at the beautiful day, the sun shining and the leaves on the trees waving at her in the breeze. Sunny closed her eyes and willed herself back to that magical afternoon in June.

Stu had arranged for her to come over after lunch. Sunny told her parents she was going to spend the day with Stu and her friends, perhaps see a movie. It was a bit of a fib, as they planned to spend the day together, alone. Her excitement was overpowering.

His parents had gone up north to the wine country and wouldn't be back until dinnertime, so Stu and Sunny would have the whole day together.

Sunny wore her best jeans, a nice, new form-fitting top, and she'd taken extra care to get her makeup and hair just so. She wanted to look fabulous for him. This was an important day in their relationship.

As Sunny drove over to Stu's that June afternoon, she felt so light, so happy. It was just after high school graduation, and she and her boyfriend were making all their plans for college. With her at UCLA and Stu at USC, they would be able to see each other often. They were both happy to have been accepted into such great schools that were so close to home.

It was a perfect day, as the weather wasn't too hot yet. The morning was foggy and damp, a perfect example of the "June gloom" in Southern California. By late morning, the bright sunshine had burned away the fog, leaving the sky a piercing blue.

Sunny could hardly contain her excitement as she drove over to the Hammands' house. When Stu greeted her at the door, tall and long-limbed, with light-brown hair and green eyes, he was so gorgeous. But the greatest thing about Stu was he was so wonderful inside, so kind, like his dad, and whip smart and funny like his mom. *He's just perfect,* Sunny thought to herself as she walked in and he enveloped her in his arms.

"Hey," Stu greeted her.

"Hey, yourself," Sunny replied as she gave him a sloppy kiss hello.

They walked in and sat on the couch, and Stu went into the kitchen to get them some cold drinks. "How cool that we have the house all day," Sunny shouted to him in the kitchen.

He joined her and put the drinks on the coffee table. "For sure. It's great how it worked out. You know how my dad is about wine tasting. I don't really think Mom was that excited about going. She always has lots of things to do on Sundays before she goes back to work. She seemed a bid edgy today, too.

"Not sure why it was so important to her that I was around for dinner, but it's no problem 'cause I knew I'd have the whole day with you," he said, smiling broadly.

Stu's mom, Gerrie, was the highest-level woman at the same company where Sunny's mom and dad worked. She was in charge of all sourcing, IT, and other administrative services for the multibillion-dollar business. She had hundreds of people in her department, made tons of money, and traveled all the time.

Gerrie reported directly to the CEO and was the only woman on his team. She was beautiful, with stylish shoulder-length dark hair and flashing green eyes. She looked a lot younger than her years and always wore the latest fashions. She had a great sense of humor and doted on Stu—when she was around. It seemed to Sunny Stu's dad was more like the mom than Gerrie, but it seemed to work for them.

Stu sat next to Sunny and put his arm around her. She settled into him, getting comfortable and winding her arms around his waist. Sunny looked at Stu and thought he was so different from the other boys at school. He seemed more serious but funny at the same time.

He was so intelligent; he had one of the highest grade point averages of anyone at school, so he had lots of choices for college. Sunny was pleased he'd decided to study premed at USC. Stu would be terrific at anything he decided to do, but he would make an awesome doctor.

The couple could talk about anything. She had some great girlfriends at school, but Sunny always felt more comfortable when she was with Stu, which was kind of weird, as the majority of girls she knew felt most at ease with their friends.

Such a big step today, Sunny thought. Just then, her phone dinged with a text message. She moved away from Stu, grabbed her phone, and put it on silent.

"No interruptions!" she said. "I just want to be with you. I've been thinking about our time together all day." She took a drink of iced tea before snuggling back in Stu's arms, gazing at him, thinking about what it would be like to make love with him. She'd prepared mentally and physically for this day.

It wasn't Stu's first time. When he was sixteen, he had sex with a girl named Rosie he'd met at a summer camp. They stayed in touch for some time but drifted apart, as she lived in the Boston area. He'd told Sunny about it; they shared everything.

"Well, we can do anything you want. We have the house to ourselves and all the time in the world. I don't mind to just hold you like this," Stu said, kissing the top of Sunny's head.

She looked up at him and touched his face, bringing it to hers. They kissed playfully for a long time, and then they both felt the passion heating up.

His kisses became more urgent, and Sunny tasted him as his tongue darted in and out of her mouth. She unbuttoned his shirt and ran her hands all over his torso and shifted her weight to bring her body closer to his.

Stu whispered in her ear, "Let's go upstairs to my room."

As they walked, they continued to nuzzle each other. Once in his bedroom, the two couldn't take their eyes off of each other, shedding their clothes slowly. As they explored every inch of the other's body, Sunny felt so much love for Stu. Being with him this way finally joined them together forever. How could she ever love anyone else?

After their lovemaking, lying in one another's arms in his bed, Stu kissed the top of Sunny's head, smiling, exhausted.

She looked out the window at the beautiful late-spring day and basked in happiness. To show her love to Stu this way, it was almost too much.

Sunny felt warm all over as she recalled that wonderful afternoon when they made love for the first and only time, but she was jolted back to reality when she opened her eyes and looked out the window of *her* bedroom. That magical time with Stu was over. She had relived that afternoon so often it almost felt as if he were actually touching her.

Every time she recalled that memory, she hoped the accident had only been a bad dream and Stu was still alive, next to her, holding her.

But the ending was always the same.

"Why? Why? Why?" Sunny screamed, but no one was home to hear the anguish and regret in her voice.

chapter three

Ted

Ted busied himself around the condo, preparing for his guests and the Green Bay Packers game. It would be good to have people over, as he spent too much time by himself now with his marriage over and his son gone. As he was an independent accountant, he did most of his work alone.

He'd set up his office in the condo as soon as he moved in, and it seemed to work efficiently enough. It wasn't as fancy as the office at the home he'd shared with Gerrie and Stu, but then it wouldn't be, would it?

Ted had asked Gerrie if he could take some of Stu's awards and honors to have on the shelves in his new home office. It was one of the few really calm and civil conversations the two had been able to have since the accident.

Other than those few things he took for his office, Gerrie and Ted had left Stu's room the same. They didn't have the heart to clear it out; their grief was still so overwhelming and fresh. Gerrie still lived in the grand house, and Ted couldn't imagine what it would be like to walk by Stu's room every day. Fortunately, he didn't go there very often.

Gerrie had made her choices, and she had to live with them.

He couldn't waste his time thinking about her, as he didn't want to admit—even to himself—how much he missed his marriage, his son, his family, his life. But that was all over now.

When he took a break from work, Ted would walk over to Stu's awards and touch them, sometimes chatting to his son about the past or some day-to-day, trivial thing, like a dumb unsolicited phone call or a funny advertisement he saw online or on TV.

Ted didn't realize it when he was alive, but his son was like his best friend. They shared so much. How lucky he was to have had a son like Stu, but how hard it was now without him.

Before Stu died, Ted kept his focus squarely on his family and work. He didn't need anything else. But now, without his family, Ted's life was pretty empty. With his brother and sister and their families in Wisconsin and his parents gone, he really was alone.

Ted knew he must rebuild his life, but he just wasn't ready yet. Could he ever give so much of himself again? His wife and son were his everything. . . .

"Get ahold of yourself," he told himself aloud. He was amazed how much he talked to himself now that Stu was gone. He definitely needed to get back to counseling, to help sort himself out.

Ted brightened when he thought about enjoying the games with Stu. They were both so knowledgeable about football, and they could discuss all the coaches, the most competitive teams, and all the best players in the league. They had discussed the possibilities for the season with great enthusiasm and had watched the draft day coverage this spring on the NFL Network and ESPN, discussing each Green Bay pick in depth.

Now that Stu was gone, Ted felt strongly that he needed to continue with the football traditions, which had been started so early in his own life. *Besides,* he told himself, *the beginning of the season is always a hopeful time, full of promise.* Ted knew he desperately needed some new possibilities in his life now, some hope of better things to come.

Ted had read that about 20 percent of parents who lose a child get divorced. Before he looked it up, he actually thought the percentage would be higher than that. It made him sad to think he was on the wrong side of that statistic. He lost his son *and* his marriage, which shattered his world into a million pieces.

Despite that, Ted never worried about surviving; he knew he would. *Just keep moving forward,* he thought to himself, putting one foot in front of the other. He was a practical, pragmatic man. Rock steady. Perhaps that was why he enjoyed being a dad so much and was good at it. His wife always told him he was an amazing father and she didn't know what she would do without him. *Well, that clearly didn't last.*

Snap out of it, Ted, he told himself. *This is going to be a better day.*

He actually did feel a bit happy, excited about Sunny and Aleen coming by to see the game. He'd shut himself away for far too long, and maybe he really was taking that first step forward, away from his grief.

Ted appreciated his encounter with Aleen earlier today, even though when he first spotted her, she was in the grass, crying her eyes out. He had days like that, too, so he understood.

Ted felt he could talk to Aleen, and that just wasn't the case with most of his friends. Everyone always seemed so uncomfortable dealing with him, like they might say the wrong thing. Always walking on eggshells.

It was awful to see the look of pity on people's faces as they approached him. Hell, he could see it in their eyes from ten to twenty paces away. Of course he knew why they looked at him that way, but he hated it all the same. Aleen didn't do that; she dealt with him with interest and concern—exactly what he needed.

And Sunny treated him the same as she did before Stu's death. The difference now was they had moments of shared grief that they didn't speak about, but just felt. No need to verbalize. When they felt like talking about Stu, they did. Sunny and Ted could read each other so well. It was the damnedest thing.

Clearly, he couldn't talk to his soon-to-be ex-wife about anything now. Yes, they had to deal with anything concerning Stu, finances, the divorce, and their former life together, but that was mechanical and without emotion. They mostly communicated through email and the lawyers, as that was much easier.

Ted wasn't able to talk to Gerrie at all about Stu; that was totally off-limits, as she just couldn't handle it. He understood why, but it was her own doing; she had made it hard on herself.

He could see Aleen was suffering, too, so perhaps they could help each other even more in the future. The psychologist Ted went to see was no help whatsoever. Maybe he was just the wrong person, as he and Aleen had discussed today, sitting in the grass. Who knew?

Ted was glad to have a townhouse-type condo, as he had a courtyard garden, which was great for the dogs. They were out there now, chasing each other around. They always brought a smile to his face. *Thank God for the dogs*, he told himself, as Hope and Cash gave him another reason to get up in the morning.

He busied himself putting out some snacks and placing Stu's favorite Packers shirt over the chair for Sunny. There was a Packers helium balloon tied to the end of the entertainment unit and the cheesehead hat was placed next to the television.

That cheesehead sure had seen better days, as Stu and he played around with it a lot, opening up a long crack along the inside. Oh well. Since it had been his as well as Stu's, it would continue to be his best football lucky charm as long as Ted had breath in him.

Ted missed his son terribly, but he also missed his marriage. He loved being married, and he always thought he was a good husband until everything fell apart. He was the one who kept the household going and handled the shopping, the cooking, Stu's school activities, and any family holidays.

His wife's job took up sixty hours a week, and Gerrie was often exhausted when she got home at night. She always tried to be at her best for Stu, talking to him in the evenings about school, social activities, and friends. Even when she was traveling, she called every night to talk to the guys, telling each of them how she loved them. Ted had to give her that, but it made him feel sad, as he believed his wife.

Gerrie had gotten along well with Sunny, always making her feel welcome in their home. Since their son and Sunny had been inseparable, that was a good thing. When the two of them weren't at the Hammands' house, or the Riddicks', they were with friends or at school.

That seems so long ago now, Ted thought, shaking his head. *A whole other life.*

He welcomed the knock on the door that interrupted his thoughts.

"Hello, Mr. Hammand," Sunny greeted Ted, and he motioned her into his new home.

"Sunny, you have to call me Ted," he insisted.

"I'm not sure I can do that," she said, smiling. "You'll always be Mr. Hammand to me."

"Well, I understand, but I'll keep bugging you about it," Ted said, smiling. "Please come in and take a seat, and I'll get something for us to drink."

"Great place," Sunny said, taking a quick look around the condo.

His unit had been totally renovated with all new appliances, and the kitchen looked out on the small but extremely functional family room.

"A lot different than the house, huh?" Sunny said, touching the back of the large leather couch.

"For sure," Ted called out from the kitchen, where she could see him putting together a tray.

Sunny looked around and saw Stu's shirt on the chair, and she went over to pick it up, smelling it and hugging the material to her.

"I thought you might want to have that shirt and wear it on game days. Of course, that's only if you want to. . . ." Ted said as Sunny slipped it over her head, and he put the tray of drinks and snacks on the coffee table.

"You didn't wash it, did you? It still smells like him." She gathered a handful of the shirt and smelled it again. "Wow."

"No, I didn't wash it. The last time he wore it was when he helped me clean up the yard just before the accident," Ted said sadly.

"I love this shirt, Mr. Hammand. I'll wear it every Sunday when the games are on. Maybe it'll bring the Packers good luck," she replied.

"Let's hope so," he said with a smile. "A win for the Packers to open the season would be just what the doctor ordered.

"Did your mom tell you I invited her to join us?" Ted peered through the opening from the kitchen to the family room to judge Sunny's reply.

"No, but we kind of missed each other before she went out grocery shopping. I think she would probably appreciate the company, joining our little party."

Ted nodded. "I know. I ran into her today at the flowers by the road. Clearly, she was upset. We actually had a good chat about everything. That's when I invited her to stop by. She won't be here until after halftime, I think. She's bringing the pizzas."

Sunny and Ted sat for a minute until he broke the silence.

"You know, Sunny, I think the three of us need to help each other," he said.

"You're probably right," Sunny said, looking down. "I haven't been very . . . How would you say it . . . ? Available, accessible? I know I've shut out my mom too much. Most of the time, I'm just in my room, studying or daydreaming."

"About Stu?"

"Yes, it's the only way I can still be with him. I saved a lot of his old texts to me, and I read them a lot, too. I know it's probably not healthy to spend so much time wishing and dreaming he was still alive."

"I think about him a lot, too," Ted admitted.

"We loved him most in the world, you and me," Sunny stated.

"His mother loved him a lot, too," Ted almost whispered.

"I'm not sure why you defend her. She doesn't deserve it," Sunny argued, acting like a little kid.

"Sunny, both of us need to work on our feelings of anger and grief. Your mom, too. We talked about it today. Maybe we all need to get back to counseling," Ted suggested as he looked at Sunny hopefully.

"I know I need to talk to my mom more about what I'm feeling. It's just been easier to shut down. Now I can talk to you. And I always worry about bringing everything up and upsetting her, too. Why do you think she was crying today? Did something trigger it?"

"You know how it is. It doesn't take much to remind us. . . ."

Ted leaned over to rummage around in the snacks, picking up a chip to nibble so he didn't have to finish his thought.

"I guess we could think about counseling again, but I hated that last guy. You didn't have any luck, either," Sunny said, putting some cheese on a cracker and wolfing it down.

"No, it wasn't very helpful, for sure," Ted said, shaking his head. "I was a bit encouraged talking to your mom today, though."

Sunny narrowed her eyes. "Hey, you aren't going to date her, are you?"

Ted chuckled. "No plans to. I'm not ready to date. When you've been married for more than twenty years . . ."

"That's a lot of years. My mom and dad were married a long time, too. . . ." Sunny looked down at the carpet to try and stop herself from tearing up. "Nothing's the same. Nothing. I'm just so sad all the time. And mad . . . sad that Stu's gone, mad that my parents broke up."

Ted moved over next to her and put his arm around her. "I know, Sunny. I know. I'm hurt and angry just like you."

"But you don't show it. You're so, like, calm and collected, and you've always been so great to me and Stu. You made me so comfortable at your house. I guess that's why we spent so much time there with you. I never saw you lose control. Well, except for that night . . ."

"It's a good act, hon. I promise I'm as torn up inside as you. I'm working on it; I know you are, too," Ted said as she leaned into him.

"That's why we—your mom, you, and me—need to help each other. We've got to pull ourselves out of all this sadness and anger, starting today." Ted glanced at Sunny, then got up to make sure the television was on the right channel for the game.

"You act more like my dad now than my *real* dad. I just can't deal with him!" Sunny took a quick drink of her Vitamin Water and stuffed some popcorn in her mouth.

"Listen. I understand, but he *is* your father." Ted gazed at Sunny. She had shut down a bit with the discussion turning to her dad.

"Look, the game's getting ready to start." He pointed to the television. "Let's have a nice Sunday afternoon and look forward, not back. We can't change the past, unfortunately, as much as we wish we could." A look of sadness overtook his face.

"I know, Mr. Hammand. I just don't think I can ever love anyone the way I loved Stu," she said, her eyes full of sadness. "And I wish my parents were still together."

"You're very young, Sunny, with so much ahead of you. I know everyone says that to you, but it's true. There's so much of your life to live. You'll never forget Stu or the time you had together. I know that. But the three of us have to drag each other forward, as hard as it is."

Just then, the dogs decided they wanted to come in and scratched against the French doors. As soon as they were inside, they ran like a gunshot over to Sunny, jumping up on the couch and licking her. She laughed out loud and petted both equally, so as to not cause them to snip at each other.

"I'm so glad you got the dogs. I just love 'em." Sunny laughed, petting the pooches, alternating rubbing them behind their ears and along their furry backs.

"Me, too, Sunny." Ted smiled. "Now," he said, addressing the dogs, "you guys get off the couch and settle down. We have a guest, and both of us need to watch this game."

Sunny turned her attention to the television as the dogs obeyed and jumped down to sit at Ted's feet.

The Packers won the toss and elected to receive. The game and the hopeful beginning of a new season were underway.

chapter four

Aleen

Rounding the corner with her grocery cart, Aleen caught a view of herself reflected in the door of the frozen food case. She stopped in her tracks, horrified. Her clothes looked a bit shabby, her hair was way too frizzy, and she still had a few too many pounds on her, despite her weight loss after Durk left.

Did he leave her because she got too frumpy and didn't pay enough attention to herself? Why did he stop loving her? What did she do wrong?

Aleen angrily banged her cart. She had to stop this. Her marriage was over. The divorce was underway. She couldn't go backward and always blame herself. She wished she had money for every time she gave herself the same pep talk. Was it ever going to work? She shook her head, as she had no idea.

She had a lot more work to do, clearly, to start her life over. She paused in front of the frozen pizzas and nodded at her reflection in the glass, agreeing with herself to make some changes. She needed to get healthy—mentally and physically—and do something positive and proactive for herself. Her daughter deserved a mother who was confident and happy and had some optimism about the future. She deserved that for herself as well.

Rummaging through the large collection of pizzas in the frozen food case, Aleen choose sausage and pepperoni for Ted and Sunny and a low-fat, gluten-free vegetarian for herself. "I've got to start somewhere," she mumbled.

She drove home to put away all the groceries for the week and then grabbed the pizzas, salad, and her homemade salad dressing and headed over to Ted's.

As she pulled the car out of the driveway, Aleen realized she was a bit anxious. *Why should I be nervous?* It was just her daughter and Ted. What was scary about that? Maybe she was taking the first few steps in creating a new life, one that was very different from the one she'd lived in the past.

When she rang the bell, Ted and the dogs greeted her enthusiastically at the door.

"That's a wonderful welcome." Aleen laughed as the dogs jumped up on her legs.

"Come on in," Ted said excitedly. "The game is well into the third quarter, and the Packers are on a roll."

"Glad they're playing well," Aleen said. "I'll put this stuff in the kitchen and preheat the oven."

As she put the pizzas on the counter, she heard Sunny and Ted scream, and then they both clapped. The Packers must have scored.

Ted rushed into the kitchen to try to get a few things ready during the commercial break, including putting two pizza stones on the racks in the oven. "The Packers just had a fantastic touchdown. Unbelievable catch in the corner of the end zone," he exclaimed.

"I'm so happy to see you and Sunny enjoying yourselves," Aleen whispered so her daughter couldn't hear. "What have you done to bring a bit of the old Sunny back?"

"Not sure." Ted got some bowls and plates out and put them

on the counter. "We did have a good chat and agreed we needed to help each other. It's also been fun to watch the game. I guess it reminds us both of the good times we had before the accident."

"Well, keep doing what you're doing," Aleen said, squeezing Ted's arm. "I've been so worried about her."

"It's written all over your face. Your worry, your doubt, your sadness . . ."

"I know—I'm part of the problem. I get that now. Clearly, I've not invested any time in myself because of my concern about Sunny and my own anger with the end of my marriage. I resolved to change that today when I saw my reflection in the glass of the frozen food section."

Ted laughed. "That's a story I want to hear. I have some ideas for both of us as well, but that has to wait until after the fourth quarter." He rushed back into the family room and to the game.

Aleen got a big bowl for the salad, set out some utensils, and found napkins and the salt and pepper. Amazing how she just walked into Ted's kitchen and made herself right at home. She loved to cook but hadn't been spending much time in the kitchen lately. Sunny seemed to have lost her appetite since the accident, and Aleen just couldn't find the energy to cook for just herself. That had to change. From now on, healthy eating for Sunny and herself.

Perhaps she could make some meals for Ted as well, especially if they were going to continue to come over for the games.

Aleen grabbed a sparkling water for herself and went into the living room to join Ted and Sunny. They were so engrossed in the game and talked about everything: the pass interference penalty, the officiating, the players for both teams, and the coaching staff. Aleen was impressed that her daughter knew so much about football. Durk liked sports a lot, and he probably contributed to their daughter's appreciation of the game.

Once the oven was up to temperature and the game was winding down, she put the pizzas in. Ted and Sunny were so focused on the game, they didn't even notice.

"What a great game," Ted gushed. "I enjoyed that."

"It's always a great game when the Packers win!" Sunny shouted, putting her arms up the way the officials did to signal a score was good.

"Well, the pizzas should be about done," Aleen said, "so I'll get everything ready."

"Wait a minute," Ted said, pulling his attention from the television and game highlights. "You're the guest here. I should be doing that."

"Understood, but I'm the only one who can stand to take my eyes off the Packers, so I'm happy to help." Aleen went into the kitchen to pull the pizzas out of the oven.

"I'll cut them. Precise slicing is one of my unique skills." Ted smiled as he joined her, cutting the pepperoni and sausage pizza into perfect slices.

"That little dinky, boring one is mine," Aleen said. "It's low fat since I've resolved to begin to take care of myself a bit better than I have been lately."

Sunny joined them and slid a piece of the pizza on her plate, gobbling it down in a few bites. "Mom, you *do* need to take better care of yourself."

"I promise I will if you will," Aleen said, looking at her daughter hopefully, dishing up some salad on the plate with her low-fat pizza.

"I will if Mr. Hammand will, too," Sunny said, glancing at both the adults.

"Well, I guess it will be a new start for all of us." Ted agreed, nodding at Sunny and Aleen. "See, your mom brought salad so we could have something healthy!"

Sunny took the last few bites of her second slice of pizza and finished up her salad. "I've gotta get going in a minute. I promised Nikki I'd stop by after the game."

Sunny took off Stu's Packers shirt and handed it to Ted. "Will you keep it here for me? Then I know it's always here and ready for game day."

"You got it," Ted said. "Have a good time with your friend."

"Thanks again for today, Mr. Hammand," Sunny said. "See you later, Mom." Then she grabbed her keys and ran out the door.

"Ted, I haven't seen her like this for ages. This is great," Aleen cooed.

"It's a long road. I'm sure there will be plenty of bumps along the way for all of us, but it is a start. A good start," Ted said.

"Maybe we should make Packers Sundays a standing date," Aleen said. "If that's okay with you, of course."

"Absolutely." Ted was genuinely pleased. "There is something else I need to talk to you about. My idea is perfectly aligned with your renewed commitment to your health."

"What are you thinking?" Aleen looked at him quizzically.

"You're going to think this is weird coming from a guy, but I think we both need makeovers."

"Makeovers?!" Aleen almost shouted.

"I've been looking into it. Trying to be objective, I look at myself and I see a boring, suburban dad in khakis. That's what I was; it's not what I am now. My hair is wrong. My clothes are wrong. Everything about me screams my old life. I've got to change. Shake things up."

"Go on," Aleen said, clearly not convinced.

"You said earlier that you looked at your reflection and didn't like what you saw. You're an attractive woman, but you've put all your attention into your daughter and your marriage.

Isn't it time you focused on yourself? You said you were planning to devote more time to your physical and mental health in the future. . . ."

"Do you have any wine?" Aleen asked, eyebrows shooting up.

"Sure. Red or white?" Ted inquired, moving over to a small wine rack on the counter.

"Red." Aleen opened the cabinet and took out two large wine glasses. She'd spotted them earlier when she was looking for plates for the pizza.

"I have a nice pinot noir. Does that work for you?" Ted asked hopefully.

"Pinot noir just happens to be my favorite. Thank God!" Aleen put her hands together as if she were praying. "If we're going to talk about makeovers, we better have a good glass of wine. It's late enough in the afternoon." She giggled.

"I totally agree." Ted popped the cork and filled their glasses less than a quarter full. He swirled the wine around and sniffed it. "Smells perfect."

After they both took a drink, he decided to plunge in on his makeover plan.

"I have a client who does makeovers and is a personal shopper. Monica is fantastic. I called her today and asked if she could give us a discount rate, working with both of us in one day—me in the morning and you in the afternoon."

"You already talked to her about *me*?" Aleen asked, shocked.

"I didn't say who you were, of course, just a friend."

"You did all this after I saw you today?" Aleen asked.

"We'd been planning my makeover, and it just came to me after we ran into each other that you might want to do it, as well. I guess I thought if we're starting our new lives, we should try and look the part."

Aleen took another sip of her wine and walked around the

kitchen island, contemplating this makeover. Did she really want to do this? With Ted?

"What would this 'makeover' entail?" Aleen queried, stopping and staring straight in his eyes.

"Well, it would be a little different for you than for me. For you, she'd take you shopping and buy at least two outfits: one casual and one for work. She'd also have your hair and makeup redone. It would take all afternoon.

"In the morning, she would take me out, help me buy some new clothes, and have a hair stylist redo my hair. I'll get new glasses, too," Ted said, studying Aleen's reaction intently.

"Money is a bit tight right now. How much will all this cost?" she asked.

"That's the good part. I'm bartering my services as her accountant, so all we have to pay for are the clothes and hair. She has a great rate with the hair and makeup stylists, so it should be reasonable," he replied, still hoping for a positive reaction.

"Hmm." Aleen was clearly considering it, and Ted remained hopeful. "Just when were you thinking to do this?" she asked.

"Next Saturday."

"That soon!" Aleen was surprised, walking around the kitchen island again, considering the possibility of having herself "made over." She stopped and remained quiet for a bit, thinking it through.

"Okay, I'll do it," Aleen declared. "I hope I don't regret this."

"You won't. I promise," Ted said, beaming.

Ted

When he got up Monday morning, Ted had a bit more pep in his step after the Packers's win and the afternoon he spent with Sunny and Aleen. Perhaps they all could have a fresh start.

After he had his coffee, Ted leashed up Hope and Cash for their morning walk. It was early September, and the afternoon temperatures could still reach ninety degrees. At night, however, it cooled down considerably, and the early mornings could be crisp and comfortable. Today looked to be a perfect day in Southern California.

Ted felt lighter this beautiful morning and actually was looking forward to the week, particularly the weekend and the makeovers. Perhaps Aleen and Ted could have dinner afterward. Her friendship meant a lot to him. She and Sunny were helping him more than he was helping them; he was sure.

Walking along the beautiful boulevard, Ted decided to take a long stroll with the dogs. The large, old trees lined the street and provided a good bit of shade along the sidewalk. They were lucky to have these beautiful trees on their main street, as there sure weren't as many here in California as compared to the Midwest where Ted grew up.

He was glad to get in a mile walk because he knew Monica would discuss exercise programs as part of the makeover. He neglected to mention the exercise part to Aleen, as he was focused on making the "sale." Ted smiled to himself, hoping she wouldn't be upset with him later.

As he walked back toward the condo, he thought he would swing by the tree and check the flowers. As he got close, Hope and Cash broke free, running over to a man sitting in the grass. As usual, they jumped all over the guy, licking him and demanding he pet them. He complied, and the dogs clearly loved the attention.

"Sorry about that." Ted apologized to the stranger, smiling down at him. "The dogs really get a kick out of making new friends."

He looked to be a bit younger than Ted, with blondish, sandy hair. He was wearing jeans with a light-blue shirt. When he looked at the stranger's eyes, he could see an incredible sadness; something was troubling him. Something was terribly wrong.

"They are wonderful dogs," the man said. "You don't see that many corgis around. I guess I always think about the Queen of England when I see them. What sweet and fun personalities they have. I did notice you got the dogs fairly recently."

"Oh?" Ted said, thinking it was odd this stranger knew so much about him.

"I come here quite often, but I try not to bother you when you're here. I leave flowers just about every time," he told Ted, getting up and brushing off his jeans. "I brought these today." The man pointed at a lovely arrangement of flowers he'd placed on the ground at the foot of the big tree.

"They are beautiful. Thank you. Did you know my son?" Ted asked.

"I, um . . . I really don't want to bother you, and I'm so sorry

I didn't see you coming. If I did, I would have left." He seemed so uncomfortable.

"Why?" Ted asked. "Who are you?"

The man looked straight into Ted's eyes.

"I'm Vincent. I killed your son."

chapter six

Aleen

It was sure tough to complete all her chores Sunday night after she spent so much time at Ted's, but Aleen got it all done, even though the laundry wasn't folded and put away until around eleven o'clock. She'd also found herself scrubbing the bathroom floor at 9:30 p.m. *Oh, the glamorous life of a working woman.*

Sunny had gotten home at about eight o'clock from her friend's house and seemed in a fairly good mood. She stayed up late studying.

In the brief conversation they had, Aleen and Sunny agreed the time at Ted's was fun and they should do it again. She didn't tell her daughter about the makeover yet. She'd save that for a discussion one evening during the week.

Thank God Durk got Sunny an old car a couple weeks ago, so she could come and go on her own schedule, particularly to school. It certainly cost less than having her stay on campus, although money wasn't the main issue. All of them agreed she should consider the dorms, but Sunny wanted to stay close to home for her first semester, perhaps the entire first year. Durk and Aleen understood.

For a long time, Sunny pretty much refused to talk to or see her father. The car was an excuse for them to actually interact. Aleen certainly wasn't happy with Durk, but she knew in her heart that Sunny needed to make peace with him so they could have a semblance of a father-daughter relationship. There just was too much anger right now, compounded with Sunny's deep well of grief.

Aleen would encourage the reunion at the right moment, but it was clear Sunny needed more time. Durk understood, too, but it hurt him deeply. He didn't need to tell Aleen; she could see it. He loved his daughter so much. After Stu died, she was sure Durk had imagined what it would be like to lose Sunny, just as Aleen had. He wanted to hang on to his daughter tight, but Sunny wouldn't let him.

Working at the same company with her soon-to-be ex-husband was trying for Aleen. They did their best to avoid contact, but they inevitably ran into each other in the hallway, the cafeteria, or at large group meetings. When she saw him, she couldn't stop herself from wishing they were still together, their little family . . .

She pushed those thoughts out of her head. Aleen needed to get some rest, as her new boss was arriving for her first day bright and early Monday morning. Trish Rendoven was the new senior vice president responsible for strategic planning and mergers and acquisitions.

Aleen's job was executive assistant, but she had broader responsibilities, as she'd been in the department so long, fifteen years now, and at the company much longer. She held deep knowledge of all the operations. People came to her for absolutely everything; her days were busy and generally went by in a flash.

She knew the staff like the back of her hand and could detail all their strengths and weaknesses. Aleen played a key role in performance reviews, as she had helped all her bosses complete them and enter the reviews in the system over the years. She was a whiz at all the company processes: performance reviews, compensation, supply chain, compliance. Staff from her department and others came to her constantly for assistance.

At least it's good to be coveted at work, Aleen thought to herself. She sure needed an ego boost and something to hang on to at this point in her life.

Aleen also was an expert at PowerPoint presentations and played a critical role in the development of all the strategic reviews presented to the CEO and his staff. She knew the exact format the CEO and his team preferred and could, with minimal input, actually develop the content for many of the charts herself. She wasn't aware of other executive assistants who had that ability.

When she took time off to spend with Sunny after Stu died, Aleen missed some critical strategic reviews, and without her assistance, the CEO hated the presentations. It was the final nail in the coffin for her boss of just over a year, as he wasn't up to the job.

Aleen knew she and other members of the team had masked some of his issues, but he was an okay guy and treated her fine, so she didn't mind working for him. He just didn't seem suited for the high-level position, so the CEO pushed him out.

Sometimes, Aleen wished she would have finished her degree, because it was clear she could do plenty of the higher-paying jobs in the company. *Another regret to add to the pile.* She sighed. *Can you please turn off your brain and get some rest?*

After a night of fitful sleep, Aleen got up early to get ready for work. She felt nervous as she drove, taking the first parking spot she saw before literally sprinting to her office with a sense of great anticipation. For the first time, she would have a woman for a leader, and she was excited. After spending a good deal of time on the phone with Trish to prepare for her arrival, she looked forward to meeting her in person.

Trish sounded so interesting and engaging. She was moving from Boston, was in her late thirties, and had an MBA from Dartmouth. Aleen was pretty sure she was single. She would work hard to help Trish get settled into the job; her company sure needed more women at the top.

When Aleen got to the office just after seven, she fired up her computer to retrieve the schedule to go over with her new boss. Trish had to leave to go to the company orientation at 8:00 a.m., so Aleen was hoping to have about thirty minutes with her before that.

When she opened her email, there were about a hundred, most requests for Trish's time. People at the company knew better than to send a meeting request to her unless it had been agreed to in advance, but the vendors were bombarding her, as they wanted to meet with Trish early in her tenure.

As she was clicking through the emails, Trish arrived. *What a beauty,* Aleen thought. She had dark-blond hair and flashing hazel eyes and wore a beautiful knit suit. Stunning. It looked like a St. John's outfit, and Aleen thought it probably cost more than a thousand dollars. She sheepishly smoothed her pants, which she'd purchased at Kohl's for about twenty bucks.

"Good morning," Trish said, sweeping in as Aleen stood to greet her and shake her hand.

"It is so good to meet you, Trish. And welcome to California. The whole team is excited you are here," Aleen said genuinely.

"Well, it's wonderful to meet you, too. And thanks for all your help so far. It's greatly appreciated," Trish replied sincerely.

"Please come in my office so we can get properly acquainted."

The women went into Trish's nicely appointed office. Trish plopped her stuff on her desk, and the two women sat at the conference table.

After reviewing the schedule and discussing how they would work together, she wanted to know more about Aleen personally.

"So you have a daughter?" Trish asked.

"Yes, Sunny is eighteen and has just started engineering school at UCLA," Aleen said proudly.

"That's wonderful. I would love to meet her someday," Trish said warmly.

"I'm sure you will," Aleen answered. "You may have heard my husband—I should say soon-to-be ex-husband—works here as well. He leads one of the largest groups in engineering," she said, tensing up.

"I had heard that," Trish replied.

"There is a story there I would rather tell you another day," Aleen said uncomfortably.

"That is your choice. If you want to tell me, fine. My main concern is how we work together, and from everything I hear, you are absolutely indispensable to this department. Off the record, the CEO told me what a great job you do," Trish said, lightening the mood considerably. "He talked more about you than anyone on the team."

"Well, thank you. I appreciate hearing that so much." Aleen smiled broadly. She needed a confidence boost, so the compliments were well received. She had huge respect for Don Parchard, the CEO, and was happy to hear he appreciated her work. "I look forward to working with you and will do everything I can to help you and the department be successful."

"I appreciate that." Trish took a quick look at her watch. "Well, I have to get going to the orientation. Look forward to spending more time with you later. See you after lunch." She grabbed her purse and headed out with the map Aleen gave her to guide her to the right conference room.

As Aleen walked back to her desk and watched her new boss make her way down the hall, she had a very good feeling about her. "I think this is going to work out very well," she said to herself, turning back to catching up on emails, even as scores of them continued to hit her inbox.

"Aleen, excuse me," Durk said as he stopped at her desk.

"Durk." Aleen was startled to see her soon-to-be ex-husband, the man who had hurt her more than she could have imagined possible. "What a surprise," she said, her eyes steely.

"Listen, I'm sorry to bother you at work, but I need to see Sunny. She just won't take my calls," he whispered so no one could hear.

"Durk, I have a new boss and so much to do. You're right that you shouldn't talk to me about this at work," Aleen retorted, angry now.

"It's hard to get ahold of you, as well." Durk looked directly in her eyes. Aleen knew he was right; she'd been avoiding his calls.

"I'll talk to Sunny and ask her to call you on your cell tonight. Now, please excuse me," she said, seething, before turning her attention back to her messages.

Durk skulked away, and Aleen watched him go with hurt in her eyes. "How did we ever get to this point?" she whispered to herself, trying like mad to focus her attention back on her computer rather than her failed marriage.

As hard as she fought it, Aleen felt tears starting to form and grabbed a tissue from the box on her desk. She could try to fool Durk into thinking she didn't care about him, but there was no way she could fool herself. She knew damn well she still loved him, even though she wanted to kick him in the balls every time she saw him.

chapter seven

Sunny

Driving to school could take forty-five minutes to two hours, depending on the traffic, so Sunny was glad she left early. This was going to be one of those awful traffic days. Unfortunately, this was the bad part about living at home and driving into school every day, because Los Angeles had so many more terrible traffic days than manageable ones.

Sunny's drive was about thirty-five miles from her house to campus, but when it started to get busy on Highway 101 as early as Calabasas, she knew she would be spending a long time in the car. The electronic sign said forty-five minutes just to get to the 405. *Great.*

She was still upset her dad had bugged her mom at work about her. *Leave Mom alone,* Sunny thought. *Haven't you hurt her enough?* She banged on the steering wheel. The last time she had a real conversation with her dad was when he bought her this car. Thank God he did, though. Sunny didn't know how she would get to school without it.

It wasn't anything fancy, but it did run just fine. A 2011 Ford Focus in electric green, Sunny's car had more than 80,000 miles on it when she got it. It had a black interior that was in very good shape. Her dad found it at work through their in-house classifieds and got a very good deal. Sunny loved her little car because it gave her so much independence.

She knew her father was trying to buy back her affection, but she let him because she needed transportation. She went with him to test drive it, and they had lunch together, but that was weeks ago. Sunny really didn't have any desire to see him now. Why did he think she could just get over what happened?

But he had to stop bugging her mom, so Sunny would call him, as promised. Maybe she could get away with a phone call rather than a get-together. *Probably not.*

Just then, someone cut her off, and she beeped the horn. She knew her mom wasn't keen on her driving in the brutal LA traffic, but what alternative did she have? She wasn't ready to move to the dorms. She needed to be home to have her time with Stu, at least in her head. She wasn't ready for a bunch of boozy college students invading her space. *No, thanks.*

The good news was she was getting plenty of practice driving under all kinds of conditions. She'd be a real pro at an early age. Thank God she got her license at sixteen so she had a few years of experience before taking on this hellish commute every day. She couldn't imagine some of her friends making this drive.

Right now, it actually was tough for her to spend a lot of time with her high school friends, even Nikki. Their concerns seemed so trivial to her: boys, clothes, social media. . . . Sunny tried to keep up with them on Instagram, Snapchat, Twitter, and even Facebook, but she found she saw them less and less, because they just didn't share a lot in common.

It's funny she didn't use Facebook that much because it really seemed for older people now—even her mom was on it. Yuck! She wondered if Mr. Hammand had an account.

The accident made her grow up fast, she guessed, so she

didn't think like her friends anymore. Sunny had always been a good student and enjoyed school, so studying engineering at UCLA was perfect for her. The school had a great reputation, too, and she was enjoying it so far. It took her mind off Stu's death and made her think about her future. She believed she would like a job like her dad's. . . .

There it was again. Her dad. The anger started to rise in her, but she tried to push it out of her mind. She was going to have to deal with him pretty soon.

Sunny could see the hurt in her mom's eyes when she described her dad's "drive-by" at work. Her mom and dad avoided each other at the office, as neither wanted to revisit all those bad feelings.

Poor Mom. Sunny resolved to try and be better with her.

She would do everything she could to help her mom and Mr. Hammand. They were both suffering, too. What a trio!

While Sunny was stuck in the quicksand of her grief over Stu, she couldn't imagine what it was like for Mr. Hammand. Father and son had been so close. Sunny knew she was biased in thinking Stu was the perfect guy, but she knew Mr. Hammand thought so, too. And he was the guiding force in making Stu the wonderful young man he was.

At graduation, Mr. Hammand was so proud as Stu gave one of the student addresses. What did he say? It was some old-school saying like "busting his balloon . . . knob . . ." No, he wouldn't say that.

Sunny smiled to herself. "Buttons," she said out loud. "I'm so proud I'm busting my buttons." Sunny laughed. *That saying must be from the Middle Ages,* she thought.

It was sad, really, as she saw the relationships many of her friends had with their parents, and it was nothing like what Stu had enjoyed with his. For that matter, the relationship she'd enjoyed with her parents had been really special as well. *Well, so much for that.* . . .

Just then, Sunny thought of a funny card Stu had given her, scrawling "PRIVATE" on the front with silly little hearts. She treasured it and kept it in her nightstand next to her bed. She closed her eyes for a second to recall his note, as she had just about memorized it.

Dear Sunny:

I just had to get you this card 'cause it was so cool and funny. I saw it at the store and thought of you right away. I think cards are mostly a waste of time and so old-fashioned, but this one just seemed perfect.

I can't stop thinking about you after our time near the hiking trail. If that other car didn't drive up, well . . . who knows what would've happened? Have I told you how beautiful you are? How I love kissing you, touching you? I dream about you all the time.

It won't be long until we graduate and head to college. Glad we'll be in the same town and get to see each other often. I can't imagine not being with you all the time. That would be torture!

I'm thinking of you now, your gorgeous smile. Looking forward to our time together this weekend. Love you!

Your Stu

xxxxx

The only good thing about her horrendous commute was it gave her time to think about Stu. Sunny became aroused thinking about that time together in his car near the hiking trail. Their make-out sessions had progressed as their relationship grew, and they explored each other further and further each time. In the darkness that March night, Stu had started to kiss her passionately, and the urgency between them continued to grow as their hands roamed. He cupped her breasts through her T-shirt and gently massaged her through her shorts.

Pushing her fingers underneath his shirt, Sunny touched Stu's bare skin, so smooth and wonderful. She stroked his chest and moved her hand farther down to the hardness beneath his jeans, and he moaned. He undid her shorts and slid his hand down her belly to stroke her, and Sunny thought she might jump out of her skin. As he continued to delve deeper, she rocked on his palm and exploded in an orgasm that shook her to her core.

Sunny grabbed Stu and hung on for dear life. The lights of another car flashed into view, and the young lovers quickly separated and fixed their clothes before driving off.

Sunny smiled at the memory, recalling how wonderful it was to kiss him, to touch him, to hold him.

She snapped out of her fantasy and back to reality when a pickup truck nearly hit her car. She swerved as the driver tried to change lanes. Honking her horn, Sunny swore under her breath.

Getting close to school, she needed to focus on her driving and finding parking, which was always a feat.

When she finally made it to class, Sunny sat next to a guy named Benjamin. He seemed really with it, always giving excellent answers. Maybe they could form a study group with some of the other students. He was good looking, too, but still being so absorbed with Stu, she wasn't interested in a relationship.

When Benjamin looked over at her, she smiled, and he smiled back, pleasantly surprised the pretty girl noticed him.

chapter eight

Ted

Vincent shocked Ted with his statement about Stu, and he studied this man standing next to the flowers that served as a memorial to his son, flashing back to that fateful night. Yes, he recalled a man that looked like Vincent standing there. Several people had tried to help, and then a few stayed around as witnesses to offer their accounts to the police.

Stu went through the stop sign and right into the path of the oncoming car. That's what the witnesses said. Once he learned that, Ted knew in his heart he couldn't blame the driver of the car, as much as he might have wanted to. . . . He hated to think about it, but anyone driving down the street could have hit his son.

The police report was clear: Stu was going over the speed limit on his motorcycle when he went through the stop sign and the impact occurred. The driver of the car, Vincent, was traveling at the posted speed limit. No charges were ever filed because the accounts from the witnesses all lined up.

"I am so, so sorry, Mr. Hammand," Vincent cried. "There isn't a day that goes by that I don't think about Stu and you and your wife. I wish I wasn't going down this street at that exact moment. I would do anything to change it, to go back in time, so your son was still alive." Vincent dropped to the ground, overcome with emotion, hiding his eyes with his hands.

Ted walked over to the tree and tied the dogs' leashes onto a small branch. He then knelt on the ground to put his arm around Vincent to comfort him.

"Vincent, it wasn't your fault. You know that. The police report and all the witnesses said the same thing. You were just driving down the street. Stu was upset and ran the stop sign. . . . It could have happened to anyone. You were in the wrong place at the wrong time. That's what happened.

"I should have never, ever gotten him that motorcycle. We can all find ways to blame ourselves, but we can't. We just can't." Ted tried his best to console the man, but he couldn't seem to pull himself back together.

"Maybe it's best to let it out, Vincent," he said gently as the man continued to cry. "Geez, I wish I could take my own advice. . . ."

With those words, Vincent pulled a handkerchief from his pocket to wipe his eyes and nose. "I can't believe I'm letting *you* comfort me. I'm such an idiot and so sorry to make you relive that terrible night. I just can't seem to get it out of my mind. It's torturing me." He paused for a minute, Ted's hand still on his shoulder. "Please accept my apology for being so out of control today. Can you ever forgive me?"

"There is nothing to forgive, Vincent. It was an accident. Believe me. I blame myself, too, and think through every detail of that day over and over. If I did this or I did that, he would still be alive. It's a natural thing to play the what-if game, but we just can't change anything. It can't bring him back," Ted said sadly.

"You are a fine man, Mr. Hammand. Stu must have been a wonderful young man if he was anything like you," Vincent said.

"You are very kind to say that," Ted replied. "Stu was exceptional, and I can say that with objectivity.

"Would you like to come in for a cup of tea? My place is right behind those trees."

"Oh, I couldn't impose on you. . . ."

"Not an imposition. I just figured out recently the way to work through my grief and find the strength to go on with my life is through others. So you're actually helping me. Let's have a cup of tea. Besides, it looks like you need to splash some water on your face."

"You may be right about that," Vincent replied as Ted helped him up.

After he untied Hope and Cash, the two men and the dogs headed to the condo. Once inside, Ted put the dogs out in the courtyard to play and directed Vincent to the half bath so he could gather himself.

Ted shook his head. He couldn't believe what had just happened outside. To see the anguish in Vincent's eyes . . . It was incredible to think of all the suffering caused by Stu's death. The pain of his passing had tentacles that enveloped so many hearts. He knew countless kids from school were still so upset— hundreds showed up to his funeral, and his classmates started a scholarship fund in Stu's name to honor him.

No one was affected by Stu's death more than Ted, but still. It shook him up to think Vincent was blaming himself. It was clear the guilt was ripping him apart. Ted had to do what he could to help him.

He put the kettle on for tea, thinking the old Ted would never invite a stranger into his home. He wasn't afraid Vincent was an ax murderer or crazy person. There wasn't anything that could happen to him that was worse than anything that had already happened.

Vincent joined him in the kitchen after cleaning himself up. "Thanks, I needed that," he said, his eyes looking less red and puffy.

"No problem." Ted waved aside his concerns. "Do you take your tea with anything?"

Vincent answered nervously, as he still wasn't totally at ease. "My partner is English, so I take it with milk and sugar. Thanks."

"You got it. I like it that way as well. My wife—I should say soon-to-be ex-wife—and I have spent a lot of time in England. Stu went with us a couple times as well," Ted said quietly.

"Oh no, Mr. Hammand," Vincent said. "Your marriage, too . . ."

"Please, Vincent, call me Ted."

"Okay, Ted. I do know these types of situations are tough on relationships. My partner and I are taking a break right now. I haven't been the easiest to live with. . . ." Vincent looked away as his voice trailed off.

"Well, I guess we have something in common there. I hope you can work it out," Ted said sincerely.

"I have some hope. Derek—my partner—said I needed to get professional help to get through this. I'll never get over it, but I need to learn to deal with it better than I have been. I know that. Maybe talking to you is a start. Even though I have no intent to make your life harder or to bring you face-to-face with your grief again because of my thoughtlessness. . . ."

"Vincent, my grief is right beneath the surface when it isn't front and center. It's always there.

"My son's girlfriend, Sunny, hasn't been able to get over Stu's death, either. Her parents' marriage broke up as well, so her mother, Aleen, is devastated. She lost her marriage *and* a young man who was quite dear to her.

"The three of us—Aleen, Sunny, and I—have started to help each other. The friendship and support we give each other is opening up a little crack of sunlight, some hope that we can live our lives again with some joy, some contentment." Ted looked down at the floor.

"I do remember seeing Sunny and her parents that terrible night." Vincent shuddered, thinking of the raw emotions he saw and experienced that evening. "I'm glad the three of you are there for each other. It means so much that you would try to help me with everything you're going through," he said, shaking his head. "And I'm encouraged that you have hope for the future."

"I do, even though it's so difficult at times. You should, too," Ted responded, looking at Vincent with concern.

He picked up the teapot and poured a cup for each of them.

"Well, here's to taking a few baby steps forward," Vincent said as the men touched their mugs in a toast to the future and took a sip of their tea.

"And to Stu," Ted added.

"To Stu," Vincent answered, taking a drink of his tea and looking at Ted with admiration and awe.

chapter nine

Aleen

What a busy week at work, with Trish settling into her new job, Aleen thought as she tried to straighten up her desk. She liked her new boss tremendously, as she treated everyone with respect, identified the great talent on the team immediately, and interacted with ease with all the executives, including the CEO. The buzz was all positive.

As it was approaching five o'clock on Friday, Aleen found herself getting excited about the weekend and the makeover tomorrow. Hope and Cash would come to their house in the morning during Ted's makeover. They were great dogs, and both Aleen and Sunny loved them and welcomed their visit.

Sunny would have to get up early to watch the dogs, as Aleen was planning to do all her chores before her makeover. As a teenager, getting up early in the morning was Sunny's least favorite thing to do. Aleen chuckled to herself about coming up with a bribe to get Sunny out of bed.

As they were planning to watch the Packers game at Ted's Sunday, Aleen wanted everything done before so she could relax and enjoy it.

She offered to make dinner after the game, so she would

have to figure out the menu. Couldn't have pizza every week! She was committed to eating healthy, so she thought about making a new recipe from *Cooking Light* that featured chicken and vegetables. She was sure Ted and Sunny would like that for their early dinner following the game.

So much to plan, Aleen thought just as her boss stopped by her desk, bringing her back to reality. Trish motioned her to follow her and take a seat at the conference table.

"So what did you think about your first week?" Aleen looked at her with interest.

"Well, I don't think it could have gone better," Trish answered. "And thanks to you for all of your work to make it go so smoothly."

"I'm so glad you feel it went well. I sure have heard wonderful feedback about you from everyone, and I'm not just saying that. As we work together longer, you'll see I'll tell you like it is. I know you always need to know what's *really* going on," Aleen said, feeling confident in the developing relationship with her new boss.

"I appreciate that and have heard from everyone that you are a straight shooter and a real gem. I'll look to you often for advice and support," Trish said.

"You got it," Aleen replied. "Well, I hope you're up for a busy weekend. You're with the realtor and relocation specialist all day tomorrow and Sunday. You *are* a bit of a glutton for punishment." She smiled mischievously.

"I want to find a house quickly and get settled. I don't want to stay very long in temporary living. I may need your advice once I get the lay of the land and understand the different areas that make the most sense for me to live in." Trish grabbed a piece of paper to make a note. "You just reminded me I need to talk to my realtor back in Boston about my house."

"That is one of the things I wanted to talk to you about. There were a few important messages while you were in the last meeting, and at the top of the list is the call from the realtor in Boston. You already have an offer on your house," Aleen told her, handing over the slip of paper with the number and information.

"Wow, that was fast." Trish was clearly delighted. "Listen, you pack up and get out of here to start your weekend. I'll return this call and a few others, and it won't be long until I follow you out of here," she added.

"Thanks so much. I am kind of excited to leave on time and begin the weekend," Aleen said, eyes shining bright.

"Well, we should try and make leaving on time, or even early, on Friday a tradition. And thanks again for everything this week," Trish said as Aleen got up to shut down her computer and rush out.

As she drove home, Aleen considered perhaps having a new boss—and a great one—was part of her fresh start.

Since Sunny was out for the night, Aleen made a salad for dinner and wolfed it down before completing a few chores. She was excited for her makeover day and began to lay clothes out on the bed to try and decide what to wear. She laughed at herself, puzzling over the outfits. Why was she going to so much trouble to pick out clothes when her makeover artist, Monica, was going to find her new ones that better suited her?

Aleen admitted to herself that she'd never put that much time into her appearance, and she wanted to look good from the start tomorrow. She did need help to look more stylish, making better choices for her clothes, makeup, and hair. She knew this was superficial, but perhaps it would be a start in improving her mood.

She'd been so down on herself since Durk left. His departure had come out of nowhere. Aleen had been stunned and felt so stupid.

While she wasn't ready to start dating, she had warmed up to the idea of getting help in the appearance department. She needed to do something for herself. It actually was a good suggestion from Ted.

He was right that they could talk about things more freely than with others, and Aleen was grateful for his friendship. She couldn't think of another man who could suggest she needed a makeover without launching her into a sea of self-doubt. He was just so matter-of-fact about it. She knew it wasn't just about clothes and hair; it was about a fresh start in their lives.

Once she settled on the right outfit, she finished the wash and some other chores and went to bed early. Aleen was happy she'd gotten a head start, as she knew she would be up at the crack of dawn due to her excitement and the 7:45 a.m. arrival of Hope and Cash.

The next morning, she woke up early without the alarm and buzzed around the house, getting herself ready. Aleen spent a few extra minutes on her makeup to show Ted, Monica, Sunny, and the hair and makeup stylist she could actually do a decent job when she put her mind to it. Why didn't she spend a little more time on it sooner? Maybe Durk would still be here.

Aleen grabbed her head to stop the negative thoughts. *Stop it! Today is a new day.*

Right on the dot, Ted rang the doorbell, and the dogs came bounding into the house, checking out the new environment and quickly making themselves at home.

"Thanks for taking care of them," he said. "Hey, you look really nice," he added, looking at her with admiration. She beamed at her friend. "I thought we should go out to dinner tonight as our *made-over* selves. What do you think?"

"Well . . ." Aleen wasn't sure she wanted to be out and about, as she had no idea what her "made-over" self was going to be.

"Come on. You've got to take some chances in life," Ted said, smiling broadly.

"All right. You're running this show, so I'll put my trust in you."

"Excellent. I made a reservation at seven thirty tonight at Amazing District, that new swanky restaurant."

"What!" Aleen gaped at him incredulously. "You already made the reservation?"

"Gotta go," Ted said, leaving quickly before she could change her mind.

Aleen shook her head and got the dogs some bowls of water. That Ted! He seemed to be guiding her life in a whole new direction.

She turned to gaze out the window at the beautiful view; it was so captivating. Aleen loved her home; it was almost like another member of the family. She and Durk had bought it fifteen years ago. They'd always dreamed of buying a house on Lake Sherwood, and they saved and saved until they were able to do so. They had taken what was an older home and totally redid it, putting in so much sweat equity themselves.

Their goal had been to have the view of the lake in as many rooms as possible. To do that in the main living areas, they opened up the kitchen and family room so it was one large room with huge windows. They added a large outdoor kitchen and expanded the patio so they could enjoy the stunning views outside as well.

The result was that the entire first floor had spectacular views of the lake, as did most of the bedrooms, which were downstairs since the house was built into a hill. They also added a large guest suite off the family room, which had French doors that opened up to the courtyard and fountain. The remodeling took them a year, but it was well worth the effort.

So many memories, Aleen thought, sighing.

She looked at the view of the lake with the small islands and abundance of wildlife. Framed by the majestic mountains behind, it was breathtaking. The dogs seemed to like it, too, as they parked themselves in front of the window.

The sound of the birds was constant; the geese were on the lake year round. Durk, Aleen, and Sunny went on a birding walk a few years ago and spotted cormorants, white pelicans, hawks, ducks, coots, moorhens, sandpipers, ravens, woodpeckers, swans, and so many other kinds of birds. Some visited only part of the year, like the cormorants and white pelicans.

Durk, Sunny, and Aleen had also seen deer, coyotes, raccoons, skunks, a weasel, and the occasional rattlesnake. Sunny went hiking in the mountains across the lake and even saw a mountain lion. Her parents were glad when she was home safe after that trek.

Overall, it was just a beautiful environment, and she couldn't imagine living anywhere else.

This was the only home Sunny could remember, and she loved it as much as Durk and Aleen. As an engineer, Durk was quite handy around the house and could fix anything. He had enjoyed being the king of the castle and especially loved working outside, often with Sunny at his side.

Durk and Aleen had found a secondhand electric boat when they first bought the house, and the three of them loved to cruise around the lake to see the wildlife and all the houses, most of which weren't visible from the street. One time, they saw a bobcat sunning himself on a rock on the edge of the water. What a gorgeous animal.

Gosh, she thought to herself. She couldn't recall the last time they took the boat out on the lake. Sad, because the three of them loved to cruise around, sharing a drink and a snack, enjoying the breeze on the lake.

There would be no way Aleen could afford the house on her salary alone, so she was glad when Durk agreed she and Sunny could stay in their home. He probably felt guilty, so he didn't plan to make them move out. She wasn't sure Sunny could handle the change, either, and Durk knew that.

Just then, Sunny came into the kitchen in her shorts and T-shirt, and the dogs began to jump all over her.

"Hey, you guys," Sunny said, laughing. "Do you think you own this place?" she asked, bending down to let them hop on her and lick her hands and face.

"'Fraid so, hon," Aleen said. "Hope and Cash just scurried in and took over this morning." She looked at her daughter intently as she played with the dogs. She hadn't seen her smile in the morning like this for ages. "Well, you're in charge. I'm off to the store to get all the shopping done this morning so I'll be ready for my makeover afternoon. And remember, tomorrow I'm cooking dinner at Ted's place after the game." Aleen grabbed her purse from the counter.

"Right," Sunny said, continuing to play with the dogs. When she stood, she addressed the dogs in a mock-stern fashion. "Now, Hope and Cash, you're going to have to listen to me."

The dogs looked at her as if they were laughing and ran around the kitchen island.

"Good luck with that," Aleen said, petting the dogs before she ran out.

As it was so early, Aleen was able to avoid the crowds and completed her errands in record time. When she got back to the house, there was a note from Sunny to let her know she took the dogs for a walk.

"Good," Aleen said aloud. "You should get out of the house more often on weekends."

She busied herself with putting away all the groceries, as it wouldn't be long until her makeover would begin. She was so nervous but excited as well. What would her made-over self be like? Would she like her new look? What would Sunny say? And Ted?

Would Durk even notice? She pushed that thought out of her mind. Her husband was part of her past, unfortunately, and she needed to look to the future.

A future without him, she thought sadly.

chapter ten

Ted

Ted stood in his bedroom, admiring his new self. Instead of his usual khakis, he had on form-fitting designer jeans. They actually looked good on him, as he'd always been trim and lean.

His typical polo shirt was replaced by a long-sleeve shirt with a thin, stand-up collar in a beautiful shade of teal that accented his eyes. The sleeves had tabs so he could roll them up in warm weather. Ted also wore a trendy looking sports coat that was a beautiful light beige and fit him perfectly.

His hair was styled in a much more contemporary fashion. He laughed. He always thought his previous hairstyle was "early out-of-control." As his hair had been wispy and a bit curly, he just pretty much let it alone. Now it was styled with gel and looked totally in-control. It made Ted a bit nervous to try and figure out how to do it himself in the future, even though the stylist walked through it with him several times.

Monica had helped him pick out a new, hip style for his glasses a few weeks ago, and they went to get them at the end of his makeover. The semi-rimless style was much more modern than his old wire rims. As he looked in the mirror at all the changes, he felt like a different man.

He hoped Aleen would like his new look and her makeover

day was going well. Ted wondered if she would look as different as he did.

What would Gerrie think? Frowning at the thought of his wife, Ted stashed away his old clothes as well as the shopping bags and headed out to pick up the dogs.

Look forward, not back, he told himself.

What would his young friend Sunny think of the new Ted? He felt surprisingly nervous as he stood on the front step and rang the doorbell. He could hear Hope and Cash barking and running to the door.

When Sunny opened it, she gasped. "Mr. Hammand, you look great!" she said, letting him step in around the jumping dogs. "Now, guys, leave your dad alone. He has these fantastic new clothes, and you can't muss him up," she said, trying to keep the dogs at bay.

Ted smiled, clearly pleased with her compliments.

"I love the shirt, the jeans, the jacket . . . and your glasses. Those are so cool!"

"Thanks, Sunny. It means a lot coming from you."

"Just turn around once," Sunny commanded, helping twirl him around. "Your hair is so nice. I can't believe how it makes you look so different. You remind me of Stu . . ."

"Stu . . ." She said his name again, hanging on to the words as she started to tear up.

"Oh, Sunny, I'm so sorry. The last thing I want to do is upset you. . . ." Ted took her in his arms and stroked her hair as she struggled to control her emotions.

Sunny pulled herself away abruptly. "I can't stain your new shirt or jacket. Especially after I scolded the dogs about that very thing." Sunny smiled a bit through her tears, grabbing a tissue from the pocket of her shorts.

"Honey, don't ever worry about shedding tears on me." Ted squeezed her arm.

"I'm okay. I'm fine." Sunny tried to assure him. "You just threw me for a minute because I never really thought of you and Stu looking much alike until you walked in here just now."

"Understand," Ted said, nodding. "I guess I always thought Stu looked more like Gerrie. I hadn't thought the 'new Ted' made me look more like my son. I'm surprised I didn't notice."

"I'm glad you did the makeover. You look more handsome now, and I know Stu would approve. He'd give you a really hard time about it—especially your new hair—but I know he would like what you did.

"I really appreciate what you're doing for my mom—and I think Stu would, too," Sunny added, regaining her composure.

Ted nodded again. "Well, I hope she's pleased at the end of the day. Stu always loved your mother."

Sunny and Ted walked into the kitchen, where the dogs were wrestling and nuzzling each other.

"Mom loved him, too. She thought of him as part of the family. Do you think Mom will look as different as you?" Sunny asked, wide-eyed.

"I don't know. I did ask her to go to dinner with me to show the world our new made-over selves."

"Are you sure you aren't dating?" Sunny narrowed her gaze with growing concern.

"No, Sunny. As I told you before, we're just friends. I'm afraid I'm not over my wife, and my impression is your mom isn't ready to move on yet either. We both have plenty to work out. This makeover is the outside, which is a lot easier than the inside."

Sunny just stared at Ted.

"The next part is the hardest. For all of us," he added softly.

"I know, Mr. Hammand. I know," Sunny said, trying to put on her best face for the new Ted.

chapter eleven

Aleen

While Monica looked through the racks and racks of reading glasses at the pharmacy, Aleen couldn't believe it was almost five o'clock. The whole afternoon had just whizzed by. They started at the mall and picked out three outfits rather than two. She just couldn't choose between them. They all looked so good, so too bad about the budget!

Next, it was hair and makeup, which were done at the same place. The makeup artist remarked on how beautiful Aleen's eyes were—luminescent blue, radiating warmth—and used the perfect shades to accent them. She purchased the same makeup in the exact tints and couldn't wait to try it herself on Monday. She also had her nails done, which was a surprise, as she didn't think there would be enough time.

Monica was fantastic, and she had everything timed perfectly. They were on the second-to-last stop to pick out new reading glasses, and she brought over three different styles for Aleen to try. Her old reading glasses had heavy, dark plastic frames and looked entirely different than the ones she was about to try on. She only used glasses for reading, but the fact of the matter was she did a lot of reading. People at work probably saw

Aleen most often with her glasses on. Updating them was an important part of her makeover.

The three styles Monica brought over for her were more rectangular and rimless on the bottom—very contemporary.

Two of them looked great, so she bought them both, not feeling guilty, as there was a special on to buy one and get the other half price.

After they checked out, Monica led Aleen down the sidewalk of the small shopping center and then stopped in front of the Pilates studio. "Our last stop," Monica declared, opening the door for Aleen.

They watched for a few minutes as the women in their workout clothes performed a series of motions, sitting on their mats with very straight backs.

"In addition to getting fit, I think Pilates will help you with your posture. You don't sit up very straight, and we don't want you to have bad posture and appear hunched over," Monica said in a professional, matter-of-fact tone. "I'd like to suggest you sign up for three classes per week. I have a discount rate here as well, so it won't break the bank," she told Aleen.

"Well, I'm not sure I can find the time. . . ."

"I think you can if you want to," Monica answered.

Aleen relented and signed up. There was no way she was going to do Pilates in the morning before work, as it would be way too early. She might have to come in twice on weekends and one evening during the week. Maybe Trish would let her go early one night so she wouldn't have to do a late-night class.

Monica was chatting with a friend who was dressed in a form-fitting workout outfit with her mat under her arm and purse over her shoulder. She was a petite, attractive blonde, and Monica and she seemed to be having a serious conversation. Aleen was surprised when she brought her friend over to meet her.

"Sandy, this is Aleen. I explained we just did your makeover," Monica said. "Sandy is a top family therapist, and I know you said the next step was for you and your daughter to get back to counseling. I'll let you two chat for a minute," Monica added, walking over to the ladies' room to give the women some privacy.

"I heard about the accident. I read about it shortly after it happened." Sandy jumped right in. "Very, very sad. Stu must have been a remarkable young man. I'm sure his loss has been extremely difficult for his family and yours.

"If you choose to go to counseling, I would do my best to help. It is totally your choice," she added, taking her card from a small slot in the front of her purse.

Aleen took the card and slipped it into her pocket. "Thanks, Sandy. It has been a hard road for my daughter and me. I know the physical makeover is the easy part." She forced a smile. "My biggest concern is Sunny. I'll talk to her about trying counseling again and get back to you. It's one thing to talk about needing help; it's another to actually reach out and get it," she said, uncertainly.

"Why don't you think about coming to see me on your own first? Then you may be able to convince your daughter to schedule a session as well. As I said, it's totally up to you," Sandy said reassuringly.

"You may be right. I'll call next week. It's been great to run into you this way and have a chance to meet. You've given me a lot to think about," Aleen said, shaking Sandy's hand.

Monica walked back up to them, and they were off. She drove Aleen back to her car and helped her load the shopping bags into the trunk. She was surprised at how much she enjoyed the day and how good Monica's advice had been. She hugged Monica goodbye before she drove away; she felt like she'd found a new friend.

Heading home to get changed for her dinner with Ted, Aleen started to get excited about revealing her made-over self. She also thought a lot about what Sandy had said and would be sure to talk to Ted about it at dinner.

When she got home, she raced to the master suite to put on her new clothes because she wanted Sunny to get the full makeover effect.

She quickly changed into the new, beautiful midnight-blue pantsuit, pairing it with the perfectly coordinated scarf. After adding her best jewelry, Aleen checked her hair and makeup in the mirror in the bathroom. She put a bit of powder on her face and smoothed her hair slightly, though it was holding its shape very well.

Her new, more modern hairstyle was a darker shade with reddish highlights and was a touch shorter, hugging her face. It was layered a bit and totally straightened. Aleen had bought a straightening iron at the pharmacy so she could replicate the style.

Wow, she thought. She really liked the reflection in the mirror. A lot better than in the frozen food section the other day. She giggled to herself.

She could hear the hair dryer, so she knew Sunny must be getting ready herself. Aleen couldn't wait to show off her new look to her daughter and headed to the family room.

"Mom!" Sunny shouted when she caught sight of her mother. "You look gorgeous. I love your hair. Great color. Let me see your makeup." She came close to examine the shades of her eye shadow. "Awesome. And I love that suit. It makes you look thinner," she added, continuing her commentary.

"Thanks so much, hon. I have to say I am pleased," Aleen said, beaming. "Let me show you my new reading glasses." She fished them out of her purse and put them on for Sunny to examine.

"Wow, trendy, Mom. These are so much better than the ugly black plastic frames. Those were the worst!"

"Thanks . . . I think." Aleen laughed and spun around, taking off her reading glasses. "I do like my new look."

"You should. A few changes can make such a huge difference. You don't look so frumpy anymore."

Aleen scoffed. "Sunny! Why didn't you tell me I was frumpy? I could have spiffed up before this, and maybe your dad—"

"Mom, don't spoil it by talking about Dad. You look great. Just enjoy it and have fun tonight with Mr. Hammand. He came by to pick up the dogs, and, wow, he really looked fantastic. You'll be quite the couple tonight," Sunny said, smiling at her mom. "*But* I know you're not a couple and not dating, just friends. That's what Mr. Hammand said anyway."

"That's right, sweetheart. Ted has just become a very good friend. You understand because you're close to him as well."

"Mr. Hammand actually looked more like Stu after the makeover, and I got a little upset. Stupid. I didn't want to ruin his day," Sunny said, looking down at the floor.

"Aww, I'm sure you didn't, honey." Aleen reached for her arm to squeeze it. "He probably loved it that you said he looked like Stu. He was so handsome."

"He did, actually. Wait until you see—" Sunny interrupted herself. "Hey, I can't say more about how he looks. You have to see for yourself! I don't want to give anything away. I know you'll be impressed, and he'll think you look fantastic."

"Thanks," Aleen said, coloring a bit, clearly pleased by her daughter's compliments.

Sunny looked at her watch. "I've gotta get going, Mom. I'm meeting some kids from school, from my toughest engineering class."

"Really?" Aleen asked, intrigued.

"We've formed a virtual study group and decided to kick it off tonight in person."

"Virtual?" her mom queried, looking a bit confused.

"When we can't meet in person, we're going to use FaceTime or Skype, since we all live pretty far apart. So we thought we'd get together tonight in person at an in-between spot for everyone to set the ground rules and get to know each other better."

"Sounds reasonable. Just be careful driving," Aleen said.

"I will. Mom, have a great time tonight with Mr. Hammand. I can't wait to hear about it tomorrow. Have fun!" Sunny grabbed her keys and headed out to the garage.

Aleen watched her daughter leave and felt light, even joyful. Sunny was moving forward, and that made her happier than any makeover ever could.

chapter twelve

Ted

Sitting at the restaurant, wearing his new clothes and glasses, Ted studied the menu. The food looked wonderful but a bit expensive. Hell, he and Aleen deserved it. This was a special night—one in which they both should have fun and celebrate their makeovers.

Their table was right in front of the large picture window, and Ted looked out to see a number of diners sitting at tables outside. It was a beautiful September evening.

Ted watched a couple of attractive women in their thirties enter the restaurant, taking the table right across from him. If he wasn't mistaken, one of the women smiled at him. He sat up straighter in his chair and thought he should have had the makeover sooner.

He took a look at the specials menu but was interrupted when the host came over to seat Aleen at the table. Ted looked up and stumbled to his feet to greet her.

"Wowee!" he exclaimed. "Let me look at you."

Aleen spun around to give him the three-sixty view.

"You look fantastic," he said, taking in her new hairstyle and flattering clothes and makeup.

Aleen had a look of wonder on her face as well. "Ted, you look ten years younger. Your hair . . . your glasses. . . . It just works so well. You must be pleased."

"Very pleased, and I'm so glad you're happy as well. Monica is a real talent," he told his friend.

"And look at this." Aleen pulled her new reading glasses from her purse, putting them on.

"Very smart, very attractive," Ted said admiringly. "I ordered some wine so we can toast our makeovers. I hope you don't mind."

"Not at all. You are the wine expert. Anything you pick is going to be fine by me," she said, excited.

"Well, I remember you said pinot noir is your favorite, so I picked an excellent local wine, Ken Brown. I'm a member of their wine club. I hope you like it."

Just then, the waiter arrived with the wine, and Ted took a taste after sniffing it and swirling the liquid around in his glass.

"Perfect," he told the waiter, who poured glasses for them both.

"Here's to our made-over selves. Let's hope this is a fresh start for us, with happier times ahead," Ted said, clinking glasses with Aleen.

"Cheers," she said, a broad smile across her face.

Just then, an attractive woman approached the table. "Aleen, is that you? I almost didn't recognize you." It was Trish, and both Ted and Aleen stood up to greet her.

"Trish, this is Ted, a good friend. Ted, this is Trish, my new boss."

Ted and Trish shook hands and then he pulled out a chair for her to join them.

"I have heard so much about you, Trish. Aleen feels so lucky to have you as her new boss. It seems like it hasn't taken long for you to understand how talented she is," he said sincerely.

"Thank you so much. I haven't heard about you, Ted, but I look forward to learning more from Aleen on Monday," Trish said with a grin.

"We haven't had time to chat much personally, have we?" Aleen felt a little uncomfortable that Trish thought she and Ted were an item.

"No, no, we sure haven't. It was a hectic first week. We'll make time next week," Trish vowed, flashing a gorgeous smile. "By the way, I found a house today."

"That's great news. So happy for you," Aleen said.

"Where is it located?" Ted asked politely.

"Behind the gates at Lake Sherwood, not too far from the country club. It's a large condo that's much more like a house. With all the maintenance covered, it's perfect for me, as I work and travel all the time."

"We live on the lake, too, so we'll have lots to talk about Monday," Aleen told her.

"I'll let you get back to your dinner," Trish said. "My realtor insisted on taking me out tonight to celebrate. Great to meet you, Ted, and see you Monday, Aleen. Enjoy your weekend."

Trish went back to her table across the restaurant. Ted and Aleen just stared at each other for a minute.

"She seems terrific. But you were uncomfortable because she thinks we're together, right?" Ted asked, already knowing the answer.

"True. Trish knows about the divorce, but I told her I'd give her the background later. Obviously, I just didn't want to get into everything during her first week, but I'll have to tell her soon. The whole company already knows what happened. And she has a 'get-acquainted' meeting with Gerrie next week."

At the sound of his wife's name, Ted tensed. The celebratory mood of their dinner started to fade away, and they both took a sip of wine—well, Ted's was more like a gulp.

"Listen, let's not spoil this evening. I have some other news to share with you." Aleen looked Ted straight in the eyes.

"Go on," he said, taking another drink of wine.

"The last stop of the makeover today was at the Pilates studio. I've signed up for three sessions a week."

"That's good, Aleen. We both know our makeovers are mind *and* body," he answered, a bit confused as to why she thought a workout program was so important.

"While I was at the studio, Monica introduced me to a family therapist named Sandy. Monica said she was top notch. I've decided to make an appointment. If she's helpful, I want Sunny to go and for you to consider it as well."

"I don't know about that. . . ."

"Ted . . . you're the one who pushed me to do the makeover, to come to dinner tonight. . . . I know you're doing this for my own good. You and Sunny need help, too. If this therapist is good, I'm going to be persistent on this."

"Okay, I get your point, but let's not get ahead of ourselves. You go, and let me know if she's any good. Then Sunny and I can make our decisions."

"Fair enough. We'll see what happens." Aleen picked up her glass to propose a toast. "Here's to new beginnings."

"To new beginnings," Ted echoed, clinking glasses with her.

chapter thirteen

Aleen

Driving to work, Aleen was thinking about the events of the last two days. The weekend went by so fast it was a blur, with the makeover and the Green Bay game at Ted's.

Sunny seemed to have a good time at her study group kick-off, and Aleen looked forward to learning more about these new friends. If they made her daughter happy, that was a really good thing.

Sunny found it difficult to relate to her high school friends in the same way since the accident. She'd been forced to grow up really fast as she faced the reality of living without Stu. Perhaps these kids from UCLA were a bit more mature and could be better sounding boards for her.

Ted, Sunny, and Aleen all enjoyed the game and the special dinner Aleen made. She wasn't near the fan Ted was, or Sunny, but it was fun to have a shared goal to support the team. It was icing on the cake that the Packers actually won.

She and Ted had a lovely dinner Saturday night. After settling down following Trish's visit to the table and their discussion on family counseling, the pair shared details of their makeover day and just laughed and laughed. They even had the waiter take a photo of them with their wine glasses raised. Maybe she would put it on Facebook.

Well, maybe not, she thought, as she didn't want others to think she and Ted were an item. They were just becoming closer and closer as they helped each other pull out of the haze they'd been in for the last trying months.

Aleen had checked Trish's online calendar and was glad there was time at the beginning of the day for the two of them to chat. She needed to tell her boss the story of her marriage breakup from her perspective before others offered up their versions. Once she did, Aleen knew Trish would fully understand the closeness she felt with Ted.

She got into the office before 7:30 a.m., and when she fired up her computer, she was surprised to see Trish was already in her office.

"Good morning," she said, sticking her head in to greet her boss.

"Good morning, to you," Trish replied. "I hope you had a wonderful weekend. It sure seemed like you were enjoying dinner Saturday."

"It was a fantastic, eventful weekend, thanks. I'm glad you're in early. I want to tell you a few things so you can hear it from me, rather than others around here," Aleen said, taking a serious tone.

"Please, come in. I actually hoped you would want to talk . . . and I brought you a latte." Trish pointed to the hot drink at the edge of her desk.

Aleen was so surprised; she'd never had a boss bring *her* a drink. "You're so thoughtful." She pulled the chair next to Trish's desk and sat down, looking her straight in the eyes. "I want you to know the whole story. Everything that happened. The whole truth . . ."

Trish stared at Aleen with keen interest. "Since this conversation will be personal in nature and difficult for you, I want you to know in advance that anything we discuss will be totally confidential. I will not repeat it or share details with anyone." She gazed at Aleen with great empathy, as she knew this topic was challenging for her new assistant.

"I appreciate that. So much of the story has been in the news, so you can even look it up. It's the personal details that are the most heartbreaking, that reveal the anguish of everyone involved. . . ." Aleen took a drink of her latte to give her a moment to gather herself before telling Trish what had happened to change so many lives.

She looked down at her hands to build her confidence. She'd never actually told the story to anyone from the very beginning to the bitter end.

"I'll start by describing the relationship my daughter, Sunny, had with Stu, the son of Ted, who you met Saturday, and Gerrie Hammand, who you will meet with this week . . ."

chapter fourteen

Stu

Stu made up his bed after Sunny left and could still smell her perfume on the sheets and on him. Wow, making love to Sunny had been so different than Rosie, the girl from camp. Maybe it was because he had more experience and he just loved Sunny so much.

As Stu thought about kissing her breasts, he felt the passion start to rise in him again.

"Whoa," he said to himself and decided to jump into the shower to cool down.

The water felt so good. Stu usually never took long showers because he was conscientious about saving water with the drought in California. He and his friends were concerned about the environment, so they didn't use plastic water bottles and tried to conserve energy whenever they could.

He laughed to himself. He thought he'd earned this long shower, just this once. It wasn't every day he made love to his girlfriend for the first time. He'd hoped it would be good, but he'd been a bit scared for Sunny, being a virgin.

It just couldn't have gone better, Stu thought, smiling to himself.

As he toweled off, he heard his cell phone ping, alerting him that he'd received a text.

Luv u.

Me 2, he answered Sunny.

U R my 1 and only. Stu chuckled, reading her text.

He threw on some jeans and a T-shirt and returned her text with four little hearts. He laughed to himself. *Do guys really send texts like that?*

Stu's phone pinged again, and he picked it up with a smile.

This text wasn't from Sunny, but his mom, asking if he was home. They would be getting back earlier than they thought. She said they were picking up Indian food and he should get everything ready.

Good thing Sunny and he had not waited—his parents might have come home in the middle of their lovemaking!

Stu sent a text to his mom and to Sunny to let her know he'd be offline for a while.

He wasn't sure why his mom was texting him. He told her earlier he would make sure he was around for dinner. *Strange.*

Stu went downstairs to get the table ready for dinner. He snickered, because he couldn't see his friends setting the table for their parents. He didn't think his friends did anything to help around their houses.

That was never an option for Stu. His parents made him do all kinds of things around the house. But he didn't mind; he often did chores with his dad. He'd learned so much from him— his mom, too, but she was busy with her job so often.

He heard the garage door open, so he knew his parents were home. His mom breezed in with the takeout. Stu noticed a false kind of cheeriness about her. She never acted this way.

His parents had picked up all his favorites: chicken tikka, saag paneer, raita, papadums, lime pickle, and garlic naan bread.

"Well, let's eat while it's still hot," Gerrie said as they sat down and passed around all the containers.

His dad still hadn't said very much, and he didn't open any wine to have with dinner, which he usually did. Both his mom and dad just had sparkling water.

Dinner went by quickly, with little conversation and Stu the only one really eating. His parents just picked at their food. After they were done, his mom took charge in putting away the leftovers and clearing the kitchen table. That was odd, too, since most of the time Stu and his dad did the cleanup.

"Stu," Gerrie said to her son seriously, "your dad and I want to talk to you."

"Okay," Stu said. "You both are acting kinda weird, so I can tell something's bothering you."

"Let's sit down in the family room," Gerrie suggested nervously.

When Stu, Ted, and Gerrie were all seated, they just looked at each other. The tension in the air was thick, and Stu didn't know what to think.

"Well, Geraldine, you start," Ted said, anger clear in his eyes. "You're the one who needs to tell him."

"What's going on?" Stu asked. "What's wrong?"

"Honey . . ." Gerrie started tentatively. "Your father and I are separating."

"What! Why?" Stu jumped up. "I don't understand."

"We've been growing apart for some time, and I believe this is the right thing for our family," Gerrie explained quietly.

"Dad, is this what you want? What's happened between you?" Stu looked at his father in disbelief.

"No, it's not what I want, son. Not at all." Ted stared directly at his wife.

"Then why, Mom? Why are you breaking up with Dad?" Stu glared at his mother, moving closer to her, desperate for answers.

"Tell him the truth, Geraldine. He can't hear it from someone else." Ted looked to his wife coldly.

"There is . . . someone else," Gerrie said. "I've fallen in love with someone else." She let her gaze fall to the ground, unable to face her son.

Silence blanketed the room for a few moments as the shocking news settled in.

"How could you do this to us? How could you betray your family like this? Don't you love Dad? Don't you love *me*?" Stu shouted.

"Of course I love you. I love you as much as ever, Stu. And I will always love your father," Gerrie said, looking up at her son and then her husband.

Ted colored red when his wife said she would always love him. There was so much he could say but wouldn't in front of his son. He wanted to hurt Gerrie as much as she'd hurt him, but he remained silent, as he saw Gerrie falling to pieces in front of both of them. She stood, trying to embrace Stu, but he pushed her away.

"Who is it? Who have you fallen in love with?" Stu confronted his mom. "Is it someone from work?"

"Yes," Gerrie said, trying to hold herself together.

"Oh, so all your sixty-hour work weeks and business trips were just a front for you to have your dirty little affair. While we were home, you were out there fucking your boyfriend." Stu was so angry now, pacing the room.

"Now, son . . ." Ted could see his son was losing control. Stu had never talked to his mother this way.

Gerrie went back to the couch, crying openly, covering her face with her hands.

"You don't get to cry. No! *You* broke your marriage vows. Who's the man that is ruining our lives? Tell me!" Stu loomed over his mother, demanding an answer.

Ted looked on, horrified, as he'd never, ever seen Stu like this. He was like a madman.

"Son, please—"Ted tried to calm him down.

"No, she started this, and she has to explain. I want to know. Answer me! Who is it?" Stu continued to shout, his face beet red.

Gerrie looked up at him, exhausted by the conversation and the damage that had been done. "It is Durk Riddick, Sunny's dad. As you know, we work together—"

"NO! Not Sunny's dad," Stu shouted, still standing over his mother. "How could you? I love Sunny. She is the best thing that ever happened to me, and you're going to destroy her family the same way you're destroying ours." He was crying now, red-faced.

"Stu . . ."Ted reached out to his son, tears running down his own cheeks.

"No, no . . . I can't stay here with *her*." Stu turned to face his mother again. "You are not my mother. My mother would never do this. I hate you. Don't you *ever* call me your son again."

With that, Stu darted out, and Ted rushed after him while Gerrie dropped to the floor, sobbing. Stu ran to the garage, grabbed his helmet, and jumped on his motorcycle, clicking open the garage door.

"Son, no, you're too upset. Please, come back!" Ted pleaded with his son.

Stu just looked at his father and then zoomed out of the garage and the driveway.

Speeding down the road on his cycle, Stu knew he was going way too fast. Tears burned his eyes. He was seeing red and couldn't get away fast enough. How could this be happening to his family? This was like something out of the movies. It couldn't be real. His dad, his poor dad. Damn his mother!

Stu's tears almost blinded him. He didn't see the stop sign as he whizzed by. He was heading to his friend Marty's house in that condo development right off the main road. Once he got there, he would call Sunny. He couldn't just head straight over to her house with the same chaos probably going on there.

Oh, God, Sunny!

He was sure she was getting the same news he just got.

He sped up and just caught a flash of light before he flew off his bike and onto the ground.

God, what is happening . . . ? It hurts so bad. . . . The pain, in my legs . . . arms. Oh, God, my chest. . . . I feel crushed. . . . Can't see. . . . Darkness, but there is some light. Different colors. Can't move.

Voices, what are they saying . . . ? I can't understand. . . . No, no. . . . What are you shouting? It hurts so much. I've never felt anything like this before. . . .

Sunny, Sunny. . . . It's so dark I can't see you, but I know you're here. . . . They're trying to move me. . . . I can hear you. Sunny!

That light is brighter now . . . but I feel like I'm fading, going to sleep. . . . No strength now. . . . The light again, so bright . . . Sunny!

Then nothing.

chapter fifteen

Sunny

Just over Three Months Earlier . . .

Sunny was in her room and could hear her parents in the kitchen, but in her mind, she was still with Stu in his bedroom. She was secretly still glowing from making love with him for the first time. God, she loved him so much. Could it have been more perfect? She smiled to herself, thinking back to their lovemaking session.

Closing her eyes, she pictured herself in Stu's room, on his bed. He spread himself on top of her and kissed her urgently. Pulling off his shirt, he reached under her T-shirt to unhook her bra and massage her breasts. Sunny slipped off her shirt and bra, and Stu hungrily kissed her breasts while she moaned with pleasure.

After she couldn't take it anymore, she pulled him up to kiss him and feel her flesh against his. He had shed his jeans, and she quickly pulled down his briefs to reveal just how excited he was. Stu helped her out of her shorts, and when he felt how ready she was for him, he gently pulled her close and parted her legs. He kissed her down there, and Sunny thought she would explode.

She pulled him up and kissed him passionately while guiding him into her. As he entered her gently, she felt white hot with pain and pleasure. Sunny clutched him to her as they made love.

"Stu, Stu," she shouted. "I love you so much," Sunny said breathlessly.

"Sunny, oh, God, Sunny," Stu whispered in her ear as his thrusts became more urgent. His body shuddered as he came and collapsed on top of her. "I love you, too, Sunny."

A knock on the door jarred Sunny back to reality as her dad asked her to come to the family room.

Something weird was happening. She hadn't been paying attention earlier, caught up in reliving the afternoon with Stu, but she could see it now. Her parents were really tense. Something was up. Something big.

"Your mother and I wanted to talk to you tonight about something important." Durk began.

"Okay, I'm listening." Sunny glanced at her dad and then her mom, trying to figure out what was going on.

Her father folded his hands together and then unfolded them again.

"Your mother and I are splitting up." Her dad said it quickly but firmly, with some authority, although he looked at his daughter with real concern.

"What? Why?" Sunny was stunned. "I had no idea anything was wrong. Don't you love us anymore?" Sunny couldn't believe what she'd just heard.

"Mom, do you want to divorce Dad? Can't you stop this?" Sunny turned her attention to her mom to try and get some answers.

"This is your father's decision, not mine," Aleen said, trying valiantly to stay in control.

"Did we do something wrong? Why would you want to leave?" Sunny faced her father, tears of disbelief running down her cheeks.

Durk cast his eyes down at the carpet for a moment, as he had trouble bringing himself to look in his daughter's eyes. "Sunny, of course you didn't do anything wrong. Your mother will always be special to me, but . . . but there is someone else, and I've fallen in love with her. I'm sorry, sweetheart." He finally looked up at his daughter, hoping for an ounce of understanding.

"Dad . . . how could you do that?!" Sunny spat the words at her father. "How could you do that to *us?*"

"Honey . . ." Aleen wanted to reach out and hug Sunny even as she was trying to deal with her own agony.

Sunny turned her attention back to her father. "I guess you love your new girlfriend a lot more than you love us."

"No, I love you so much, Sunny. You're my daughter." Durk's eyes were pleading with her now.

"I don't understand. I will *never* understand," Sunny cried as she walked over to the picture window, hugging herself while she sobbed.

Durk got up and grabbed her to face her straight on. "Sunny, you need to know something else. I'm sorry, but the woman I love is Gerrie, Stu's mother."

Without thought, Sunny slapped her father, leaving an angry red mark on his face. "No, you can't be with her. I love Stu, and the two of you are wrecking our lives. How could you do this? How!?"

She ran now and picked up her mom's keys from the counter. She had to see Stu. He would be suffering so much when he heard this news. Sunny had to get to him.

Her mother called after her, and her father was right behind her, but all Sunny could think of at the moment was getting to Stu. She got to the van and screamed out of the driveway before her dad could catch her.

As she turned out onto the boulevard, she could see flashing lights, police cars, and ambulances, so she had to slow down. When she stopped, she saw a helmet on the pavement. It looked like Stu's, and then she saw a motorcycle in the road. . . .

"NO!," she screamed out loud as she haphazardly parked the car and ran toward the flashing lights. She could see the paramedics doing compressions on someone. As she got closer, she could see it was Stu, and she called out, "Stu . . . Stu . . . I'm here!" She could see a plastic thing over his mouth to help him breathe.

A number of folks had gathered, and they grabbed her and stopped her before she got to him. "That's my boyfriend. Let me through. Let me through!"

An older couple out for an evening walk with their dog latched onto Sunny so she couldn't get any closer. "You have to let the medical people help him now, sweetheart. Stay here. Stay right here," the older woman said, holding Sunny's arm.

She grabbed her phone from her pocket and dialed home. "Mom, there's been an accident on the main road. It's Stu. Call his parents, and please come now!"

Sunny hung up, not waiting for her mom's answer. The paramedics had the paddles out now, and she could see them move away as one of them shouted, "Clear." They stood back as the shock was administered and Stu's body jumped up.

"Again. Clear." Stu was shocked again. And then again.

Nothing.

Sunny was hysterical and called out to him again and again. "Stu, I'm here. Please come back to me. Stu! Please!"

She could see the paramedics shake their heads and move away. There was so much blood. Sunny broke away from the people trying to hold her back. She ran over to Stu, but the paramedics stopped her just short of him.

"Honey, I am so sorry. We tried everything, but he was too far gone."

Sunny threw herself at the paramedic, screaming, "No, no, it's not possible. I love him. No, it can't be true!" She was inconsolable.

The paramedic closest to her took her in his arms and let her wail. He was a big man, African-American, with large brown eyes that were moist with tears as he held Sunny, crying and screaming.

"I need to see him. I have to see him. He can't be dead. He can't!" Sunny screamed and pounded her fists on the paramedic.

Her parents were working their way through the bystanders to get to Sunny as the paramedic continued to try to calm her down.

"Let it out, hon. Let it out." The man tried to comfort her as the other paramedic used a sheet to shield Stu's body. Unfortunately, the crew had a great deal of experience with death and grief. Too much, really. But when it was someone this young, with so much ahead of him, it was just so hard, and to have his girlfriend see him die . . .

Sunny's mom peeled her away. "I'm her mother," Aleen told the paramedic as she took Sunny in her arms.

"Mom, oh my God. He can't be dead. He can't," Sunny screamed as her mother held on to her tightly.

Just then, Gerrie and Ted ran up. They couldn't believe what they just heard.

Ted grabbed the paramedic. "We're his parents."

The paramedic shook his head slowly.

They both started to cry, and Durk moved over to them. "I am so, so sorry for you both." He looked at them with tears in his eyes.

Sunny broke away from Aleen and stood before Durk and Gerrie.

"*You* killed him. You two killed Stu!" she screamed at her

father and Gerrie and tried to hit them both with her fists, until Ted and Aleen pulled her away as the stunned bystanders looked on.

Gerrie was on the ground, sobbing, and Durk tried to comfort her. Aleen had pulled Sunny to the side and tried to console her, but she continued to shake and cry uncontrollably.

Ted went over to his son's body, but the paramedic stopped him. "Sir, I'm not sure you want to see him like this."

"It's my son. I have to see him. I have to say goodbye."

The paramedic moved the sheet just a little, and Ted kissed the top of Stu's head.

He collapsed into the grass, sobbing, as the lights flashed and the small crowd stood horrified but unable to help the grieving parents and the young girl who still was crying and quaking in her mother's arms.

chapter sixteen

Aleen

Trish sat stunned, staring at Aleen as she finished telling the story of Stu's death and the breakup of her marriage. "Oh my gosh, Aleen, I am so sorry. I understand now why you worry so much about your daughter and how awful it's been for you as well." She snatched a tissue to wipe her eyes.

"Yes, to say it's been the worst time of my life is a real understatement," Aleen agreed. "Yet I think all the time how horrible it is for Ted. Stu was such a great kid, and they were so close. When I think about what it would be like to lose Sunny . . ." She couldn't finish the sentence and shuddered at the thought. "There's no question in my mind if I had to give my life for my child, there would be no choice at all. I'd sacrifice myself in a second to save Sunny," Aleen said. "I know Durk would, too.

"Ted would do the same if he could bring Stu back. He puts up a good front, but he's crushed inside. To lose his son and his marriage . . . it's more than one person should have to handle. That's why Sunny and I have become so close to him.

"We can discuss everything. Lately, we've been able to talk even more honestly with each other. Sunny, too. She loves Ted;

he's like a second father to her. She barely speaks to her own dad." Aleen dabbed at her eyes with her own tissue.

The two women sat silently for a minute, emotion hanging heavy in the air.

"I can't imagine what you're going through," Trish said, touching Aleen's arm. "You're trying to help Sunny and Ted with their grief and anger, when you have your own to contend with."

Aleen nodded and ran her hand through her hair.

"I think your idea of counseling is the right way to go. You take the time you need, even if you have to do it during working hours."

What a fabulous boss she had.

"Thanks, Trish. I'm starting Pilates as well," Aleen said. "I need to get in shape."

"Do what you need to do for yourself. I mean it." Trish pointed at her. "Now go call about the counseling appointment."

Aleen nodded and stood to return to her desk. Just before she left Trish's office, she swung around. "Thank you for being so understanding. I . . ."

Trish waved her off. There was no need to say anything more.

Taking Sandy's card out of her wallet, Aleen turned it over and over before dialing the number. With an unsteady voice, she asked for an appointment. She was shocked when the receptionist told her they just had a cancellation for 4:00 p.m. and she could come in right away.

Aleen put the call on hold to ask her boss if that would be all right.

"It is perfectly fine. You take that appointment right now before somebody else snatches it up," Trish said, pleased her assistant was taking this important step.

When she hung up the phone, Aleen continued to grasp the receiver tightly for a few seconds, hanging on for dear life.

chapter seventeen

Sunny

After checking the traffic before leaving home, Sunny ended up taking the Pacific Coast Highway, as there was a terrible accident on I-405 that wouldn't be cleared for a very long time. The accident was just after the junction with Highway 101, and traffic was clogged for miles.

The good news was PCH was a much nicer way to go. Driving through Malibu Canyon and along the ocean was stunningly beautiful. The bad news was it would probably take at least an hour and a half or longer, as many drivers would be making the same route change.

She laughed, remembering a funny comedy sketch on television where the people were always talking about the traffic in LA and which roads they should take in these unbelievable "Valley Girl" accents. Now that she was driving every day in the LA traffic, Sunny sure understood that sketch so much better!

There was always something going on during her daily drive. The things she saw: people eating breakfast, women doing their makeup, people yelling at each other in heated arguments, a man reading a book while traffic was stopped dead, people texting and talking on their phones—which was illegal! Sunny had become a real LA driver, and the long commutes always gave her lessons in what *not* to do while driving and time to think about so many things.

It had been a good weekend. She hadn't been able to say that for a long time. Thinking about her mom and Ted and the makeovers, Sunny giggled out loud. They both looked so fantastic. It was good to see them both have fun and talk about how they learned so much while going through their makeovers.

Sunny enjoyed taking care of Hope and Cash on Saturday, and the dogs seemed to love their long walk by the lake. Maybe she could borrow the dogs again; they made her laugh every time she saw them. It was fun she got to visit them again on Sundays when she and her mom went over for the games. The Packers won again this week, and her mom made a fab dinner with chicken, vegetables, and rice. Mr. Hammand seemed to like it, going back for seconds.

The photo the waiter took of her mom and Mr. Hammand at their dinner was so good; they sure made a good-looking couple. But they kept telling her they weren't an item. Still, Sunny wasn't so sure.

The get-together with her study group Saturday night was excellent. The five of them really seemed to get along well—there were three guys and two women, counting Sunny. All appeared to be serious students and interested in doing well in engineering school. They exchanged contact information so they could email, call, or text any questions to each other.

Sunny wondered if they could be friends outside of class. She really needed someone her age to talk to about everything. She couldn't talk to any high school friends. They knew Stu, too, and would break down crying every time she tried. That just didn't help.

Her mom told her about setting up the appointment with

the family therapist. Sunny didn't need to make a decision yet, as her mom had to see her first. It probably was the right thing to do.

Neither her mom nor Sunny was sure Ted would want to see a female counselor. He still was so angry with Stu's mom. Who knew if he'd agree to see her?

Of the students in her engineering group, Sunny thought Dawn and Benjamin might be the best bets to be friends outside of class. Luckily, Dawn lived in Calabasas, which was only about twenty minutes away. She was really smart, serious about her engineering education, and had a great sense of humor.

Benjamin was living in the dorms, so that wasn't convenient for getting together. Sunny shook her head. There was no way she could spend time alone with him. While she thought he was cute, Sunny wasn't ready for any kind of relationship, and if she suggested getting together, he might get the wrong idea. She did kind of think he liked her. She'd caught him looking over at her a couple times the other night.

She wouldn't encourage him, as she was far from ready to think about anyone other than Stu. Sunny still loved him so much and ached for his touch.

How could she ever go on without him? Sometimes the pain was just too much, and Sunny did find herself during her worst moments thinking about a way she could end it all. . . . But she couldn't do that to her parents and Mr. Hammand.

She saw the agony Stu's death had caused. Her parents and Mr. Hammand literally couldn't take it if Sunny were to die, too. No, that wouldn't be what Stu would want, either. She knew that.

Pulling into the parking structure was actually a relief; she needed to get her mind off of death and dying. School helped her push the agony she felt over losing Stu to the background, until it surfaced again, gnawing at her heart.

chapter eighteen

Gerrie

There would be no façade today, no way to fake it through the next meeting. Gerrie looked out the window at the stunning view of the mountains. No, she was going to play it straight with Trish Rendoven in their first one-on-one meeting. Sure, she had met her before, as they were both on the CEO's staff, but that was formal, with lots of others around.

Today, it would be just the two of them for the first time. It was good to have another woman on the team, but as Aleen worked for Trish . . .

She would most certainly know the whole story about Durk and Gerrie and her breakup with Ted. And of course, her son's death.

God, how she'd loved Stu. . . .She would never get over it, ever. She thought of him every day; he filled her thoughts constantly.

Sunny's words from that night were seared into her brain. *"You killed him. You two killed Stu."* Gerrie couldn't disagree. She had the affair with Durk, and it was her admission that made Stu rush out into the night, blinded by hurt and rage. And then . . . he was dead. She didn't need anyone to tell her; she knew her son's death was her fault.

She and Ted had stayed together in the house until after the funeral. They were both just numb. He stayed in the spare bedroom, and they kept their communications focused on the services for Stu. There were just too many things they needed to do together as a couple. They agreed that once the funeral was over, they would separate. Gerrie would stay in the house, and Ted would find some accommodation nearby.

She wanted so desperately to reach out to Ted, to hold him and grieve for their son, but she didn't. She just couldn't with that cold look in his eyes. Gerrie couldn't blame Ted. *She* was the one who caused Stu's death.

Durk had to leave his home immediately after the accident, and he moved into one of those long-stay hotels. Gerrie didn't see him again until the funeral. He came on his own, and Sunny and Aleen stayed far away from him, as did Ted. It was awful.

Ted's family came in from Wisconsin but wouldn't really speak to her very much, other than to tell her how sorry they were for Stu's death. The anger in their eyes made it clear they held her responsible. But truly, no one could make it worse. She lost her son, and it was her fault. As she was an only child and her parents were dead, Gerrie was truly on her own now.

Stu's friends gave her the cold shoulder as well. Their condolences felt forced and hard-edged. They blamed her, too.

Durk was the only one she could talk to about everything. After a period of time, he moved into the house with her. They told Ted and Aleen, but what could they say? Of course they didn't like it, but Durk and Gerrie needed each other.

Thank God Gerrie had her job. She always worked long hours, but now she truly buried herself in her work.

Everyone at the company knew what had happened. They all expressed their sorrow at Stu's death, but she could see in their eyes the distance, the disdain. Her son rushed out after he heard of his mother's affair with his girlfriend's father, and he was killed. The facts could not be denied.

If her son could be alive again, Gerrie would take it all back, the affair, everything. It killed her to see Ted torn apart, too. He was a good man who didn't deserve the hand he was dealt. Of course she knew he would be devastated by the divorce, but she never dreamed they would lose Stu as well. Now Ted was a broken man. Another burden upon her shoulders.

That's the thing about life, isn't it? It throws everything at you—love, passion, warmth, pain, resentment, joy, tragedy. . . . Gerrie couldn't feel anything at all now. She crawled into her protective shell and became the person everyone expected—the high-level, confident corporate executive, jetting around the world. *What a joke.*

The truth was she, too, was a broken woman, hanging on by a thread. Somehow, she knew Trish would see through her façade, so she wouldn't try to pretend she was all right.

Just then, her assistant, Penny, interrupted her thoughts, bringing Trish into her office.

"Can I get you anything?" Penny asked as Trish walked in.

"You know, I would love a cup of tea, English style with milk and sugar."

Gerrie looked up at Trish and smiled. "That sounds perfect. Penny, I'll have the same, thanks."

Trish took a seat at Gerrie's desk, directly across from her. "I'm very glad we have this time together," she said, looking her directly in the eyes.

"I am, too, Trish, as I hope we can have a good relationship, particularly as the only women on Don's staff," Gerrie replied sincerely.

"I see no reason why we can't have an excellent relationship."

Penny came in and brought them both the tea, setting down the steaming mugs right in front of them.

"Thanks so much," Gerrie said politely.

After Penny exited and closed the door, Gerrie looked back to Trish. "There is a reason we may not be able to have a good relationship, and I want to put it on the table right now."

Now it's getting interesting, Trish thought.

chapter nineteen

Aleen

As she drove over to meet with Sandy, the family therapist, Aleen felt nervous. She just hated talking about herself and her feelings, preferring to focus on others. She still had a bad taste in her mouth about counseling after meeting with that other guy. *What was his name . . . ? Samuel.*

Hopefully, it would be different with Sandy, as she certainly seemed to be caring and empathetic when they met at the Pilates class. She was surprised she hadn't run into Sandy again, as Aleen was religious about going to the class three times a week, as promised. She was proud of herself, really, as she looked and felt so much better.

When she walked into the receptionist area, she found it much different than a doctor's waiting area. She signed in, but no one else was in the room. At the appointed time, Aleen was buzzed in. *Privacy,* she thought. *Good idea.*

Sandy's office had a relaxed feel, with a series of comfy couches and funky lamps. The light was actually low, as bulky, thick curtains covered the windows and plush carpets blanketed the floor. Aleen guessed she was trying to create a kind of welcoming and comfortable atmosphere to help her patients open up. So far so good.

She was also glad the counseling was covered by her company's insurance. Aleen's budget did not have any room for extras at the moment.

Sandy was talking to someone on the other side of the door. It sounded like she said goodbye, and then she opened the door and came into the office to greet Aleen. "I'm so glad you decided to set up an appointment," she said. "I'm sure it wasn't an easy decision."

Aleen looked at Sandy intently. "No, it wasn't. Both Sunny and I know we need help, but we've been reluctant to take the first step again after our bad counseling experience."

"Well, let's get started. I'm here to talk about whatever you want to talk about."

"That's the problem." Aleen cast her gaze down at the colorful oriental rug, "I really hate talking about myself. It's much easier for me to discuss my daughter or, in the past, my husband."

"While I totally understand that, today is about you: your feelings, your concerns, your fears, and your hopes for the future." She got up to offer Aleen a glass of water.

She grabbed it and gulped down a few mouthfuls. This wasn't going to be easy.

Aleen walked over to the curtained windows, the heavy drapes pulled shut to provide privacy. She stared at the folds in the velvety material cascading down to the carpet and then touched them lightly.

"My feelings . . . I guess I try not to have feelings. I'm just . . . numb. One day, I have a fantastic and successful husband, who I love very much and believe loves me. The next day, he tells me he's leaving me because he's in love with his daughter's boyfriend's mother."

Aleen walked back over to the couch and sat down, tracing the pattern in the rug with her eyes once more. Reliving that painful time was like a punch to the gut.

She cleared her throat to continue. "Hearing the news, our daughter flips out, as does her boyfriend, Stu, and he runs out in a rage, goes through a stop sign on his motorcycle, and is killed. My daughter, Sunny, comes on the scene as he is dying and watches the whole horrifying thing.

"When his parents, Ted and Gerrie, arrive to find their son dead, our daughter shouts at her dad and Stu's mom, screaming that they killed him. Sunny was desperately trying to hit them, but we were able to restrain her." Aleen pauses to gather herself, wiping at her eyes with a tissue.

"I'm so sorry, Aleen. I know how difficult it is for you to talk about all of this," Sandy says gently.

Aleen shook her head at the very unpleasant memory and took a minute to compose herself.

"It must have been awful for all of you, Aleen," Sandy said, trying to comfort her.

"Yes. We have lived through a nightmare that we could have never imagined possible." There was no hiding the pain in Aleen's eyes as she looked at her counselor, who nodded so she would finish her story.

"Sunny was almost catatonic for the first month or so. My husband and I separated immediately. Stu's parents stayed in the same house in separate bedrooms through the funeral and then split. The adulterous couple live together now, and Sunny rarely speaks to her father."

Sandy looked at Aleen intently. "And what about you?"

"I plod on with anger and doubt . . . and pain that feels like a knife through my heart. I go on because of my daughter; she is the center of everything for me. To have seen and experienced what she has in her young life . . ." Aleen grabbed another tissue before taking a sip of her water.

"Take your time," Sandy told her client.

"As hard as I try not to, I cry for Sunny and Stu almost every day. And I wish my husband hadn't left. I rack my brains about what I could have done differently to have stopped all of this from happening.

"Why did Durk leave me? Was I unattractive to him? I had put on a few pounds and didn't dress like a million bucks. Should we have had sex more often? Is that why he strayed? Was I just so uninteresting to him—a boring glorified secretary?" Aleen covered her face with her hands. "If Durk didn't leave me, Stu would still be alive!"

Sandy gave Aleen another tissue from one of the many boxes situated around the room. "You may never understand why this happened, but it isn't helpful for you to try and find fault with yourself."

"Easier said than done, for sure. . . . I believe women, more often than men, look to find blame in themselves in situations like this, as wrong as that may be. What did *I* do . . . ?" Aleen asked without finishing her thought.

"I'm not saying it's the right thing to do, but you are correct that many women do just that," Sandy answered.

"Sunny and I have been doing a bit better lately, though; I can feel it. We've spent time with Ted and talked openly about our feelings, which I believe has helped all three of us. There's a positive for you." Aleen tried to brighten a bit.

"That's good, Aleen. Very good," Sandy said, trying to encourage her. "Can you think of another positive thing?"

"Ted suggested we do makeovers, and we both did. That's when you and I met at the Pilates studio. If I'm honest, the makeover and the exercise have done wonders for me.

"Ted also got these great corgi dogs, Hope and Cash, and they've been a godsend in lifting his mood. We just love those dogs, too."

"Do you see Ted and the dogs often?" Sandy asked, studying her.

"We have lately, and it's been fun. Ted and I have an easy rapport and can talk about anything, including our marriages and children. It's hard to do that with anybody else. As Ted would say, people walk on eggshells around us because of what happened. He also despises the pity he sees in people's eyes." Aleen put the tissue in her pocket.

"When Ted and you are together, what do you enjoy doing?"

"Well, we watch the Green Bay Packers on Sundays." She smiled at the therapist, as she knew this would surprise her.

"I guess that isn't what I thought you would say." Sandy chuckled.

"Ted is from Wisconsin and is a lifelong fan. Stu inherited his dad's love for the team and brought Sunny into the fold. I didn't think I could be a football fan, but I am. I've learned more about the games, and I've been cooking dinner or lunch afterward, so we all sit down, share a meal, and rehash the game."

Sandy was pleased Aleen was actually animated and enthusiastic when she talked about the games and the time with Ted and Sunny.

"I love to cook but really got away from it after the accident and when Durk left. Sunny never seemed to have an appetite, and I just couldn't find the energy to cook for just me. It was a really unhealthy time for us.

"That's why the games are so much fun. We get out of the house, always have a good meal, and laugh and enjoy each other's company. And the Packers are having a really good season so far." Aleen surprised herself with a laugh.

"That's wonderful, Aleen. It sounds like the games have been a help for all of you."

"While I agree with you, there are always reminders of our

sorrow, but sometimes that isn't a bad thing. For example, Ted saved Stu's favorite Packers T-shirt for Sunny, and she wears it on game day. That shirt is the way we keep Stu with us. . . . It's not really a downer, if you know what I mean. It's more like a positive way to remember him."

Sandy nodded. "It's helpful to have good memories of Stu that don't always bring on the grief and pain. That's actually healthy."

"Stu was such a remarkable young man; we will never forget him." Aleen folded her hands in her lap.

"I think perhaps you don't give yourself enough credit for making some progress in moving past your anger and grief," Sandy said sincerely.

Aleen took another drink of water; talking about her feelings seemed to leave her throat very dry. "Well, I'm glad it sounds that way, but I can tell you, when I'm alone in bed at night, I cry out for my husband and my marriage, and I dream of my daughter happy and Stu still alive. . . . So I may not be moving forward as much as you think."

"I understand," Sandy said quietly. "I do understand."

chapter twenty

Ted

As he leashed up the dogs to get them ready for their morning walk, Ted felt a bit uneasy. Time was marching on, and he knew the divorce papers would be signed any day now. It had been six months since the accident when his world was shattered to pieces. God, how he missed his son and his marriage.

He longed for the intimacy, too. Ted thought he should have known something was wrong when their sex life changed and their lovemaking sessions dwindled. Gerrie and he had always had a wonderful sex life prior to that, and Ted wrongly surmised his wife was just overworked and overtired.

It was another beautiful day in Southern California, and Hope and Cash were their usual selves, sniffing and chewing on anything they could find on the ground. Ted was constantly making them stop and spit out any awful thing they found in the grass.

Eventually, his mind wandered back to sex. What to do? The idea of dating was so unappealing to him. Just then, another dog got free of his leash and ran toward Hope and Cash. All three were barking and jumping around. What a ruckus!

When the woman was able to get her dog under control, she

apologized and was off. Maybe he would meet someone walking the dogs, Ted thought before dismissing the idea. "Probably not," he said to himself.

Hope and Cash kept looking back at the woman's pup longingly, and Ted shouted, "Forget about it, guys. Keep your eyes straight ahead."

What characters they were. He was so glad he had the dogs; they did the funniest things.

As he walked along, Ted's good mood soured when he thought about the one-year anniversary of Stu's death coming up. Thinking about the day terrified him, as he knew he would relive every agonizing moment. He was glad he'd set up an appointment with Sandy to try to talk through it.

Well, on a more positive note, Ted was looking forward to his lunch with Vincent; it would be good to see how he was doing. Hopefully, he wasn't blaming himself as much about the accident. Perhaps counseling would help him, too.

Ted hurried the dogs along, as he needed to get back and complete some important work assignments before his lunch with Vincent and counseling appointment with Sandy.

Later, when he walked over to the restaurant, he saw Vincent was already there and had snagged a great table outside.

"Lunch al fresco sounds like an excellent idea." Ted shook Vincent's hand in greeting.

"I thought so, too. How are you?" Vincent looked at his new friend with keen interest.

"Okay. Making progress, I guess, but I find myself missing my marriage and intimacy today." Ted got right to the heart of his feelings.

Vincent nodded sadly.

"I hope I'm not being too direct." He looked at Vincent with some concern, as this was a pretty personal conversation to have, particularly with someone he didn't know well. But Vincent and he had a unique and personal connection because of Stu's death, and Ted felt he didn't need to pull any punches with him.

"Not at all. I'm actually glad you brought it up, because I'm having the same feelings. My partner and I have been on our 'break' for months now." Vincent took a sip of water that the waiter had just given to them.

"Have you talked to him lately? Any new developments?" Ted asked his new friend.

"Well, I have been thinking about some things lately that I've never really articulated before. It's scary to say out loud . . ." Vincent was struggling to get the words out.

"Just say it, Vincent. It's no help to you to hold it in. I speak from experience," Ted said.

"I deserve better. When you love someone, you support them, and Derek hasn't even tried. We've been together four years. After the accident, he pulled away from me, didn't try to comfort me. It was like I was damaged goods. I needed him so much then. I was dying inside, blaming myself for your son's death."

Ted patted Vincent's arm. "Vincent, we know it was an accident. It wasn't your fault; you must know that now."

"I'm getting there . . . frankly, by getting to know you. You've helped me tremendously. So much more than Derek."

Ted looked at his friend with concern. "I'm glad I've helped. You're probably right about Derek. If he wasn't there for you with the first sign of adversity, perhaps the break is a good thing.

"You are right that you deserve better. You do," Ted said confidently.

"It's a hard thing to face, but I do believe it's the right decision for me. I need to think through the next steps, which will be difficult . . ." Vincent couldn't finish his thought.

"Perhaps you should consider counseling. I have my first appointment today, this afternoon, after our lunch. I'm steeling myself for the divorce. It'll be final soon," Ted said, his voice dropping to a whisper.

"Oh, so sorry, Ted. I know signing those papers will make you very sad." Vincent put his hand on his shoulder to comfort him just as some birds landed on the table next to them, stealing some leftover food. "And in a few months . . ."

The men looked at each other and nodded. They both dreaded facing the anniversary of Stu's death.

"You may be right about the counseling. I need to build up my courage to have the conversation with Derek, but in so many ways, I think he's moved on, even though that's not what he says to me."

Ted nodded just as the waiter came to let them know about the specials. After ordering, he looked around at the beautiful blue sky, the fountain with the sleek waterfall, and the vibrant flowers in planters next to him. At that moment, he felt hopeful for the future for his friend and himself, even with the difficult moments ahead.

"I'll see how it goes for me today with the counselor. If I feel she's helpful, I'll pass along her contact info," Ted told Vincent.

"You're a good friend, Ted. Ironically, you're the only person who truly understands how I feel."

There was nothing he needed to say to Vincent, as he agreed with his friend. He glanced around at the people at the tables outside, laughing and enjoying their food and conversations. He ventured a guess that no one sitting around them would deduce the tragedy that brought them together and bonded the two in friendship. It was too incredible to believe.

Life sure had unpredictable twists and turns.

chapter twenty-one

Sunny

As Sunny and the other students filtered out of her engineering class, Benjamin was at her elbow.

"Hey," he said. "Would you like to grab a drink at Starbucks?"

Sunny eyed him warily, just as Dawn joined them.

"Got to run, guys. And, oh, can't wait to see you tonight, Sunny," Dawn said, rushing off to her next class.

"Looking forward to it," Sunny called after her friend.

"So you guys are getting together?" Benjamin looked at her, a bit confused. "You're not having a mini study group, are you?"

"Not really. Dawn lives about twenty or so minutes from me, and I wanted to get to know her better. The plan was for it to be more social, just girls chatting." Sunny glanced at Benjamin. He almost seemed put off or jealous he wasn't invited.

"Well, let's head over to the Starbucks, and maybe *we* can have a more personal, social conversation," Benjamin suggested, looking at her hopefully.

"Okay . . . but I'm not sure how personal it will be." Sunny stiffened.

When Sunny was driving over to Dawn's house much later, she felt really stupid. She'd been terrible to Benjamin while they had their drinks. He was just trying to be friendly, and she wouldn't give him an inch. She just didn't want him to think she was interested in him.

She wasn't ready to date anyone, and she didn't want to mess up the relationship with Benjamin because the study group was working really, really well. He was so smart and a great help to everyone.

Instead of making friendly talk with him, Sunny froze up. She could tell he thought something was wrong with her.

Could she do anything right? When she was with Stu, everything was right. *Now everything is wrong.*

Oh, she was so mad at herself! Sunny pounded her fists on her legs, trying to cause some pain.

As she pulled into the driveway at Dawn's house, she tried to calm herself. Perhaps her new friend could help her figure out how to make things right.

Dawn's house was impressive from the outside. The homes in Calabasas could be very grand, and this one was a large, Mediterranean style with beautiful landscaping and what looked to be a fabulous pool area out back. When Dawn answered the door and led her in, they passed a spectacular spiral staircase that overlooked the living and dining rooms.

The room was huge, with very contemporary, lighter-colored furniture and a coordinating dining room set. Walking behind her, Sunny was reminded Dawn was a beautiful girl. She had flawless tan skin and the most amazing brown-green eyes. She was tall, about five feet eight, with long legs and a fantastic figure. Her dark hair was tied up in an attractive bun.

"Come and meet my parents," Dawn said, taking her in the kitchen. Her mom and dad were just getting everything in order after dinner. Once she saw her mother and father, Sunny understood why Dawn was so stunning.

Dawn's dad was tall, well over six feet, and he was very handsome and incredibly fit. He was African-American with close-cropped hair and an extremely warm smile. He had on his workout clothes, as he must have done some exercising when he got home from work. Mr. Pircell was a lawyer in one of the top LA firms.

Dawn's mom was petite, perhaps five feet four, with long, sandy hair and sparkling blue eyes. She worked at a local high school with kids with special needs. They also had a son, Jeremy, who was away at college, hoping to be a lawyer just like his dad.

"So nice to meet you," Mrs. Pircell said, shaking Sunny's hand.

Mr. Pircell came up to her and hugged her. "Any friend of my daughter gets a hug." He laughed, first looking at Sunny and then his daughter.

"Boy, I needed that hug!" Sunny laughed, too. "Thanks for letting me hang out here."

"Not a problem," he answered. "Dawn's friends are always welcome in our home. You two have better things to do than hang out with the old folks, so you're free to head upstairs and do what you want." Mr. Pircell smiled as he shooed them off.

With that, Sunny and Dawn went up the spiral staircase to a large open area just off the foyer that was set up as a game room. There was a big television, a pool table, and a large, built-in cabinet that looked to have lots of other fun things waiting inside.

Sunny went over and sat on the couch and got right to the point. "I need your help," she told her friend seriously.

"I had this feeling you wanted to talk about something." Dawn sat next to her.

"Not sure where to start," Sunny said, scrunching up her forehead, trying to figure out how much of the story to tell.

"Wherever," Dawn said, looking squarely at her friend.

"Well, first of all, you have to help me with Benjamin. I went to Starbucks today with him, and I was a real brat. Didn't treat him well at all."

"Why?" Dawn seemed confused. "He likes you a lot. I can tell you that."

"That's exactly why!" Sunny shot up, pacing over to the window that looked out on the pristine valley and other beautiful houses dotting the hillside.

"You're not making sense," Dawn said. "Can you help me out here?"

"I'm just not ready for anyone to 'like' me." She came back to sit on the couch next to her friend and dropped her face in her hands.

"Please tell me, Sunny." Her look of concern was growing.

"Stu was my boyfriend. I loved him so much. We made love for the first time last June, and it was perfect. He was perfect. That same night, we both found out our parents were having an affair that was breaking up both families." The words came pouring out of Sunny, and she couldn't stop, even though this was an extremely difficult story for her to tell, and Dawn had a look of shock on her face.

"After his mom told him she was leaving his dad, Stu flipped out. Ran out on his motorcycle and was so upset he went through a stop sign and was hit by a car. I was upset, too, and ran out of the house, driving up just in time to find Stu on the ground, dying. I watched him die, Dawn. I watched Stu die!"

Dawn put her arms around her friend, and they rocked back and forth as Sunny cried on her shoulder.

"Oh my God. I am so, so sorry." Dawn kept her arm around her friend. "I knew there was something bothering you, but I had no idea."

"Nothing has been the same since that day. Nothing." Sunny

took a tissue from her pocket to dry her tears. "That's why I was so bad to Benjamin." She looked at Dawn with tears still streaming down her face, despite her best efforts to try and regain her composure. "He is a great guy, but I'm just not ready for a relationship. I still love Stu." Sunny stared down at her feet. "But how do I make it up to Ben?"

Dawn reached over and grabbed some more tissues from the side table. "Don't worry about Benjamin. I'm sure he'll understand. I'll talk to him. Everything will be all right."

Sunny sat up straight and stared into her friend's eyes. "But, Dawn, that's just it. I know everything won't be all right. Ever again."

chapter twenty-two

Durk

Durk took a detour driving home from work to stop by his old home, the one he'd shared with Aleen and Sunny. *Such a great house*, he thought, stopping at the curb for a minute. While Gerrie's house was much grander, it just wasn't as magical as the bungalow Aleen and he bought and then fixed up themselves.

He loved Gerrie, but Durk couldn't fool himself into thinking he didn't miss his old life. If they could all return to the way it was and bring Stu back, they would in a minute. Losing him was horrible, and it took his daughter away from him, too.

Check that, Durk thought. *I caused the split with my daughter by having an affair with Stu's mother. And I contributed to his death.* He shook his head. As Sunny had said, *"You two killed him."*

She was right. The guilt Gerrie and Durk felt was like iron weights, dragging them down the same as Marley's chains. Doomed to carry around this burden of their own creation the rest of their lives, Gerrie and Durk clung to each other and their shared misery.

Time had marched on, and it was about six months from the time Stu was killed. The divorces would be final soon. Gerrie and Durk would get married; they were all each of them had left.

His daughter would never attend, so Gerrie and Durk would just elope. Not very romantic, but their lives had little romance.

They had sex, yes, and it was good, but it was almost brutal, like two people trying to hurt each other. Maybe they were. Part of him felt he needed to punish himself for having sex with Gerrie, particularly after everything that had happened. She probably felt the same.

They both traveled and worked so much that they didn't see each other every day. In addition to domestic travel, they both had international trips that could take them away weeks at a time.

When they were home, Gerrie liked to go out or get takeout, as she hated to cook, and he was awful in that department. He sure missed Aleen's cooking and the way she'd cared for him. She nurtured people, and Sunny and Durk had been spoiled. He wasn't sure "nurture" was even a word in Gerrie's vocabulary.

Durk found himself stealing glances at Aleen at work over the last few months, as he had heard through the grapevine and then from Sunny about her makeover. She looked fantastic.

He guessed Sunny was talking to him a bit more so he wouldn't bug Aleen. He could see the hurt in his daughter's eyes when she agreed to get together, and he wanted to kick himself. The disruption the affair had caused wasn't worth the pain and suffering it had inflicted on both families. Life was very tough now . . . and lonely.

Durk had lapped up the details of Aleen's makeover from his daughter. He didn't know it had been Ted's idea. He wondered if they were an item. It wasn't his business if they were, but it nagged at him. He was actually jealous!

His soon-to-be ex-wife seemed to be doing well and moving on with her life. She got in shape by doing Pilates and seemed to really enjoy it, according to Sunny. Aleen also returned to counseling, as she found someone better suited to help her on the second try. She'd convinced Sunny to go for sessions with this new counselor, Sandy, as well. Good for her. Aleen needed to create a new life and help Sunny recover and move on from Stu's death.

Durk was proud of her, and he wished he could tell her himself. *That's not happening,* he thought glumly. Aleen made it clear that all communications were to be about Sunny. The ice in her eyes and voice made it crystal clear what she thought about him.

At least his daughter was talking to him now. They actually had gone out to lunch a few times, too. A little progress, but she still didn't look at him the way she used to. No, that time was over and done.

While he knew he was respected at work, Durk also understood he wasn't held in high regard. Everyone knew the tragic story, and even though no one would say it to their faces, most blamed Durk and Gerrie for Stu's death and the failure of their marriages. He couldn't change that.

He still loved his work, though, and took great pride in it. He particularly liked to mentor the junior engineers and help them solve tough design problems. He was so proud his daughter had decided to pursue engineering, just like him. He just wished they could talk about engineering and science the way they had in the past.

How Sunny used to sparkle when he brought her to the office to get a feel for the real work of engineering. It was killing him that he couldn't spend more time with his daughter, talking about her classes, her career aspirations. But he would never give up trying. Never.

Durk turned on the car, figuring he should get home to Gerrie. He'd been sitting outside the house for about fifteen minutes.

On second thought, he didn't need to rush, as Gerrie was most likely still at work.

He was really worried about her, as she blamed herself for Stu's death and thought burying herself in her work would help. It wouldn't. Durk knew she needed help. Hell, he did, too. If he was really okay, he wouldn't be sitting outside his old house, pining for his old life.

You've made your choice, he thought as he drove over to the grand house that would never feel like home and would constantly remind him of the fine young man who died because of Durk's affair with his mother.

This was his life now.

chapter twenty-three

Gerrie

She just wasn't feeling well physically, so Gerrie made an appointment with her primary care physician. It was probably the stress of the last six months taking a toll on her, but she was feeling so out of sorts that she made an appointment and snuck out of work early. She didn't even tell Durk.

Her doctor planned to do a few tests and a physical exam. Gerrie arrived right on time, and after chatting with her doctor, the assistant took her blood pressure and temperature, drew blood, and then directed her to the ladies' room to fill up the little container. After some poking and prodding and more tests, including an EKG, Gerrie sat in the exam room, waiting for Dr. Allen.

She had plenty of emails to answer, so she didn't mind the wait. Gerrie always liked to make sure all her emails were answered before she went to bed at night.

And Dr. Allen was worth waiting for. He'd been her physician for fifteen years and was a very good doctor and a kind and caring man. She appreciated that so much now, as kindness directed at her had been in short supply since the accident.

After about twenty-five minutes, Dr. Allen joined her in the exam room.

"Well, am I okay? Is there anything I should be concerned about?" Gerrie looked at Dr. Allen, waiting for his reply, which seemed to take ages.

"Gerrie, all the tests show you are perfectly fine. There are no health issues," Dr. Allen replied.

"That's great news. I didn't tell Durk I was coming in. I didn't want to worry him. He'll be pleased everything is fine." She smiled at Dr. Allen.

"But there is something I know you will be concerned about," Dr. Allen added.

"Oh?"

"Gerrie, you're pregnant."

"Dr. Allen? I am forty-six years old. I *can't* be pregnant," Gerrie said, her voice rising.

"You *are* pregnant, and we need to know how far along you are. Please try to be specific. When was your last period?"

Gerrie looked at Dr. Allen in a daze. "There has to be some mistake. I don't *want* to be pregnant. This can't be happening."

"Gerrie, calm down. I know you've had a terrible year and there's a lot going on in your life, but you need to slow down and think about the baby."

"Oh my God . . ." She looked down at the floor in disbelief. "A baby."

"Gerrie, please answer my question. How long since your last period?"

She put her face in her hands. *Think . . . think,* Gerrie told herself.

After the shock of Stu's death, she didn't have her period for about eight weeks, so she got it again in August. Was that the last time? She just didn't pay attention to her periods because she thought she was starting menopause, which she mentioned to the doctor before all the tests.

"I think it was sometime in August. That's the last time I remember."

"Please set up an appointment with your OB-GYN. It's Dr. Lebamon, right?

Gerrie nodded.

"She'll be able to tell just how far along you are. Of course, at your age, it is a high-risk pregnancy, so we must proceed with caution."

She sat in the chair next to the exam table in shock.

Dr. Allen came over and touched her arm. "Gerrie, you need to take care of yourself now. Cut down on the hours at work and the travel. This pregnancy could be hard on you at this age. And as we've discussed, I really believe you need to start counseling. It's clear that everything that has happened has taken a toll."

Gerrie was immobile, trying to take in this unbelievable development.

"Please take a few minutes if you'd like to gather yourself. You are welcome to stay in this room for a while. It looks like you need to adjust to the news."

Gerrie looked at Dr. Allen and nodded, but she had no idea what to say. Or what to do next.

After a few minutes, she pulled out her phone. It was before five o'clock, so she called Dr. Lebamon's office to see if she could get an appointment as soon as possible. The receptionist said she could come over on Friday at noon. Gerrie took the appointment without even checking her calendar. This was too important.

A baby . . . a baby!

Gerrie was finally able to leave the exam room and head back to her car. She decided to stop at the grocery store on the way home. If she was pregnant, she needed to drink milk. Maybe she would get some ingredients to make a nice dinner for her and Durk.

Pregnant? How could this be? Then it hit her as she came around the corner into the next aisle. She was being given another chance to be a mother. What if it was a boy, like Stu? He could never be replaced, but another boy . . .

Oh my God, she thought. *I'll be almost seventy when this baby finishes college. Durk, too. What will he say?*

Standing in the bread aisle, Gerrie made her decision. She was having this baby, no matter what. God was giving her another chance to be a better mother, and she would be. She had to atone for the loss of Stu, and this was her chance.

Durk would be a fabulous father. She knew it. He was excellent with Sunny before the accident. She had idolized him.

But what if Durk didn't want the baby? Gerrie grabbed her head as if she were in pain. She could never have an abortion. Not after Stu. . . . No. If she had to be a mother alone, then she would.

Gerrie picked up freshly baked bread and some chicken and potatoes for dinner and marched to the checkout. She was making dinner for her soon-to-be husband and telling him he would be a father . . . again.

As she waited in line, she touched her belly and said silently to Stu, *You are going to have a brother.*

chapter twenty-four

Aleen

Trish had asked Aleen to come into her office at the end of the day to go over a few things. After they talked about the schedule for the upcoming European trip and went over the presentation on an acquisition target, Trish pushed aside everything on her desk.

"I want to talk about you and your career," Trish said.

"Well, I love my job; that's for sure," Aleen said. "And working for you is fantastic. I can't tell you how much I appreciate all of your encouragement."

"Well, good, because I have a suggestion for you."

Aleen shifted in her seat. "I'm all ears."

Trish continued. "As you know, Mary has gotten a promotion and is moving over to marketing, leaving her analyst position open. I think you should post for it, as you could do it in your sleep."

"Well, I'm flattered, but that job requires a degree, and I never finished mine." Surprise was written all over her face.

"If you agree to pursue your degree part time to finish it, I don't think that will be a problem at all," Trish said confidently.

"Gosh, I know I could do the job, so if you think I'm qualified,

I'll go for it. The promotion and boost in pay would be fabulous, as I'm a soon-to-be single, working mother." She beamed at Trish, so pleased her boss was placing her confidence in her.

"Now, you'll have to make sure you help me find a first-rate assistant to replace you if you get the job,"Trish said, smiling at her.

"Of course I would. I sure would miss working with you, however, as the job reports to Terry. He's a great guy, but he's not you!"

"Well, thanks for that, but you'll still be in my department, and you'll be involved in all the critical assignments. I learned early on that if there is a presentation to the CEO, you must be included on the team."

Aleen soaked in the praise and encouragement from her boss. "I'll look into the college courses right away and be sure to say I plan to finish my degree when I post for the job. And thanks for your confidence in me."

"You deserve it for everything you've done for this department over the years,"Trish said. "What's your question for me?"

Aleen felt a bit uncomfortable asking her boss about her meeting with Gerrie, but she decided to come right out with it.

"How did your meeting with Gerrie go?" Aleen looked at her boss with keen interest.

Trish got up and walked over to the large window that looked out on a beautiful view of the mountains.

"It was very interesting. We know it's important we work well together and that there is an added responsibility for both of us as the highest-level women in the company," Trish said, turning to face her assistant.

"I wouldn't say she has been a good role model," Aleen mentioned, sneering her distaste.

"Was she before the affair and the death of her son?" Trish asked, coming back to sit across from Aleen, sincerely interested in her answer.

"I would say yes, she was. She was one of the most highly respected executives here."

"Hmm." Trish looked at Aleen but didn't say anything further.

"Did she mention me?" Aleen got right to the point.

"Yes, she did. She brought up the whole situation, as she thought, correctly, that you and I had discussed it. And just as I told you, I assured her any conversation she would have with me would be confidential."

"I totally understand," Aleen replied, shifting in her seat uncomfortably.

"To be clear, we laid the groundwork for a good and cooperative working relationship, which I hope we can have. I have to put aside any personal feelings I might have about her life or her actions. Particularly where you are concerned," Trish said in her most professional manner.

"She is an important executive here, and you have to work with her. I get it. I didn't mean to pry," Aleen said, getting up to leave.

"You didn't. It's human nature to want to ask the questions you did. Just as it was human nature for her to speak frankly to me about the situation. While I don't respect her past actions where your family is concerned, I do respect you both. I must."

Trish watched her assistant walk out but turn to face her as she reached the doorway.

"I know you're right. It's just that it's impossible for me to think about Gerrie without emotion. I am human. I know there's a day coming when we have to deal with each other civilly and perhaps even with compassion. I'm just not there yet." Aleen continued back to her desk.

She wondered to herself if that day would ever come.

chapter twenty-five

Durk

When he arrived home, Durk was surprised to see Gerrie's car in the garage. He was even more shocked when he saw she was in the kitchen, cooking dinner.

"Well, this is a pleasant surprise," he said, gathering her in a hug and kissing her passionately. She had already changed into her jeans and a T-shirt.

"What? You act like I'm never home early, cooking dinner." Gerrie laughed as she stroked his face.

"Well . . ." He was trying hard to bite his tongue. "I was just trying to remember the last time I came from work and you were here, in your jeans, cooking dinner."

She pointed at him, laughing. "Okay, okay, you win. I know it doesn't happen very often." Gerrie took a fresh salad she made and put it on the table.

Durk thought about Aleen's homemade salad dressing and how much he wished he had some for this beautiful salad.

"Are you impressed?" Gerrie asked, stirring some potatoes.

"Absolutely! Let me get changed. I'm starving." Durk rushed out of the kitchen to their bedroom and quickly changed into his comfortable sweats.

When he walked back in the kitchen, he picked up a bottle of wine and held it up for her approval.

"No thanks, hon. My stomach feels a bit funny, but you go ahead."

Durk opened the bottle and poured himself a glass.

"Rough day?" Gerrie asked, observing the very large glass of wine.

"A bit. That's why it's nice to be here with you, getting ready to have a wonderful dinner."

Durk helped Gerrie get everything on the table, and they started to eat.

"This is very good, Gerrie. Thanks so much for getting home early to make us dinner." He regarded her with affection.

She beamed at her soon-to-be husband. Now that she was pregnant, she would have to get home and make dinner more often. Maybe she could learn to be a good cook. She frowned a bit, as she knew she would never stack up to Aleen when it came to domestic life.

When they finished, Durk and Gerrie worked together to clean everything up. He kissed her tenderly as they put the last dishes in the dishwasher.

"Thanks, hon. I really enjoyed that." Durk folded the dish towel and put it on the counter.

"Let's go into the family room. I've got something I need to talk to you about." Gerrie took his hand and led him over to the couch.

"What's going on?" He looked at her with concern.

"Well, I didn't tell you, but I went to the doctor today because I just haven't been feeling well lately."

"I noticed you seemed very tired the last several weeks. I think that last international trip took it out of you," he said, taking her hand in his. "Everything is okay, isn't it?"

"I'm fine, darling. I'm fine. But I did get some very unexpected news."

Durk's eyebrows shot up. "What is it?"

"I'm pregnant."

"What!" He jumped up. "Are you *kidding*?"

With their cozy mood broken, Gerrie became concerned. "I'm not kidding, Durk. I am totally serious. I'm pregnant with your child."

He walked over to the window with the beautiful view of the valley, his back to her.

"Durk. Don't you have anything to say?" Gerrie felt fear rising in her.

"I didn't expect to be a father again . . . and in my late forties. God, we'll be so old when the child gets out of college!" Durk turned to face her, and it was clear he was unhappy about the pregnancy.

"But don't you see? This is my chance to be a mother again. My last chance. I loved Stu so much. I know I wasn't around as much as Ted, but I was a good mother. I was!" Gerrie looked at her partner defiantly.

He came over to sit next to her on the couch. "You were a good mother. I know that." Durk comforted Gerrie, grabbing her hand.

"No one questioned I was a good mother *before* the accident. Everyone has since."

He squeezed her fingers. "You were a wonderful mother. I saw it firsthand."

"But I'm *not* a mother now. Don't you see? It's like God is giving me another chance to get it right. To make up for what happened to Stu . . ."

"This baby is *not* a substitute for Stu. This is a huge decision for us. A baby at our age . . ." He nervously ran his hand through his thick, dark hair specked with grey.

121

Gerrie's mouth was set in steely determination. "I *am* having this baby, Durk, with or without you."

Durk looked at this woman who was his whole life now, and he just didn't know what to say.

chapter twenty-six

Ted

The divorce papers sat in front of Ted on his desk, and he looked at them warily. Gerrie had asked to come by to talk to him, and he assumed it was about the final divorce agreement. As she had been his wife for twenty-one years, he thought he owed her this, to have a civil conversation just before their marriage was officially over.

She would be here soon, so he made sure Hope and Cash were out in the courtyard. As entertaining as they were, Ted knew there wasn't anything that would make him smile today.

Just as he clicked the French doors shut, Gerrie rang the bell.

When he let her in, Ted noticed she looked beautiful as always, though a bit tense and tired. Something was different about her, and he knew that look.

"Hello, Ted," she said, slipping in as if he would change his mind and shut the door in her face if she didn't get inside quickly.

"Gerrie." He eyed her up and down, as he rarely got the chance to see his soon-to-be ex-wife lately, much less be alone with her.

"May I sit down?" she asked, aware she was being studied.

"Sure. Let me get you something to drink. What would you

like?" Ted was trying so hard to appear calm and unaffected by the presence of the woman who had not so long ago been the center of his life.

"A sparkling water would be perfect."

Gerrie watched Ted walk out to the kitchen. He looked fabulous since that makeover. She dreamily thought back to the early part of their marriage, right after Stu was born. What a wonderful and good baby he was—slept through the night so young. And Ted was an extraordinary father, so caring.

Stu loved sitting in his bouncy chair, before he could walk, and would just smile and laugh, playing with the plastic toys hanging in front of him and using his chubby legs to jump up and down. . . .

"Here you go." Ted handed her the sparkling water with a lemon slice, gazing down at the carpet.

"Thanks. You know the way I like it." Gerrie took a sip, as her mouth was becoming dry, thinking about what she needed to tell her soon-to-be former husband.

"You looked like you were a million miles away just now. What were you thinking about?" Ted cocked his head, clearly interested in her answer.

"Oh, Ted, I was thinking about when Stu was a baby and he would just bounce and laugh in that little chair. And how he was so wonderful, such a good boy . . ."

"Listen, I know it's hard today with the divorce papers ready to be signed," he told her gently. "I think about our marriage and our son every day. It's natural to relive our lives together."

Ted glanced over at Gerrie, and she seemed unsettled, nervous. He knew they hadn't spent much time together over the last six months, but he always felt they could have civil conversations about legal matters.

He caught himself, as a divorce was hardly a cut-and-dry

legal matter. It was the end of the most important period of his life. And Ted had been so happy.

He walked back into the kitchen to try to get a handle on his emotions. "Just getting a water for me, too. Be right back."

Gerrie knew something was wrong, so she followed him into the kitchen. When she saw he was upset, she wrapped her arms around him and gently put her cheek against his back.

"I am so, so sorry, Ted. You know that, don't you?" she whispered and continued to hold him. She couldn't see his face, but she was sure tears were rolling down his cheeks.

"I know, Gerrie, but it doesn't take away the pain of Stu *and* you."

He was clearly so upset now that Gerrie turned him around so she could see his face. In the last months, Ted had appeared so controlled. She guessed it was a front, just like the one she put up every day. She wiped away his tears with a napkin she picked up from the counter. They stood there holding each other for a long time.

She looked at him with such affection that Ted couldn't help himself. He kissed her.

Gerrie pulled back and tried to stop him. "You know this isn't a good idea, even though I will always love you—"

When he heard those words, he grabbed Gerrie and kissed her passionately. She resisted at first but quickly gave up and kissed him back. Ted led her to the master bedroom, which was nothing like the one they shared at their grand house. As she lay back on the bed, all Gerrie could think about was the danger she and Ted were unleashing, but she did want him and couldn't stop.

He continued kissing her and quickly took off her blouse and unhooked her bra before she could try and pull back again. Ted felt out of control as he kissed her breasts.

"Ted . . ." When Gerrie tried to protest, he covered her mouth with his own and unzipped her pants, quickly stroking between her legs. She started to respond, and he could feel she was becoming excited.

He took off her slacks and panties and peeled off his jeans and briefs as quickly as he could.

"Ted, oh, Ted . . ." Gerrie said passionately, and her words made him want her more than he'd wanted her in his entire life.

She took him in her hand and felt how ready he was. Ted parted her legs and plunged into her, and they rocked together for a long time, never wanting their lovemaking to end.

Ted screamed her name as he came, and she grabbed onto his shoulders, hugging him close as her climax matched his.

When he slid over to her side, she turned to him, stroking his face and kissing him all over—on his cheeks, his nose, his forehead, his neck.

"Ted, Ted, Ted . . . we shouldn't have made love. It was wrong. We're signing divorce papers. I am committed to Durk." Gerrie put her head on the pillow as Ted pulled himself away from her.

"Why, Gerrie? You said you loved me. I still love you. You know that! If you're committed to Durk, why did you make love with me?" He was so upset.

"I'll always love you. But our time together is over. I'm so sorry. I tried to stop. I should have never let you kiss me to start all of this. . . ." How could she have let this happen?

"Listen, I admit I didn't want to take no for an answer and was quite aggressive, but I thought you wanted it, too. I thought you were giving us another chance!" Ted was pleading with her now.

Gerrie covered her face and started to cry. "Ted, I don't want to hurt you again. I don't, but I know I just have. I am so stupid."

"You're not stupid, Gerrie. You just love me, too. Just give us a chance." He stared at his wife, hoping and praying she would come back to him.

"We can't be together again, Ted . . . because I'm pregnant. I'm pregnant with Durk's child." Gerrie cast her eyes down, as she could not face her husband.

"What?! Pregnant!" He jumped up and away from her, stark naked. "How can you make love to me when you're carrying another man's child?" Ted quickly pulled on his pants and shirt. "Are you crazy? Haven't you hurt me enough?" He was in such a rage that it scared Gerrie, and she covered her face, starting to sob.

"Please get up and get dressed and leave. Don't you *dare* cry in front of me. I can't stand the sight of you."

Ted walked out and slammed the door. Gerrie tried to stop crying and put her clothes back on as quickly as she could. She knew she had made a terrible mistake.

When she came out of the bedroom, Ted had the divorce papers in one hand and a pen in the other. "Here's why you came by," he said. "You wanted me to sign these papers, so here you go!" He signed the papers angrily and threw them at her.

"Ted, you don't understand. This is my chance to be a mother again. To make up for—"

"Don't talk to me about making up for Stu's death, you bitch! Don't you dare mention our son. Sunny was right when she said you and Durk killed him. You did! And Stu was right when he said you weren't his mother anymore . . . and now you aren't my wife. GET OUT! GET OUT!" Ted was enraged as Gerrie grabbed her purse and the divorce papers, running through the doorway of the condo when Ted threw it open.

Once she was gone, Ted crumbled onto the floor, wishing his life was over, because he wasn't a father, wasn't a husband; he was nothing now.

chapter twenty-seven

Aleen

It wouldn't be long now until Durk arrived at their house; well, it was actually her home now. Aleen knew Ted was seeing Gerrie today, too. When they had chatted about it earlier, he and Aleen both tried to help each other prepare for the visits by their soon-to-be ex-spouses that confirmed the end of their marriages.

Final divorce papers, she thought to herself. *How did we ever get to this?* She shook her head sadly, walking around her well-appointed and comfortable home.

Sunny was dreading Durk's visit as well. It was odd he insisted she be home when he stopped by. The divorce was between her parents; Sunny didn't need to be involved in the legal process. Perhaps he wanted to express his love to his daughter. Aleen just didn't know.

Glancing around the house she and Durk had lovingly made into their home, Aleen sighed, thinking about all the wonderful times they enjoyed. When they remodeled the major living areas, he and Aleen did most of the painting and wallpapering themselves; they spent many days covered in paint and wallpaper glue. *What a chore,* she thought, running her hand over the kitchen wallpaper, which they had picked out together.

She looked out the window and saw the boat, recalling the first time they went out on it—Sunny was just three. To this day, their daughter loved going on the water. They hadn't been on the boat for so long.

She gazed at her herb and vegetable garden, which had helped her make so many wonderful meals. Durk had dug up the patch years ago to create it, with his little assistant, Sunny, always at his side. There was nothing that had made her happier than to see her husband and daughter enjoying a meal they all contributed to in some way.

Those happy memories made her feel warm all over. It was when Aleen thought of signing the divorce papers that she felt the cool breeze surround her, changing her mood from happiness to dread.

Right on cue, the doorbell rang. It always seemed odd when Durk rang the bell, as this had been his house for so many years and his imprint was everywhere.

Aleen let him in with a forced smile and led him over to the couch. Sunny must have heard him arrive, and she came down the hall to join them.

"Hello, Dad," she said as she sat in the overstuffed chair across from him. The view out the window onto the lake was spectacular as usual, but that wasn't the focus of their attention, as Durk, Sunny, and Aleen sat uncomfortably together.

"It's good to see you, sweetheart," Durk said, nodding at his daughter. "And your mom, too," he added, looking over nervously at Aleen.

He couldn't think of the right words to start, so he looked down at the floor.

Aleen jumped in to get the conversation started. "Durk, we know this is hard, as the divorce is final when we sign the papers. We don't need to make it any more difficult by drawing this out."

"I understand," he replied quietly, "but there is something else I need to talk to both of you about."

Aleen and Sunny gazed at him quizzically.

"This will come as a surprise to you, as it did to Gerrie and me. It certainly wasn't planned." Durk stopped for a few seconds, and Aleen and Sunny continued to look confused.

"Gerrie is pregnant. We will get married right away, obviously, after the divorce papers are signed. I wanted you to hear this news directly from me." He had forced the words out before he looked at Aleen and his daughter for their reactions.

Sunny shot up, walking right over to her father, pointing in his face. "Oh great! She thinks she can have a baby now to replace Stu, to make it all okay for you and *her*." She spat the last word with disdain.

She couldn't stop herself now. "No! It isn't okay. It's the opposite of okay. You make me sick." Sunny ran out of the room, and Durk got up, calling after her.

"Sunny, please. Don't act this way . . ." But his words fell on deaf ears, as his daughter stormed to her room and slammed the door, locking it.

Aleen looked at her soon-to-be ex-husband with no idea what to do or say.

"I'm sorry, Aleen. I know this news is a bit of a shock. It was to me as well. I'm struggling, and I just didn't know how to tell you, so I just came out with it." Durk rubbed his hands together nervously, waiting for her reaction.

"Durk, just when I felt you couldn't hurt Sunny and me any more . . ." she responded softly, more to herself than to him. "But my feelings aside, you have really set Sunny back again. She was doing so well."

Aleen put her head in her hands, and the tears started to

form. The news that Durk was having a baby with Gerrie hit her hard. She struggled not to cry; she didn't want him to see how much she still cared.

He had moved over next to her, kneeling on the ground, putting his hand on her knee. "Aleen, I know you won't believe me, but the last thing I wanted to do was upset you and Sunny again. You're both so important to me. Gerrie is committed to this baby, as she thinks God is giving her a chance to be a mother again and get it right."

She moved his hand off her knee and stood. Aleen felt like she was in another bad dream, and she desperately wanted to wake up.

Her husband stood, too, looking her in the eyes, and took her hands in his. "Aleen, this was totally unplanned. If it were my choice—"

She threw his hands away from hers. "No, you don't get to explain or comfort me or touch me anymore. You are my *ex*-husband, and this is no longer your home. The damage you have done is immeasurable, and I have to ask you to leave."

Aleen moved away from Durk but looked him straight in the eyes. Her anger was raging out of control. "You've said what you came here to say. I'll send the signed divorce papers over. Go and live the life you've chosen with your new family. I am done with you."

Durk was stunned by her coldness, taking one last look at her before he headed for the door. She saw the pain in his eyes as he walked out of the home that once had held so much happiness for him.

Aleen stared at the door after Durk left. She *would* hold it together.

Just then, Sunny came back into the living room, as she must have heard her father depart. "Are you okay, Mom?" she whispered as Aleen enveloped her in a hug.

"Your dad's news was very upsetting for both of us. It's hit me hard. I can't lie to you." Aleen smoothed Sunny's hair and wiped away the tears beginning to dry on her cheeks.

"I hate Gerrie. I hate her. She thinks she can replace Stu. She can't. She just can't." Sunny was so angry and hurt.

Aleen observed her daughter and saw a little girl, not the young woman that stood next to her.

"She planned this. You can see Dad didn't want this. He wasn't happy at all." She pulled away from her mother and sat on the couch, and Aleen joined her. "Mom, I heard you shout at Dad that you were done with him. Did you mean it?" Sunny, the little girl, looked straight at her.

"Honey, I was very, very angry, and I'm sure your dad has been devastated by his visit here, just as we are. I believe you're right that he wasn't really happy about the baby. At their age, it won't be easy. But we can't change it; a baby *is* on the way. You'll have a new brother or sister."

"A baby . . ." Sunny appeared to be in shock. "A brother or sister . . ."

"It certainly was a bombshell. I know Gerrie was going over to talk to Ted . . ." A look of horror spread across Aleen's face. "Oh my God, Ted . . . I have to talk to him. He must be in such a state after hearing this news." She ran to grab her purse and keys.

"I'm going with you." Sunny came after her mom.

"Honey, no. I know how I feel right now, and it must be absolutely devastating for Ted because of the loss of Stu. Let me go alone. I think this is going to have to be an adult-to-adult chat. One that's going to be very difficult." Aleen hugged her daughter.

"I get it. Mom, please just let me know he's okay," Sunny called after her as she rushed out to the garage.

Making the short drive over to Ted's, she felt panicked for her friend, as Aleen couldn't imagine his state of mind after hearing this news from his ex-wife and the mother of his dead son.

chapter twenty-eight

Ted

He wasn't sure how, but Ted found the strength to gather himself and get up from the floor after the totally unexpected encounter with Gerrie.

Peeling off his crumpled clothes, he jumped in the shower, trying to scrub the smell of his now ex-wife off of him. His skin turned pink from all the scouring.

When he got out of the shower and dried himself off, Ted buried his face in the softness of the towel. How could Gerrie do this to him? Make love with him and give him hope, only to destroy him *again*. And a baby? She would have the chance to be a mother again, but not him. No, he would never be a father again.

Ted threw the towel angrily on the floor. He never did that, had always been such a neatnik. Well, his life wasn't very orderly right now, was it? Ted couldn't control the thoughts buzzing around in his head.

Aleen and her ex-husband had Sunny, and now Gerrie and Durk would have a child. Ted thought about taking a drink, but he ruled it out, as he needed to keep his wits about him.

As he finished dressing, his thoughts were interrupted by

Hope and Cash scratching to get in from the courtyard. "Sorry, guys. I forgot about you."

When he opened the door, the dogs ran in like a shot. Ted sat on the couch, and the dogs jumped on him, licking and nuzzling him. "Boy, do I need you both now. I'm sure you don't understand just how much." He hugged and petted the dogs, and they clearly loved it.

"Well, I am your dad, aren't I?" The pair answered by continuing to give him the love he needed at that precise moment.

The doorbell rang, and he didn't move, but the dogs leapt up and ran, barking. He couldn't see anyone, and if that was Gerrie again, he just couldn't open the door. Ted was frozen in place. The bell rang again, and then there was a knock. The dogs went crazy.

"Ted, it's Aleen." He could hear the muffled voice of his friend. "You gave me the key in case of emergency, so I'm coming in." She turned the key in the lock and walked into the condo, the dogs jumping all over her.

Ted stood. "I'm sorry, Aleen. I really didn't want to see anyone, and there was no way I was answering the door if it was Gerrie again."

Aleen came over and sat next to him on the couch.

"Can you believe their news?" he said dejectedly.

"It was a real shocker. Sunny was hysterical, as you can imagine. She told Durk that Gerrie was trying to replace Stu with this baby. . . ." Aleen grimaced, as she thought this might be difficult for Ted to hear. "Sorry, I don't want to make it worse, but I needed to check on you. I was so worried." She grabbed a tissue from her purse.

"I wish I could tell you I took it well. I didn't." Ted got up to go in the kitchen to gather himself. "I'm going to grab some sparkling water. Want some?"

"Yes, please." Aleen observed her friend with growing unease.

He handed her the water, took a long drink of his own, and sat down facing her. "I, um, need to tell you something that I won't tell another soul. You must promise me."

"Okay, I won't tell anyone, but you're worrying me," she said with increasing concern.

"What happened this morning was almost surreal. I felt like I was in a good dream, then a really, really bad dream. . . ."

Aleen was so confused. What was he talking about? "Ted, I know how difficult all of this must have been for you."

"I snapped, Aleen. You know how really sane people just lose it under stressful circumstances? That was me. I think I went crazy for a few minutes; I was so angry and hurt." He folded and unfolded his hands and couldn't look at Aleen as he tried to tell her his shocking news.

"I became upset about the divorce being final, so when Gerrie tried to comfort me, I kissed her. I just wouldn't take no for an answer, even when she tried to discourage me. . . . And then we made love. Mad, passionate love. And I thought she was giving me another chance.

"But, no. Just after I made love to my wife, she told me she was pregnant. Pregnant with your husband's child!" He spat out the words, staring right at a shocked Aleen.

"Oh my God . . ."

"When she told me about the baby, I went crazy, signed the divorce papers, and threw them at her as she rushed out. I was wild, and I could see she was scared. I don't think she knew what she was doing, either. How could she hurt me again like that? How could I be so *stupid*?" Ted was on his feet now, pacing back and forth.

"Oh, Ted . . ." Aleen looked horrified as he continued.

"You and Durk have Sunny. Now Gerrie will have this baby.

You will be parents, but not me, no. I will never feel that joy again . . . only the pain of visiting the site where my son was killed. My son is dead because of the affair between Gerrie and *your* husband."

Aleen was crying now, for her friend, her daughter, Stu, and her failed marriage. She'd never seen Ted like this and wasn't sure what to do, how to comfort him. He was lashing out at her as well. *Best to let him finish.*

"I told her I blamed her for Stu's death. No, *told* isn't technically correct, as I literally *shouted* it at her."

"I'm sure Gerrie was crushed." Aleen tried to envision the scene in her head.

"She was devastated. She looked distraught as she ran out of here. As angry as I am with her, I shouldn't have acted like that. It was terrible, and it is *not* who I am. It just isn't." He ran his fingers though his hair and kept holding his head for a minute.

Dabbing at her eyes, Aleen looked straight at him. "Ted, most people would have reacted exactly as you did. If it's any comfort, I took the news like a knife to my heart, and I was very harsh with Durk as well, trying to hurt him.

"Sunny ran out, but not before spewing hate at her father once again. Durk was so uncomfortable the whole time. Ted, I don't think he wants this baby."

"Would you want to have a baby again at our age?" He looked at Aleen intently, waiting for her answer.

"To be brutally honest, no. But as a woman, I do understand why Gerrie would want to be a mother again, particularly with the events surrounding Stu's death."

The two friends looked at each other, a bit in shock.

"God, life is messy, and we are up to our necks in the really messy part." Aleen took a drink of her water to try to calm herself. Her blood pressure had to be sky high. Ted's, too.

"Sunny and I were both so concerned about you. She wanted to come over, but I convinced her not to. I thought we needed to have an adult conversation. Little did I know how adult." She glanced at Ted.

"I'm sorry. I didn't mean to act out so much, but I feel like I've been cut into pieces. Honestly, I feel as if I'm in shreds on the floor." He took a gulp of his drink. "And thanks for convincing Sunny not to come over. I wouldn't want her to see me this way."

Aleen tried to smile at her friend, but it was a feeble attempt.

"You've had an awful time as well. Are you okay?" Ted looked down as the dogs chased each other around the couch before directing his gaze at his friend.

"The thing that really threw me was the way he looked at me, like he still cares so much for me. Durk has hurt me so badly and continues to do so. The wounds are very deep. I have to try to protect myself, *but a baby . . . ?*"

"Yes, a baby. What if it's a boy?" Ted gazed out the window, the pain and hurt clear all over his face.

"I feel you're part of our family now, and so does Sunny. As family, there are moments of anger, frustration, and, yes, bad behavior. So if Gerrie's baby turns out to be a boy, we will handle it . . . together. So you're stuck with us."

"You and Sunny are the only good things in my life right now." Just then, Hope and Cash took a break from running around and chasing each other and jumped up on the couch and all over Ted.

"Sorry, guys, you're both pretty special to me, too. Didn't mean to exclude you." Hope and Cash nuzzled Ted, almost as if they understood him. "You two are the reason I get up every morning—literally, 'cause you jump on me in the bed!" He actually laughed at his own comment.

Cash came over and sat on Aleen's lap, licking her face. "Thanks, Cash, I know you're the one male I can always count on for a kiss." She gave the dog a big hug.

After all they'd been through that day, the two friends sat together for some time in silence, interrupted only by the happy and playful sounds of the dogs giving and soaking up the love.

chapter twenty-nine

Gerrie

Gerrie wasn't sure how she'd gotten home after the disastrous meeting with Ted, as she was in a panic. *What was I thinking?*

She dropped her keys and handbag on the kitchen counter and sprinted up to the master bedroom. After stripping off her clothes, she made the water as hot as she could stand and jumped in the shower.

Covering her face with her hands, she sobbed as the water hit her head and enveloped her in warmth. "Why did I make love with him? How could I hurt Ted again? What is wrong with me?" she shouted, water streaming down her face.

"Stop it!" Gerrie hissed as she tried to come up with what she was going to tell Durk about her visit with Ted. "You're going to have to tell a convincing lie to the man who'll be your husband and father of your child."

She could do it. Gerrie would put on an act and tell Durk a credible story.

Frowning as she soaped up, she had to admit she didn't like washing away the smell of her former husband, as it was such a wonderful and familiar scent. If she were honest with herself, she loved the intimacy with Ted; she had missed it.

How can I love two men? My life is with Durk now . . . and our baby. My old life is gone, just like our Stu.

Gerrie shook her head to snap out of it, the water falling around her. She was fairly confident Durk hadn't recently had sex with Aleen. "No, I'm sure you didn't, my dearest Durk. You're a much better person than me. I don't deserve you. I don't! I don't deserve Ted, either. I'm a terrible person. Terrible!"

Gerrie turned off the water and opened the shower door as she raged at herself. Reaching for the towel, her foot caught on the shower step, and she began to fall. "The baby!" she shouted as she instinctively turned to fall on her backside and protect her unborn child.

She cried out again as she hit the floor with a thud, just as Durk entered the master bedroom suite and came running into the bathroom.

"Gerrie! Gerrie! Are you all right?" Durk rushed to her side, kneeling on the floor, concern etched on his face.

"I'm okay. I just hope the baby . . ."

He grabbed a towel and wrapped it around her and snatched her robe from the nearby hook, helping her put it on.

"Oww," Gerrie moaned as she tried to get up, rubbing her hand over her backside, which was already beginning to bruise.

"Honey, I'm sure the baby's fine. Let me help you dry off and then come sit down," Durk said, helping her up.

She walked gingerly over to the bed and sat in an unusual position, as she didn't want to put pressure on the bruising on her buttocks. "Could you get me some of the pain reliever the doctor said I could take? It's on the counter in the bathroom. This really hurts." Gerrie fidgeted to try to get comfortable.

She quickly swallowed the pills with the ever-present glass of water at the side of the bed. "Oh, what a day," she declared, turning to Durk.

"I was going to ask you about your visit with Ted, but perhaps we can get into that later, when you feel better."

Gerrie nodded. "Thanks, darling. I just need to clear my head and deal with this pain a bit before we have that conversation. Frankly, I'm just not up to reliving it right now."

Durk put his arm around Gerrie, and they sat quietly for a minute.

"You know, when I knew I was falling, I tried to come down on the most padded part of my body to protect our boy."

"You seem so sure it's a boy." Durk stared into her eyes.

"I can't tell you why I feel that way, but I know it's true. We're having a son. I just hope my fall didn't hurt him. He just has to be all right." Gerrie buried her face in Durk's shoulder, sending up a silent prayer for their son.

chapter thirty

Sunny

After the events of the afternoon, Sunny wasn't sure she wanted to go through with the planned evening with Benjamin and Dawn. She told herself to calm down; the last thing she needed was to act like a jerk *again* with Benjamin.

Sunny was grateful to her friend for passing along the story of the tragedy to Benjamin—she wasn't up for reliving the accident again, particularly after the upsetting encounter that afternoon with her dad. She'd had her fill of drama for the day.

Picking up her phone from the bed, Sunny started to text Dawn to cancel, but she stopped.

Maybe I do need to talk about everything. That's what Sandy would say, Sunny thought, recalling advice from her counselor. And better to talk to neutral parties like her friends. She confided more and more of her feelings to her mom and Mr. Hammand, but they were hardly impartial and shared her hurt and anger.

Oh well, maybe she should go see her friends. Sunny threw her phone back on the bed.

A baby, a brother or sister. . . . Sunny would be more like another mother, as she would be almost twenty when the baby was born. She couldn't imagine spending time with Stu's mother and her dad and the baby. *Horrible!*

She worried about Mr. Hammand. He would think the same thing she did; Stu's mom was trying to replace him with the baby. But Stu was irreplaceable. Mr. Hammand and Sunny knew that.

It was no use to try studying, as all she could think about was Mr. Hammand, her mom, Stu, and this new baby. When she got home from the condo, her mom had tried to assure her that Mr. Hammand and she were both fine, but there was an edge in her voice, something . . .

Sunny understood her mom wanted to have an "adult" conversation with Mr. Hammand, but there was something Aleen was holding back; she could tell.

She wondered if she had to be over twenty-one to have an adult conversation—at what age would she qualify?

Maybe she could find out what was going on tomorrow, as the Packers game day at Mr. Hammand's was still on. Good. The last thing he needed was to be by himself after hearing the news today about the baby. Canceling football Sunday was not an option, and he had agreed.

Sunny hugged herself, trying to turn off all of her thoughts about the day's jarring events.

After a few minutes, she jumped up to get in the shower, as she knew the best thing was to spend the evening with her friends.

When Sunny arrived at the Pircells', Benjamin's car was already outside. Mr. Pircell gave her another much-needed hug, and she said hello to Mrs. Pircell, who was getting some things together for them in the kitchen.

"Honey, Dawn told us about what happened to your boyfriend and your family, and we wanted you to know if you ever need anything, you shouldn't hesitate to ask." Mrs. Pircell came over and embraced her.

"You're always welcome here," Mr. Pircell said, touching her shoulder lightly.

"You guys are the greatest, thanks," Sunny said as Dawn's father led her upstairs. *How nice it would be to have my parents together.*

Dawn jumped up to embrace Sunny but left quickly with her dad to get the drinks and food her mother was preparing. Conveniently, she would be gone for a while, which gave Benjamin and Sunny some time to talk.

"I hope you know I'm sorry for being such a jerk to you the other day," Sunny said, settling into her seat next to Benjamin on the couch.

"Listen, Dawn told me why and all about Stu, so please don't worry about it. You've been through enough. Let's just start again, and if you ever want to talk about it . . ." Benjamin looked at her with his kind blue eyes.

"Thanks," Sunny said, fidgeting a bit in her seat because she wasn't sure if she should just plunge in. "I had a really upsetting day today. I actually thought about not coming. I didn't want to screw up again."

"Why? What happened?" Benjamin watched as she got up and walked to the window.

She just wasn't sure how to start.

"My mom and dad's divorce is just becoming final. My dad stopped by today to tell us he's having a baby with Gerrie, the mother of my boyfriend who died, and they're getting married right away. It was terrible for my mom and me, not to mention Mr. Hammand, Stu's dad."

"Sunny . . ."

"I sort of flipped out, too. I thought Gerrie was trying to

have this baby as a substitute for Stu, and that just sent me over the edge."

"Wow. Your life is, like, really complicated right now," Benjamin said. "It's almost too much to handle. You have so much to deal with."

"Yeah." Sunny agreed, staring out the window. "I'm a real mess right now. That's why you should probably steer clear."

Benjamin joined her and put his hand on her arm. "That's not what I meant," he said softly. "You need your friends, and that's why Dawn and I wanted to get together tonight. You can't do this on your own. We want to help."

She turned to look at him. "I know. I can't always predict my feelings, when the anger and grief hit me. It was so bad right after Stu died that my mother couldn't believe I was the same girl. I thought I wanted to die, too. I'm doing better, really. Sometimes it just gets really hard, like today. It shook me up."

Benjamin wiped a tear from her face, gently taking her in his arms to comfort her. "Sunny Riddick, you are so special. I want to be here for you and help."

Sunny pulled back and took his hand in hers. "Can you just be my friend for a while?"

"I'll do my best." Benjamin touched her hair gently.

"Okay, deal," she said just as Dawn walked up the stairs with a tray of chips, nuts, and drinks. They broke apart to help their hostess put everything on the coffee table.

As they all dug into the snacks, Sunny looked at Dawn and Benjamin with affection. Just some friends hanging out on a Saturday night. She smiled to herself as they grabbed their drinks and munched on the goodies.

chapter thirty-one

Aleen

The months whizzed by at work. Aleen got the promotion and loved her new job. Trish made sure to stop by her new office often, making her feel special. The new job and pay raise were fantastic and much needed.

As she promised Trish, Aleen had signed up through a local college to finish her degree. She actually enjoyed the school work and could do a great deal of it online.

By her estimation, Aleen would be able to finish up her degree in business in about eighteen months. Between work, school, and Sunny, her plate was full. She also made plenty of time for Ted. He was part of their family now. In many ways, Ted was more of a father to Sunny than Durk.

Sunny did relent and agree to see her father a little more frequently, but the closeness they once shared just wasn't there, as she continued to hold him at arm's length. She did talk to him about school and engineering as a career, and that made Durk happy. He scooped up the crumbs of affection he could pull from his daughter and cherished them.

Aleen couldn't quite figure out what was going on with Durk and Gerrie, as they didn't seem to be on the same page. Gerrie obviously had to stop traveling with her advancing, not to mention high-risk, pregnancy, but Durk kept up his usual schedule.

She was a bit embarrassed to admit she kept track of her ex-husband through the online calendar at work. She could always claim it was for her daughter's sake, but she knew the reason had a lot more to do with her own feelings and concerns.

Based on what she saw on Durk's calendar, Gerrie had to be spending a lot of time alone. In the few conversations Aleen had with her ex-husband, he didn't seem at all excited about the baby. She just didn't get their relationship at all. Aleen wondered if Durk knew Gerrie had made love with Ted. Unlikely.

Durk had been very helpful and supportive when Aleen was pregnant. He wasn't the best at helping out when Sunny was a tiny baby, but as soon as she started to form words and explore, he loved spending time with his daughter. Before the breakup of the family, he was a wonderful father, which Aleen tried to get Sunny to admit when she expressed continuing anger toward her dad.

Could they ever get back to a really healthy and normal father-daughter relationship? Aleen certainly would do whatever she could to facilitate that, as it was best for both of them, but she had to admit the anger and hurt both mother and daughter still felt got in the way. They both needed more time.

The fact of the matter was she wasn't over her ex-husband. More than twenty years of marriage was a long time. It was just that she did miss so many things about being married, including the physical intimacy. *Lord,* she thought. She hadn't had sex in how long? She stopped herself from figuring it out.

As she recalled some of those wonderful lovemaking sessions with Durk, Aleen thought about what a fantastic thing it would be to be physically in sync with someone again, to touch them in a familiar way. Would she ever have that again? She didn't want to hazard a guess, because what if the answer was no? Too depressing.

Aleen was surprised when one of the guys in marketing kept stopping by her desk and then asked her out. Dating at her age was so scary! While he seemed like a very nice guy, she politely declined. *Just not ready,* Aleen thought, shaking her head.

She wanted to encourage Ted to date, but she didn't see that happening, either. His ability to move forward took a huge hit after he made love to Gerrie when she came over to give him the news about the baby. He still loved her, even with all the baggage. Aleen and Ted were just plain stuck; they admitted it when they had their really honest conversations.

They couldn't fool each other, so they didn't even try to fib. It was wonderful to have a confidant like him; he had actually become her best friend.

When Stu was killed and the divorces followed, so many of her so-called friends just went away. As these friends were all married and the couples were friends with both Aleen and Durk, the basis of the friendship was destroyed with their split. *When tragedy happens, it's easy to find out who your real friends are,* she thought sadly.

She blamed herself as well, as she had focused her attention on her husband and daughter and work; friendships were secondary. So when Aleen really needed her friends, they weren't there for her, with rare exceptions. Ted was the same, as his priority had always been squarely on his family, his beloved wife, and son. With Stu's death and the divorce, he found himself adrift.

Aleen had gotten back to cooking on a regular basis, which was like therapy for her and seemed to be appreciated by those who enjoyed her delicious meals. She'd hosted dinners for Ted and Vincent, some work colleagues, and even members of Sunny's study group. She thought the world of Dawn and Benjamin and was glad her daughter had found wonderful new friends. It was clear Benjamin cared deeply about Sunny, but as far as Aleen knew, she was still holding him off.

He was a lovely young man, and Aleen hoped her daughter would finally let her guard down and give him a chance. But that was Sunny's choice; Aleen couldn't advise her what to do, just as she couldn't tell her mother to move on, leaving her marriage with Durk behind.

Ted, Aleen, and Sunny were making progress, each in their own way. While they didn't discuss their individual counseling sessions, the three agreed Sandy had been a huge help. They were all pleased that Vincent had started seeing Sandy as well, and it seemed to be beneficial for him.

It still was difficult for Aleen to see Durk, so she avoided him at work. She spied Gerrie from time to time, waddling around, as big as a house now. The baby would come soon. It was a boy, and both Ted and Sunny handled that news fairly well.

Trish had developed a very good relationship with Gerrie. They got together for one-on-one meetings frequently, and Aleen believed they might have gotten together socially.

There was a wall between Aleen's relationship with Trish and Gerrie's relationship with her, so she didn't ask Trish about her after their earlier conversation. Trish had made it clear she respected Gerrie, and Aleen had to leave it at that.

She knew it was important the two women executives got along. While Trish wasn't an overly political being, she was smart enough to make sure the relationship with Gerrie worked and worked well. There was a goodness and kindness in Trish that made Aleen think her attention toward Gerrie was more than job-related.

Get back to your *work*, Aleen told herself, as she only had one more thing she needed to get done for her boss, Terry, and then she would be free to enjoy the weekend. It was Friday night, and she had plenty to do, with schoolwork, plans to see Monica, her makeover artist, and dinner on Sunday at her house for Ted, Vincent, and his new partner, Richard. No game Sunday, as the Packers had a bye.

When she finished her project and emailed it to her boss, Aleen closed down her computer and headed out to enjoy the weekend. She actually looked forward to it.

chapter thirty-two

Sunny

After class, Sunny stopped Benjamin in the hallway, because she wanted to ask him to come over to dinner on Sunday at her house.

"Hey." She grabbed his arm. "Are you doing anything right now? Do you want to grab coffee?"

"Sure," he said with a chuckle. "As long as you aren't going to be mean to me." It was a running joke they had about their first get-together at Starbucks. That time was well behind them, and their friendship had grown considerably since. Dawn, Benjamin, and Sunny were like the Three Musketeers; they spent a lot of time together, particularly on campus.

Dawn had to rush off to meet her new boyfriend, Andrew. He was a great guy, premed. The two of them had met at a UCLA basketball game.

We're going to have to incorporate Andrew into our activities, Sunny thought, smiling to herself.

"What are you thinking about?" Benjamin asked as they headed across campus to the coffee shop.

"About Dawn and Andrew and if he'd want to join our little group."

"Well, that's up to Dawn and Andrew, I guess," Benjamin answered as he opened the door for Sunny. She slid through into the Starbucks.

"And I was thinking about Mr. Pircell." Sunny laughed. "It must be hard to get his stamp of approval when it comes to Dawn. He just adores her. Can you imagine coming face to face with him to try and convince him you're good enough for his daughter?"

They cracked up. They could just picture Mr. Pircell eyeing Andrew and not so subtly asking about his intentions in relation to his daughter.

"Good luck to Andrew is all I can say." Benjamin chuckled.

Changing the subject, Sunny felt a bit apprehensive about asking him to dinner. It represented a big step in their relationship. "I was hoping you were free this Sunday. My mom's cooking for Ted, Vincent, and his partner, Richard. It's kinda like a family dinner." She played with her hair, anxiously waiting for his response.

"Sounds great," he answered, smiling broadly and giving her shoulder an affectionate squeeze. "I'll get the drinks. Be right back."

Sunny grabbed a seat while Benjamin ordered their usual. When she looked over at her friend, she sighed with relief that he'd accepted her dinner invitation. She also realized how much she cared about him. He was a good guy—kind, generous, intelligent, and so cute! Sunny smiled to herself, calling Benjamin cute. *Am I back in high school?*

In many ways, he did remind her of Stu, but he wasn't him. She liked him for who he was. Sunny knew she wasn't trying to make Benjamin a stand-in for Stu. *Progress.*

She continued to watch him at the counter and began to reflect on her true feelings for him. Was it time she let him in?

Sunny toyed with her phone, considering the possibilities, smiling at him when he sat down with their drinks.

On Sunday, Sunny felt herself getting nervous about seeing Benjamin that evening. What if their friendship got all screwed up if the nature of their relationship changed? There was no way she could imagine her life without him in it. She depended on him more than she'd realized before.

It was May now; early next month was the one-year anniversary of Stu's death. How things had changed for her, her family, and Stu's in the last year. He would hate the aftermath of his death, all the anger, hurt, and bitterness.

Mostly, Stu would be sad their families were totally broken apart. Would he approve of her moving on . . . with Benjamin? Sunny shook her head. She would never know.

She combed her hair and put on some lipstick before heading downstairs to see if her mom needed any help getting dinner ready. As usual, Aleen had everything in hand, and Sunny just helped put out a few snacks.

The table looked beautiful, and the food smelled so delicious. Aleen had prepared her special Italian meatloaf with roasted red-skinned potatoes and heirloom carrots. Her homemade mushroom gravy was on the warmer and ready to be poured into the server. Sunny wasn't much of a meat-eater, but she loved this meatloaf because it was loaded with breadcrumbs, spices, onion, garlic, and Parmesan cheese.

Ted was the first to arrive, and he brought some beautiful flowers and a fantastic bottle of wine—a pinot noir, her mom's favorite. Next, Vincent and Richard arrived with another bottle of wine, a wonderful Italian Barolo.

After Ted greeted Vincent and Richard, he grabbed their wine. "Wow! This is an excellent Barolo. Impressive."

Aleen gave both Vincent and Richard hugs. "If Ted is impressed with the wine you brought, that means it's really good. Thanks so much." She took the bottle from Ted to admire it. "I don't know as much about wine as you guys, but I do know we should start with the pinot, as it is lighter, and then move to the full-bodied Barolo."

"Absolutely correct, Aleen." Richard praised her. "You may know more than you think."

Sunny liked Richard instantly. Vincent had met him not long after he broke things off with Derek. He seemed to make Vincent happy, and she was glad.

She'd never blamed Vincent for Stu's death and made sure he knew that soon after they met. It didn't take long for them to become close, and she couldn't imagine football Sunday or any other family gathering without him now. They'd both been through hell, so she could talk to Vincent about anything, as could her mom and Ted. They all wanted the best for him, and that's why meeting Richard was such a big deal.

Vincent came over to Sunny and put his arm around her, whispering in her ear, conspiratorially, "Big night, tonight, eh?"

Sunny laughed and pointed her finger at him. "Don't make me more nervous than I already am. You know *way* too many of my secrets! And, hey, it's a big night for you, too. All of us get to meet Richard." Sunny linked her arm through Vincent's and then cupped her hand around his ear. "I liked him the minute he walked in."

Richard walked over, smiling, and touched Vincent's arm. "Why do I get the feeling you're talking about me?"

Vincent and Sunny giggled and didn't get the chance to answer, as Ted waved everyone over to the get the drinks started.

"Well, let's get the pinot open right now." Ted retrieved the corkscrew from the counter to open the wine and then poured glasses for the adults. He sniffed it and swirled it around before taking a small taste. "It's great for a pinot, but I have to say I'm getting excited about moving on to the Barolo." He raised his glass to propose a toast. "Here's to good friends and family." He stole a look at Vincent, Aleen, and Sunny. "And for surviving the last year."

"Cheers," they all said and clinked glasses, Sunny using her Vitamin Water for the toast before she ran to the door when Benjamin arrived, giving him a big smile and a kiss.

"That's a nice welcome. Thanks." Benjamin observed her with a mixture of surprise and affection, and Vincent smiled at the young couple.

After everyone welcomed Ben, Richard got a chance to chat with everyone before the group took their drinks on the patio to enjoy the view. The guests continued to chatter as Aleen and Sunny put the finishing touches on dinner, and soon, all were ready to sit down for their meal.

The meatloaf and vegetables were delicious, and the diners clearly enjoyed the food and conversation. Aleen was pleased when she looked around to see everyone's plates were empty and the serving dishes held very few leftovers.

"That was just fantastic, Aleen." Vincent raised his wine glass to toast the hostess.

"I have to agree. My mother used to make meatloaf, but it wasn't even in the same league." Richard joined his partner in raising his glass.

Aleen glanced around the table, soaking up the compliments. "Well, contrary to what you may think, I do have some Italian blood, even though my name is not an indicator," she told the group. "My grandmother was a fantastic cook, and her mother was an Italian immigrant to this country.

"My grandmother did something that most people don't—

she transcribed all the recipes she could before her mother died, writing everything down, noting each ingredient as she cooked. My great-grandmother had very little education, so her reading and writing skills weren't good, forcing her to prepare all kinds of marvelous food straight from her memory.

"Most American meatloaf recipes have ketchup or tomato sauce." Aleen continued. "But that's all wrong for Italian meatloaf. You'll never find ketchup in any of my great-grandmother's recipes. I know she had a word for that."

"I'm sure she did!" Richard interjected, and the whole group had a laugh.

Sunny got up and helped her mother clear the dinner plates.

"All of you stay right here. Dessert is on the way." Aleen hustled out and came back with a lemon tart perched atop a beautiful but simple white stand. The tart was garnished with ribbons of lemon rind on top.

"Another of your great-grandmother's recipes?" Richard asked, eyeing the dessert.

"No," Aleen answered. "This is a creation of mine, combining several recipes I found online. I wanted to find a way to use all the fruit from our lemon tree, but didn't want to use all the fat and sugar included in most recipes.

"Ted has to cut it. He's the precise slicer." Aleen smiled and handed him the knife.

After everyone finished their perfect triangles of tart, savoring every bite, Richard placed his knife and fork on his plate with an expression of great satisfaction. "Aleen, if I lived here, I would be as big as a house. I didn't think you could top dinner, but that tart was heaven on a plate."

Aleen beamed at her guests. "I'm so glad you liked it."

"'Like' is not the word I would use," Richard said. "That is better than any tart I've had at a restaurant."

As Aleen gathered the dessert plates, she smiled. "You guys are spoiling me. Just stay put, and Sunny and I will bring out the coffee."

While rinsing some of the dishes in the kitchen alongside her daughter, the hum of the conversations of her guests and the warmth of the friendships wrapped around Aleen, and she felt, well, almost happy, surprising herself. Glancing over at Sunny as they worked in tandem, she felt such love for her daughter and an incredible connection to those in the next room, just as if they were family.

When she walked back to rejoin her friends and the spirited conversation, she smiled at Ted, and the recognition in his eyes said he felt the same way about all those gathered around the table.

Once the coffee, cups, and cream and sugar were on the table, Sunny asked if she and Benjamin could be excused. "Benjamin and I need to do a little studying, so we'll skip the coffee."

"Of course." Aleen looked at her daughter and Benjamin with great interest.

"Thanks for that awesome meal, Mrs. Riddick." Benjamin smiled broadly at his hostess.

As they went off to Sunny's room, Ted watched them and broke the silence. "It is so good to see Sunny happier, like a normal college student. Benjamin is a fine young man, too."

Richard nodded. "Did you see how he looks at her? He's in pretty deep."

Aleen acknowledged Benjamin's keen interest in her daughter. "Sunny doesn't talk about it, but from what I understand, she's held him at bay while she tries to get over Stu. Amazingly, he's been patient with her, as I'm not aware they're dating yet."

Vincent laughed. "They will be soon, I think. She's confided in me a bit about her feelings for Ben."

"I think she talks to you more than anyone about her love life," Aleen said, eyeing Vincent, and he just smiled. He treasured his relationship with Sunny, as all around the table understood. While Ted was happy for Sunny, he also felt a bit sad. "Benjamin reminds me of Stu—smart, kind, thoughtful. Perhaps he is a good match for her."

"Hey, she's only nineteen; we don't have to marry her off yet!" Aleen said, lightening the mood and pouring off the last of the Barolo into her guest's glasses before filling her own. "Let's go back on the patio to finish our wine."

Once Benjamin and Sunny got to her room, she closed the door. She heard a good deal of what the adults said about them as they left. She was listening closely, but she wasn't sure what Benjamin heard. It was really embarrassing.

"I didn't know we were doing any schoolwork tonight." Benjamin looked at Sunny, trying to figure out if she was finally going to let him get close to her.

"We aren't. I just wanted some time alone with you." Sunny sat on the bed, and he joined her, sitting so close their thighs touched.

"Hmm," Benjamin said, gazing straight in her eyes. "I like the sound of that."

Sunny stroked the side of his jaw and smoothed his hair before bringing his face to hers.

Benjamin didn't need much encouragement. He took her in his arms and kissed her, soft and light at first, as they were just getting to know each other. But soon, they became more passionate as they explored each other.

Sunny broke away first. "Wow, that was . . . I haven't kissed anyone like that since Stu. . . ."

At the sound of his name, Sunny darkened a bit, and Benjamin tilted her face to him so they looked directly at each other.

"Sunny, we can take it really slow. I've waited this long, but you are so worth it."

Sunny rested her head on his shoulder and put her arms around him. She just held him, savoring the feeling of being in his arms. She was scared; she had been so in love with Stu and was devastated to lose him. Could she ever love anyone like that again?

She kept all her doubts to herself. It was so wonderful being in Benjamin's arms, and she just wanted to enjoy it, trying not to think beyond the moment.

chapter thirty-three

Gerrie and Durk

As she felt so exhausted, Gerrie went to bed right after dinner, even though it was still relatively early in the evening. When she got under the covers, she moved with considerable effort onto her side—the only way she could sleep now that her pregnancy was nearing its end.

Gerrie couldn't believe how big she'd gotten. She felt like a balloon, swollen all over—her feet and ankles were so puffy. Her pregnancy with Stu had been so different; she gained much less weight, and she didn't remember feeling so drained all the time.

Don't be an idiot, she told herself. *You were in your twenties with Stu. Now you're in your late forties. What did you think it would be like?*

Gerrie tried to stop dwelling on her difficult pregnancy. If she were honest, Durk hadn't been very supportive. Yes, he helped her get around, like holding her arm as she walked and being sure to open all doors for her, taking great care when she got in and out of the car. But he didn't ask her about the baby or put his ear to her stomach to feel the baby move and kick as Ted had constantly while she was pregnant with Stu.

There was no question the pregnancy had driven them apart, not brought them closer, as Gerrie hoped it might. She prayed he would warm up to the baby once he was born. The problem was she felt creeping doubt about the baby as well. Was Durk right? Were they too old to have a baby? It sure seemed her creaky and bloated body agreed with him, and her intrusive dark thoughts scared her.

Gerrie couldn't fool herself; she knew she was a wreck. She still blamed herself for Stu's death. She thought she could plunge into her new life with Durk and everything would be just fine, but she was wrong. And the hurt she'd caused Ted nagged at her every day. She'd literally ruined his life. She could hardly live with herself, and now a baby . . . ?

As she always did, Gerrie pushed the negative thoughts out of her mind. There was no going back now; the baby would be here very soon. She already knew she wanted to call him Michael Stuart Hammand Riddick. Yes, it was a mouthful, but she never took Durk's name, so she wanted her new son to carry both names. And she had to pay tribute to her first son; she wouldn't budge on that.

She thought about her ex-husband. She would have to tell Ted about the name so he wasn't blindsided, but she just couldn't take another tongue-lashing from him. She just couldn't.

Gerrie missed the old Ted now, because if this were his child, he would be so excited. *Maybe I'm giving him too much credit,* she thought sadly. Maybe he would resent the intrusion a baby would cause in their lives at this stage, just like Durk.

No, she thought. Ted would embrace this child; she knew he would.

Just then, a steady wave of discomfort gripped her abdomen. After several more painful "cramps," Gerrie was sure she was having contractions. "Mmm," she groaned aloud. Then another pain shot through her, stronger this time. "Durk, Durk, the baby's coming!" she called out.

Gerrie tried to sit up a bit in the hospital bed. It had been a very difficult delivery, lasting all night and into the early hours of the morning. It just about took everything out of her, but she did it. As the painful labor dragged on into the dawn, the doctors had been worried about both mother and son, but Michael made it into the world. And he was perfect. Her son. She was a mother again.

Durk had stepped out to go to the nursery with their son for a few simple evaluations. He didn't seem overjoyed with the name, but he agreed because Gerrie had gone through so much to deliver him. In fact, she was exhausted and fell into a deep sleep as soon as she was alone.

When she woke, Durk was in the room with her. Once she slowly opened her eyes, he jumped up and came to sit on the side of the bed to hold her hand.

"Hey, how are you feeling?" Durk brought her fingers up to his lips and kissed them. "We were getting worried about you."

"I'm a wreck, but I'll be fine. How's the baby? Michael's okay, isn't he?" Gerrie sat up straighter as her concern for the baby grew.

"Gerrie, relax. The baby is perfect, fine." He nodded toward a rolling bassinet near the foot of her bed. "He's sleeping, like you should be. You had a very rough night, and, frankly, you look terrible. You need rest." Durk rubbed her arm.

"You're right. I know I need to sleep. Can you call the nanny and tell her we need her as soon as we're home from the hospital?"

Durk stroked her hair. "I will. Just rest now."

Gerrie looked into the eyes of her second husband. "Will you promise to go home and get some rest yourself? You've been up all night. I feel like I could sleep for days right now."

"Okay, before I leave, I'll tell the nurses to keep an eye on you both." Durk kissed his wife's forehead as she shut her eyes.

Gerrie fell fast asleep, but her last thought before she dropped off was of her husband telling her she looked terrible. Weren't husbands supposed to lie and tell their wives—even when they were too old to have babies—they were beautiful and glowing? Gerrie's head fell to the side as she slipped back into a very deep sleep.

When he saw she was sleeping soundly, Durk left her room, stopped by the nurses' station to let them know mother and baby were resting, and went down the hallway to try to find a decent cup of coffee. It was too early to call Sunny, but he planned to contact her later so she knew about her brother. He understood she wasn't pleased about the baby, but she needed to know he'd entered this world and was healthy. He wondered how she would react to Michael's name.

As he continued down the hall, he remembered Gerrie's request to call the nanny. It irked him a bit, as he and Aleen didn't have a nanny when Sunny was born. She had extended her leave to have more time at home with the baby and then enrolled Sunny into their company childcare center.

The onsite childcare worked so well for their little family because Aleen could stop by on breaks or at lunch, which was particularly handy when she was breastfeeding. Durk loved to pop in to see Sunny as well.

He remembered one time when he had a really tough day at work, he stopped by the center to see her. Sunny was about three years old and such a doll. He spotted her in the corner with a couple other kids, playing with some building blocks. When she looked up and saw him, her little eyes lit up and she shouted, "Daddy!" and came running toward him. Durk got down on his knees as his daughter jumped into his arms and gave him a big hug.

That one moment with his little girl totally changed Durk's mood and made a bad day wonderful; he never forgot it.

Thinking of that memory brought tears to his eyes. He grabbed a handkerchief from his pocket to quickly wipe them dry. Even though he was in the hospital to welcome his new son, the tears he cried were for his grown daughter who he missed and loved so much.

Instead of leaving for home, Durk stopped in the hospital cafeteria for a pretty terrible cup of coffee and a stale donut. He just didn't want to go home to the empty house and knew he wouldn't be able to sleep with so many things on his mind.

He'd been watching his newborn son, Michael Stuart, sleeping peacefully. He was beautiful, but Durk still had serious misgivings about being a new father at his age. His son was living and breathing now, so he would deal with the situation just as he had dealt with everything over the last year.

His mind drifted back to the events of the last twelve months, and it was painful. God, he wished he could tell everyone he knew what NOT to do in life. Hurting the people he loved most in the world, his wife and daughter, had been the lowest point in his life. And literally seeing that wonderful young man die . . .

Durk shook his head. He had to focus on taking care of his new family now. Gerrie hadn't been the same since the accident, and now there was a baby to think about. They would have to plan their lives around Michael. That was what he and Aleen did when Sunny was born. *Look how well that worked out.*

"And whose fault is that?" He admonished himself and threw the cup of coffee and the remainder of the donut into the trash. No, Durk couldn't go home. He knew exactly where he was going.

When he pulled up in front of his old home, he sat in the car for a minute, as it was so early. He and Aleen would always sleep in a bit on Saturday mornings, but generally, Aleen got up to make the coffee and get going by 7:00 a.m. Sunny, well . . . she was a teenager, so Durk and Aleen had to blast her out of bed sometimes. He smiled at the memory.

When he got to the door, he knocked quietly, not wanting to wake his daughter.

Aleen answered with a look of total surprise. "Durk. What are you doing here so early?"

"Good morning to you, as well. Can I come in?" he asked, still a bit apprehensive about his visit.

"Sure. Yes. Is something wrong?" her expression now changed to one of concern.

"No. I just wanted to tell you in person that Gerrie had the baby. Michael Stuart Hammand Riddick." Durk watched intently for her reaction.

"Congratulations. Come on in. I'll make some coffee." Aleen closed the door behind them, and they walked into the kitchen a bit awkwardly. "If I knew you were coming, I would have dressed up a bit more." She looked down at her worn, stained sweats. "But you look horrible as well. I assume you were up all night. Is Gerrie all right?"

Durk sighed, weary in every way. "She had a very rough delivery. Very rough. She needs lots of rest. The whole pregnancy has taken it out of her. I've never seen her like this."

Aleen regarded her ex-husband with a mixture of concern and anger. She couldn't believe she was having this conversation with him. About his wife and new baby!

Durk read her expression. "I realize this is highly unusual—coming to see your ex-wife to tell her about your new baby—but I wanted you and Sunny to hear it directly from me. And I need to ask you a favor."

"Durk . . . I guess I've given up trying to figure out what's the . . . appropriate thing to do. We're all stuck in this situation together, unfortunately." Aleen busied herself with getting the coffee going.

"Even though it hurts like hell, this is a big day in your life, the birth of your first son, so I'm going to make your favorite breakfast." She gave him a crooked smile.

"Scrambled eggs with ham and vegetables and hash browns?" Durk looked so excited, like he might jump out of his skin.

"Exactly." Aleen got the ingredients from the fridge and set out her food processor to speed the chopping and dicing of the vegetables.

"I have a photo on my phone if you want to see the baby. I thought Sunny should see her brother as well."

Aleen looked over as he held up his phone. "He's beautiful, Durk. I just can't imagine having a baby again at our age. Sorry, I guess I'm too honest this early."

Durk smiled. "Well, I do recall you were pretty straightforward first thing in the morning."

"Straightforward." Aleen laughed out loud, surprised at how much she was enjoying this time with her ex-husband, celebrating the birth of his and Gerrie's son. "That's a very nice way of putting it.

"So what was the favor you wanted to ask me?"

"Well, I know Gerrie really wanted to tell Ted herself, but she's in no shape right now to have a serious conversation. Frankly, I think if the exchange got intense at all, she just couldn't handle it. She is totally physically and mentally spent."

"Hmm." Aleen started cooking the hash browns, which she made with onions and green peppers.

"So I was hoping you would tell him. I would, but I don't think he'd appreciate hearing it from me." Durk looked at his ex-wife intently, hoping she would agree.

"You're right about that. I could run by on my way to the store to see if he's home. This isn't a phone call kind of conversation." As the potatoes were cooking, she poured Durk another cup of coffee and refreshed her own.

"This is *so* much better than the sludge I had at the hospital." Durk took a sip and closed his eyes, enjoying it and savoring being in his old home with his former wife.

Aleen studied Durk. Even though he was exhausted, he still looked so handsome with his hazel eyes and beautiful dark hair, now flecked with grey.

She was pleased she could do something to help him, but she was confused; her emotions were so jumbled up. Shouldn't she hate him right now? Why was she happy to see her ex? And especially today, when he just had a baby with another woman!

When the potatoes were almost done, Aleen started sautéing the vegetables for the eggs, and she grabbed a glass of orange juice for Durk and herself. He watched with great interest as she whisked the eggs and poured them into the pan with the ham, vegetables, and fresh herbs she always used. Such a simple thing, watching her cook. He missed that, too.

"Bring your plate over here, and we can get this breakfast going," Aleen said with a surprising amount of cheer as she filled his plate with generous servings of the eggs and potatoes.

Durk dug in as if he hadn't eaten in a long time. "This is so good. You have no idea how much I've missed your cooking."

She smiled, so pleased he liked the breakfast. She saw the strain on his face and was worried about him, despite everything. He had a tough road ahead; she could see it.

Aleen took some eggs onto her plate, along with the piping-hot hash browns. "You know, I didn't cook for a while after . . ." She faltered, and Durk gazed at her knowingly.

"I understand why. You don't have to say it."

There were many things that could go unsaid between the two when they were married, because they understood each other so well. She missed that, and so much more.

"I can't thank you enough, Ali, for making this breakfast and welcoming me when I showed up on your doorstep with no warning." Durk's eyes shone with great affection for his ex-wife.

Aleen was momentarily thrown by the use of his pet name for her and the warmth in his eyes. She opened her mouth, but nothing came out.

Just then, Sunny padded into the kitchen in her pajamas. "Dad, what are you doing here?" She seemed shocked to see her father sitting with her mother at the kitchen island, finishing his breakfast as her mom started to dig into her full plate.

"Good morning, honey." Durk stood and wanted to hug her but held himself back. "I came by because I wanted to tell you in person that you have a brother. Gerrie had the baby early this morning. His name is Michael Stuart Hammand Riddick."

Durk waited for his daughter's reaction, but Sunny just stood there staring at her father.

chapter thirty-four

Ted

Just as Ted was leashing up the dogs for their morning walk, the doorbell rang. He thought it was strange; he wasn't expecting anyone, particularly early on a Saturday morning.

When he opened the door, he found Aleen standing there in her workout clothes.

"I was just on the way to Pilates and shopping and thought I would stop by," she said a bit nervously. Ted thought her smile seemed forced.

Hope and Cash ran to greet her, jumping on her and demanding attention. Aleen complied, rubbing and petting the dogs so they calmed a bit.

"Well, this is a surprise." Ted gazed at Aleen, still a bit confused. "I was just going to take the dogs for a walk. Do you want to come?"

"Sure. Maybe I'll get some extra Pilates credit for the exercise." She giggled. "It's a beautiful morning as well."

They walked out into the sunshine and headed down the long boulevard.

"So what's up? I can tell this isn't just a spur-of-the moment visit." He turned to his friend as the dogs stopped to sniff around a tree.

Aleen nodded, fussing with the strap of her bag. "You're right. I came by with a specific purpose in mind, because I had an unexpected visitor this morning, too."

"Oh?" Ted's interest was piqued.

"Durk came by early today. Gerrie had the baby. . . . His name is Michael Stuart Hammand Riddick." She slowly looked to Ted.

"Is Gerrie all right?" He stared at the ground.

"She is, but she had a terribly rough time. She was in labor all night. At her age, the pregnancy and delivery took a lot out of her. Durk says she needs rest now."

"Well, I hope she's okay. . . ."

"Durk said she would have wanted to tell you herself, but she's just too worn down and couldn't take any kind of—"

"I could have talked civilly with her. I'm not an idiot, Aleen."

She gently placed a hand on his arm. "No one thinks you are, but Gerrie isn't herself and needs lots of rest. Durk is quite worried, to be honest. He looked like hell."

"Sorry to get upset, but this kind of news is unsettling, isn't it?" Ted said, walking along the path again.

"It does bring up painful memories for us both." Aleen agreed as the two friends strolled along. "When Durk came by so early this morning, I was surprised, of course, but when I saw how much he needed to talk, how exhausted he was, and worried, I guess my nurturing instincts kicked in. I made him his favorite breakfast."

Ted was silent for a few moments. "Well, you're a better person than me. I guess I've always known that." He seemed sad as he moved down the path, dragging the dogs along when they tried to chew on something they shouldn't.

"Not sure about that." She shook her head slowly. "I felt a real pang of anger or jealousy or something when Durk showed me the photo of the baby, so I'm no saint."

Ted stopped in his tracks. "You have a photo of the baby?"

Aleen pulled her phone out of her pocket, found the photo Durk had shared, and held it up so he could see.

"Gosh, he does remind me of Stu." He looked intently at the photo, studying the infant.

They continued on in silence for some time.

"You okay?" Aleen glanced over at her friend with real concern.

Ted rubbed the back of his neck. "When you said the baby's name, Michael Stuart, I think my heart stopped. I know Gerrie meant it as a tribute to Stu, but it just stunned me for a minute. And then when you showed me the photo, the resemblance to Stu . . . well, it just took my breath away."

"I understand," she said, rubbing his arm affectionately.

"I'm racking my brain, trying to figure out what to do, but I think I know the answer, and it isn't easy."

"What are you thinking?"

"I've got to see Gerrie and the baby. There are so many things that went unsaid between us after Stu died. I know it almost destroyed me, and Lord knows what it's done to her. She puts on this tough exterior, but I know my wife—" He stopped himself. "Ex-wife, of course."

He walked on for a few moments.

"Gerrie needs to get back on her feet. I wouldn't attempt to have this conversation until she is absolutely ready, but we must have it." Ted's jaw was firmly set, his mind made up.

"I would like to make a suggestion, if you'd allow me," Aleen prompted as gently as she could.

Ted nodded.

"I believe you should go and see Gerrie and the baby when she is well and have an easier conversation first. Don't come straight out of the box and talk about your shared grief. Sandy would have ideas about the best way to approach it." She stopped to gauge Ted's reaction.

"Good ideas. Thanks." He pulled at the dogs' leashes. They'd gotten ahold of something plastic they found in the grass. "Guys, put that down. Put it *down now*."

The pups finally obeyed and ran ahead.

"The irony is I believe Gerrie needs this conversation as much as me, perhaps more so. Let's hope she can get back on her feet physically as soon as possible. Knowing her, she's going to want to get back to work right away, and that's the worst thing she could do."

Aleen nodded. "For sure."

"I need to make peace with Durk, too," Ted continued. "That's going to be really hard."

"And I need to figure out a way to have a civil relationship with Gerrie." Aleen grimaced at the challenge. "She is the mother of Sunny's half-brother, and my daughter is going to want a relationship with him."

Ted nodded as they followed after the dogs. "I know Sunny well enough to know you're right. There's no question in my mind she will want to spend time with her little brother. Perhaps not right away, but soon enough."

"It may take her some time, but she's going to want to be a great big sister to him. I know it. If she sees Stu in him, as you did . . ."

Ted didn't say anything, but he knew Aleen was exactly right. Sunny would love that little boy so much, even if she didn't know it yet.

"What are you thinking?" Aleen asked as the dogs stopped to sniff around some flowers.

"This baby may help us all. We can't continue to focus on our own grief and anger."

Aleen didn't answer, but instinctively, she knew he was right. Things would change now, for all of them, and they needed to be ready.

chapter thirty-five

Sunny

After her mother left to see Ted, Sunny grabbed her phone to call Benjamin.

"Did I wake you up?" she asked after he answered, sounding a bit groggy.

"Well . . ." Benjamin laughed on the other end.

"Sorry," she said. "I wouldn't have called if it wasn't important."

Benjamin was concerned now, hearing the tension in Sunny's voice. "What's wrong?"

"When I got up this morning, my dad was having breakfast with my mom. He stopped by early. Mrs. Hammand had the baby. I knew it was a boy, but she's named him Michael Stuart Hammand Riddick."

"Wow, that *is* big news." Benjamin was all ears.

"When I heard his name, I kind of froze . . ." Sunny couldn't finish the sentence.

"Listen, Sun, we were going to get together later today anyway. Why don't I come early?"

Sunny found herself nodding, even though he couldn't see her gesture. "I think that would be good, Ben. I don't want you to worry. I'm really okay, trying to sort it all out, but I'm not sure what I'm supposed to do now."

"Hang on, Sunny. I'll be there as soon as I can." They hung up quickly so they could be together.

The sooner the better, she thought to herself.

Sunny took her shower and got dressed with one thing on her mind—her new little brother. She tried to study, then made an effort to check in on friends on social media, but nothing could distract her from thoughts of Michael.

She sent a quick text to Vincent to let him know Gerrie had the baby and that she had a new brother. He answered immediately, checking to see if she and Aleen were okay.

What a great guy. I need to introduce him to my dad someday.

Sunny surprised herself with that thought and her concern for her dad. She'd spent the last year hating him, but he seemed so drained and sad; he was hardly rejoicing in the birth of his new son. He'd loved that her mom made him breakfast. Sunny heard Mrs. Hammand was a terrible cook, so her dad must really miss all her mom's homemade meals. But it was more than that really.

What's going on?

Sunny jumped up when she heard the garage door opening and her mom coming in. She ran to the kitchen to greet her. And she needed some answers.

"Mom, I didn't expect you home so soon. I thought you were going to Pilates and shopping after you saw Mr. Hammand."

Aleen put her arms out for her daughter, and Sunny walked right into a much-needed hug. "I wanted to come back and talk to you. I know everything that went on this morning is probably on your mind." She smoothed Sunny's hair. "I can go to class and do the shopping later when you get together with Benjamin."

"I actually called him, and he'll be here in a bit. I guess I just needed to hear his voice." Sunny was still rocking in her mom's arms.

"I understand, hon. Let's sit down in the family room. I need a glass of water. How about you?"

Sunny nodded, and Aleen got them each a glass and sat down across from her.

"How did it go with Mr. Hammand?"

Aleen could tell Sunny was very interested in Ted's reaction to everything. "I'm not sure what I expected, but I think it went as well as it could. Like you, when he heard the baby's name, it kind of stopped him in his tracks, and when I showed him the photo and he saw a resemblance to Stu, that really got to him as well."

"I didn't see the resemblance," Sunny said, confused.

"Well, you didn't know Stu when he was a baby. Ted spent more time raising him than Gerrie did, so seeing a baby that looked like his son brought up so many memories." Aleen was quiet for a minute, thinking about her friend.

"Do you think we should go and see him together?" Sunny eagerly looked to her mom for an answer.

"You have plans, hon. Spend time with Benjamin. Try and get your mind off of this today. I told Ted we should get together tonight. I think I'll make him dinner here. I'll call Vincent to see if he and Richard are free to join us. Perhaps you'd like to see Ted tomorrow."

Sunny picked up her phone. "I'll text him and see if that's okay."

She quickly typed the request to Ted, and Aleen watched her daughter with so much pride she could burst. The fact that she was thinking about Ted right now, not just her own feelings, made Aleen happy.

We raised a wonderful daughter, Durk.

Thinking of her ex-husband caused her to pause. Something happened this morning, and she wasn't quite sure what.

It wasn't long before Ted's answer came with a ping on Sunny's phone. She glanced at it and smiled. "He said 'yes', so I'll stop by tomorrow. But not as early as you did today!" She smiled at her mother. "Did he say anything I should know about when I visit him tomorrow?"

"Yes, he did. He actually said the baby may be a good thing for all of us, because he can help take our focus off our own pain and grief." Aleen stared directly at her daughter to gauge her reaction.

"Mr. Hammand is a smart man; he may be right.

"Do you have any idea how many times I dreamed of having a sister or brother when I was growing up?" She laughed halfheartedly.

"Well, honey, you know we tried, but it just didn't work. I had one miscarriage about four years after I had you—"

"Mom, I never knew that. Why didn't you tell me?" Sunny seemed hurt.

Aleen regarded her daughter seriously. "Because you're a young woman now, and we can have adult conversations. I chose *this* moment to tell you."

Sunny nodded. "Okay, I buy that, but if we're having adult conversations now, I need to ask you something. What is going on with Dad?" She took a drink of her water, all the while keeping her eyes on her mother, who seemed to find her question difficult to answer.

Aleen walked over to the window. "I wish I knew, honey. He seemed so happy to be here for breakfast, to see you—"

"And you," Sunny interjected.

"Yes, I felt that, too. I don't know how to explain it, but when you've loved someone as much as I loved your father . . ." She had trouble completing her sentence. "Seeing him so unsettled really shook me up. Perhaps Ted is right that the baby will help us sort things out. As much as your father hurt me, I can't really stand to see him so stressed and unhappy . . . especially on a day that should be joyous for him."

Aleen walked back over to the couch and sat down.

"I don't want Daddy unhappy, either," Sunny said, tears pooling in her eyes.

"There's something else Ted said that you would find of interest. He knows he has to make peace with your father, as I must with Gerrie now that she's the mother of your new little brother.

"But first, you have to develop a real relationship with your father. He misses you so much. He actually told me he was thinking about you today at the hospital, rather than his newborn son. You've got to try and make it right with him."

Sunny hung on her mother's every word.

"Don't think for a moment that you're being disloyal to me by having a good relationship with your father and his new family. It's been a year since the accident, and your dad left me for Gerrie. We all have to move on. There's a new baby to worry about."

Sunny stared at the ground, grinding her fists into the tops of her knees. "I'm not sure I can do that."

"You have to, Sunny. You must go to that house and see the baby when the time is right. Start thinking about how you're going to do that." Aleen came and sat next to her, putting her arm around her. "For a young person, you've had to face way too much adversity in your life."

Sunny leaned her head on her mom's shoulder. "I know, and I don't always know the right thing to do."

"I get it, honey, but your brother is counting on you now. You said earlier that you always wanted a brother or sister; now you have one.

"I understand this isn't the way you wanted it to happen. It's not what I would have wanted, either. But life throws a lot of curves at you. You have to understand I'm making this speech as much for me as for you. Going forward, I have to do a lot of things I'm not really comfortable with, too."

"I know, Mom. I know," Sunny said with great sadness in her voice.

Just then, the doorbell rang, and Sunny sprang to her feet to welcome Benjamin. She jumped into his arms before he could get all the way into the house. "I'm so glad you're here," she said, hugging him.

Aleen stood to greet Benjamin, and he broke free from Sunny to say hello. "Good to see you, Mrs. Riddick."

"Benjamin, I'm so happy to see you. Sunny is anxious to talk with you about her new brother, so I'll leave you two alone. I have my Pilates class and some errands to run. See you later." With that, she grabbed her purse and keys and went out the door to the garage.

Sunny slipped back into Benjamin's arms with no plans to let him go.

chapter thirty-six

Gerrie

Gerrie could hardly move her head off the pillow. She'd been home from the hospital for weeks but had spent most of her time in a state of total exhaustion. Thank God Durk had talked to Don, her boss, and asked for an extended leave from work. Work? She couldn't even take care of herself, much less a new baby.

Michael. He would be better off without her. This hope-lessness, this emptiness she felt was crippling her. The guilt over Stu's death was eating her alive. There was no way she deserved to have another baby. What was she thinking?

The nanny was here as much as she could be to take care of the baby. Gerrie was so out of it. *What a useless mother I am, an utterly worthless human being,* she thought. *Kill your first son and ignore your second.*

She knew Durk was scared for her, simply based on the way he looked at her when they talked. There was so much fear in his eyes. He wanted her to get well, regain her strength, be a wife and mother again.

Remember, you were the one who wanted to be a mother again, she thought. *Your husband didn't want this baby. Well, be careful what you ask for.*

God, where was the old Gerrie? The one who could solve any business problem, travel around the world by herself, lead a team of hundreds, but still be a good wife and loving mother to her beautiful son? She closed her eyes and tried to summon that woman, because Michael deserved better. Durk, too.

The old Gerrie would have been able to handle seeing Ted and then Sunny when they came by to see the baby. Durk had said they both wanted to say hello to Gerrie, but she just couldn't do it. She was so exhausted she couldn't get out of bed and face the hate in their eyes.

The last time she saw Ted had gone horribly. Again, a situation of her own making. *You betrayed him. Then you made love with him, only to reveal you were pregnant with another man's child. Who does that? You are a horrible person, Geraldine, and everything you do is wrong.*

Even though she was always in bed, she wasn't resting, as these terrible thoughts dogged her constantly. It was such a vicious cycle, trying to grab some rest when the baby slept, only to relive every mistake she'd ever made and then fall into a fitful sleep, then to be awakened to feed the baby. She felt like a zombie.

Gerrie was losing weight because food had no appeal, which certainly wasn't helping her produce milk for Michael. *Is there anything else you can be a total failure at?*

That's it, Gerrie. Get ahold of yourself. Get out of bed now. Get dressed and go downstairs. Eat something and see your baby. There seemed to be a crack of light as she made her way to the closet to get dressed and went slowly down the stairs, hanging on to the railing for dear life. The old Gerrie was trying to take over. Boy, she really needed her now.

When she got to the kitchen, Meg was preparing a bottle for Michael. "Mrs. Riddick, so glad you're up. Are you feeling better?"

"Meg, I'm doing my best to feel better. I can't thank you enough for everything you've done to take care of Michael. I'm afraid I've done a lousy job as his mother so far." Gerrie sat on one of the counter stools.

"You've had a very hard time, and you have to get better first. Glad to see you're up and around. Do you want to feed Michael?"

"I do, but I think I'll grab a quick bowl of cereal while he's sleeping. I realize I haven't been making enough milk. My eating habits have been terrible since I had the baby." She got up to get herself a bowl of Cheerios and cut up some strawberries to put on top.

Meg poured her a glass of milk and set it down in front of her. "Try to get this down. It will help."

Gerrie ate her cereal and drank the whole glass of milk. She felt so proud of herself for doing such a simple thing. "Okay, I'll go up and feed him. I'll take this formula in case I don't have enough breastmilk to satisfy him."

As she walked up the stairs to head to Michael's room, she passed Stu's old room and stopped to talk to him. "I'm trying, Stu. I'm really trying to be the mother your brother deserves. But don't think for a minute he has replaced you in my heart, as he never could. I love you so much, Stu, and I think about you every day. If only . . ."

Gerrie stopped talking, as she couldn't finish the sentence and began to worry Meg would hear her and think she was crazy. She touched her lips to her fingers and then planted the kiss on the closed door of Stu's bedroom. She was in no shape to go inside. Perhaps she could later, when she was stronger.

Continuing down the hall, she slipped into Michael's room. He was still asleep, so she sat in the rocking chair next to his crib. The steady sound of his breathing calmed her. *Why don't I feel like this all the time?* The negative and self-destructive thoughts seemed to dominate her every waking moment. She shook her head to try to keep her focus on the beautiful baby sleeping beside her.

When Michael started to fuss, she picked him up and put him to her breast. "Hey, little one . . . you beautiful boy. Let's see if there's enough there for you." His tiny lips locked around her nipple, and Gerrie rocked in the chair as her son ate greedily.

After a very short time, he started crying, and she gave him her breast again. He tried but couldn't seem to get any more milk. She switched breasts, with the same result.

Gerrie sighed, closing her shirt and retrieving the bottle. God, she was so useless; she couldn't even breastfeed her own baby. Life never seemed to be this hard before. She stared out the window as the baby sucked on the bottle.

Stu, Stu, why did you have to die? It's all my fault. God is punishing me now. That's why nothing is going right. Gerrie continued to rock her baby as he had his dinner, but she felt so tired, so hopeless.

chapter thirty-seven

Sunny

A couple weeks after the baby was born, Sunny set out in the morning to see Mr. Hammand. As she drove over, she thought of Benjamin.

Whenever they could steal a private moment, Sunny and Benjamin were in each other's arms. Sunny thought it was wonderful to have someone to touch again. She wasn't quite ready to make love with him yet, but this was becoming more serious. She knew what she had to do, especially today of all days.

Her mom understood she needed to do this on her own. Sunny could see the concern in her mother's eyes when she hugged her before leaving the house this morning. She didn't need to tell her mom what day it was or how she was feeling. Aleen knew reliving that day was going to be unbearable for all of them.

Sunny parked near Ted's condo and walked back onto the boulevard near the tree. She never went to the cemetery; she knew Stu wasn't there. The last time Sunny saw him alive was right here, next to the tree where the flowers served as an ever-present tribute to him.

She'd brought a bouquet of bright spring blooms much like one

Stu brought for her not long before he died. *What kind of teenager brings flowers for his girlfriend? That was my Stu.* Sunny laughed.

Using a long ribbon, she tied the bouquet to the tree, looping it around and finishing with a beautiful bow. Then she knelt down to have a conversation with her beloved Stu. She'd thought about it all week and came to the conclusion the best thing to do was write her thoughts down in a letter.

Dear Stu,

I know you're probably laughing up there in heaven because you know none of us write letters anymore. (Well, maybe our moms and dads do.) We only text now, not even email. . . . That is so old! I guess writing a letter like this is what it was like in the 1800s. (That's a joke!) So you must be really special for me to actually write a letter on paper.

Somehow it didn't seem right to type this note, even though I can type a lot faster than I write. This is really hard to do for many reasons, so I hope you appreciate it.

I can't believe it's been a year since you died. It's been pretty rough for all of us you left behind, which I'm sure you know. We've suffered because we loved you so much. Thinking of that last afternoon we had together, when you made love to me for the first time, kept me going for so long. It was just so amazing that I'll never, ever forget it my whole life.

Mom said I've had to go through so much for someone so young. I feel it, Stu. I do. Losing you was the worst thing that could have ever happened! Do you think we would have gotten married? Had children? I have so many questions, and I know I'll never have the answers.

Stu, I thought I was going to die, too, when you were killed. I actually thought it would be better if I died so we could be together.

But I didn't die. I couldn't do that to my parents and to your dad. Mom and I have become very close to him. We've really helped each other, and I thought you would like that. Your dad is the greatest, but you know that. He's been more of a father to me lately than my own dad, but I share some blame in that. There's just too much hurt and guilt around here.

We actually went to counseling to try and learn how to live again without you. Sandy, the counselor, actually suggested I write my thoughts down on paper. It does help, and I thought I might look a little crazy sitting in the grass by the side of the road, talking to a tree!

You probably heard we have a new brother named Michael Stuart Hammand Riddick. He'll grow up with constant reminders of you—his name just one. We'll talk to him about you all the time, even before he can fully understand. He'll love you as much as we did, I'm sure. Your dad says he looks like you. I don't see it yet, but maybe I will later.

I promise you I will look out for Michael and your dad. They're both family to me now. Your father says the baby may help us focus on something else rather than all our pain and anger. I really hope so.

We've met the man who drove the car that hit you. He is so sorry, Stu. He was in agony after you died, almost as bad as us, and he didn't even know you! When you went through the stop sign, he couldn't avoid hitting you.

His name is Vincent, and we've all tried to help him. We didn't meet him that night; your dad ran into him when he brought beautiful flowers to the tree as a memorial to you. He's a great guy; your dad, my mom, and Vincent are really close. We've all helped each other. I think you'd be proud of us, really.

There is something serious I need to tell you now. I've met someone. You should know I couldn't look at anyone for so long because I missed you so much. His name is Benjamin, and we were just friends for the longest time. He's in my engineering study group. The group has helped me a lot, and I really like studying engineering, just as we thought I would.

Anyway, back to Benjamin. He reminds me of you. He's smart, sweet, kind, and has been so wonderful, because he waited a long time for me. Stu, I think I'm ready now for him to be my boyfriend. (He isn't as handsome as you, but he's very, very cute! Don't tell him I said you were more handsome. He might not like that!)

He will never take your place in my heart 'cause there is a special section just for you, always. It's just so hard today, on the one-year anniversary of your death. To think you were so alive and well and loving me a year ago, it still breaks my heart, Stu. But I have to go on with my life and move forward.

I hope you understand and love me enough to know this is the right thing for me now.

I love you, always.

Sunny
xxxxx

Sunny kissed the letter and put it behind the flowers. When she looked up, Mr. Hammand was heading toward her with Hope and Cash.

She bent down to give the dogs a proper greeting, and they jumped all over her. "Hey, you guys, I'm glad to see you, too." Sunny laughed and petted the dogs. "Especially on *this* day."

Ted walked up and gave her a hug. "I thought you might stop by here today."

Sunny hugged him extra hard. "I had to come here to ask Stu something, something really important."

"Do you want to tell me?" he waited, keenly interested in her reply.

"Well, first I told him we had a brother now, and I promised I would always watch over him. And you, too. I explained we're all trying to get over our anger and pain and that you said the baby may help us do that."

Ted nodded and gazed with affection at the wonderful young woman before him.

"I said you, my mom, and I were close and were trying to help each other move forward. I told him about how sorry Vincent was and how we're all good friends now. But the main reason I really needed to talk to him was to ask—or tell him—that I really liked Benjamin and hoped he could be my boyfriend now."

Ted didn't say anything, but just listened with interest to what his young friend had to say.

"I told Stu I would always love him and no one could ever replace him, but I felt Benjamin was special, just like him." Sunny paused to check on how he would react to this.

"Sunny, Benjamin is a fine young man, and I think of you as a daughter, so I have more than a casual interest in anyone you go out with."

She hung on Ted's every word.

"And I can tell you without doubt that Stu would approve and want you to be happy. We all do, honey. We all do."

Sunny jumped into his arms. "It means a lot coming from you. You know how hard this day is. I've been dreading it for months," she said, pulling away from him to take a tissue out and wipe her tears.

"It's right what you said about all of us moving forward. You took a big step today, and I'm proud of you. You deserve the most special young man in the world, and I think you have him in Benjamin."

She smiled at Ted; his words made her so happy.

Just then, Vincent arrived with his flowers. "Not sure how I knew you both would be here right now . . ."he said, greeting his friends with warm embraces. He placed his flowers at the base of the tree, stood silently for a few moments, and then looked over at Sunny and Ted.

Sunny walked into his arms and held Vincent for a minute and whispered in his ear, "Vincent, I told Stu about you and how sorry you are and how we're helping each other. And how proud he would be of us."

When they broke apart, Vincent had tears in his eyes as he gazed at Sunny. Ted put his hand on Vincent's shoulder.

"Should we go for a walk?" he asked his friends, gently pulling on the dogs' leashes to get them moving.

Vincent, Sunny, and Ted headed up the street, walking together and enjoying each other's company as well as the beautiful spring day.

chapter thirty-eight

Gerrie

Gerrie could not believe how nervous she was to see her ex-husband. She kept straightening the same pillows on the couch to distract herself. She hadn't been able to get out of bed when Ted had come by previously to see her and the baby.

While her progress was slow, Gerrie was making small steps to recover, spending more time out of bed and trying to eat a little better.

She hadn't seen much of Ted over the last year, for obvious reasons. Gerrie hadn't been alone with him since that afternoon they made love and she told him about the baby. *What a disaster,* she thought. *Can't focus on that right now.* She needed to be cool and calm when he arrived.

Would Gerrie holding the baby bring back too many memories for Ted, particularly as the baby grew to look more and more like Stu every day?

Sometimes, she dreamed about the baby, and it was Stu. She shook her head back and forth. *Just think positive thoughts right now. He'll be here shortly.*

Durk made sure he wasn't at home so they could have some privacy.

Walking over to the hallway mirror, Gerrie took in her reflection. While she still appeared tired, she had done her makeup and hair, so she thought she looked at least half human. It was important to her to look nice for Ted.

Peering through the glass surround of the front door, she finally saw him walking up. Waiting until he rang the bell, she opened the door. "Ted, so good to see you. Please come in," Gerrie said a bit formally, swinging the door open for her ex-husband.

"Gerrie, you look well. I'm glad you're doing better. I know it took some time for you to recover from your very tough delivery." He looked at his ex-wife warmly but matched her formal tone and kept his distance.

"Thanks, Ted. I'm trying my best to get back to normal. Whatever *normal* is." She half chuckled, nervous. "Please, come into the living room so we can sit down."

Ted followed her and was glad she didn't choose the family room, the scene of that terrible night where she told Stu of the affair and their failed marriage. He blanched as he recalled that evening and wondered how she could cope with all the memories in this house.

He sat in the chair a bit stiffly, while Gerrie made herself comfortable on the couch, adjusting the cushions behind her to combat her nervousness.

Clearing his throat a touch too loudly, Ted made a start on the speech he'd practiced over and over in his head. "Gerrie, I want you to know it's important to me that you and I have a cordial relationship. I'd like to try to put the anger and bitterness behind us. It doesn't help anyone, and I think the baby should be everyone's focus now. He deserves to have people around him who can get along and who have his best interests at heart."

She nodded and looked at her ex-husband with great affection; what a wonderful man he was.

"Aleen, Sunny, and I have discussed the relationships we all want to have with Durk, you, and the baby. Michael is Sunny's brother, and she wants to be a big part of his life. And I must make peace with Durk, just as Aleen must have a workable relationship with you. All of this will help Sunny have a better relationship with her dad and establish a good connection with her brother."

He watched Gerrie to gauge her reaction.

"Ted, I'm happy you feel this way. You're so important to me. Not having you in my life has been terrible, and having Aleen and Sunny hate me has been awful. But it's not like I don't understand why . . ."

Ted came over to sit next to her. "We have to put all of that behind us, Gerrie. We've got to, for Michael's sake, as well as our own."

Gerrie was so overcome with emotion that she couldn't speak. She just grabbed Ted's hand as the tears rolled down her cheeks.

"It's okay, really." He squeezed her hand.

"I don't deserve you. You amaze me. With everything I've done to you . . ." She stared at her ex-husband and wouldn't let go of his hand.

They both could hear the nanny coming down the stairs with Michael, so they stopped holding hands, and Gerrie quickly tried to wipe away her tears.

The baby was fussing a little bit as Meg brought him over. "I think he wanted to say hello," she said.

"Can I hold him?" Ted glanced first at Meg and then at Gerrie. She nodded, so Meg put the baby in Ted's arms before going back upstairs.

"What a good boy you are. And so handsome," Ted said, and the baby smiled. Michael seemed to take to him right away.

"Now, you have to be a good boy for your mother so she can get her rest. She's still a bit tired, you know." He let the baby grab his finger and hang on.

Gerrie watched and felt like she was falling in love with her ex-husband again. He'd been so wonderful with Stu, and he was the same way with Michael. As he bounced Michael around, the two of them smiled and laughed. She couldn't stop looking at the two of them; she felt she could sit like this for hours.

"Mommy's a bit quiet, Michael. Wonder what she's thinking." Ted looked over at Gerrie, who still couldn't take her eyes off them.

"Mommy was just thinking she is so lucky to have both of you in her life," Gerrie said so quietly it was hard for Ted to hear.

He moved closer to her again, putting the baby in her arms. He gently touched the baby's head and cheek. "Michael Stuart, you are the most beautiful boy and remind me so much of your brother . . ." With that admission, Ted found it impossible to control his emotions.

Gerrie was crying now, too, and wiped her own tears before wrapping her arm around Ted to comfort him.

As she held the baby in one arm and tried to support Ted with the other, the three of them stayed linked, rocking together on the couch for some time. She knew this was a big step for them, and Gerrie wished this moment could last a very long time.

chapter thirty-nine

Sunny

Sunny drove over to her appointment with Sandy, full of trepidation. She needed to talk to her about things she found difficult to put into words and could never discuss with her mother or Ted. *No way*, she thought to herself.

As her mother was leaving today for her first business trip, Sunny had invited Benjamin over after school for a boat ride. She couldn't remember the last time she'd been on the boat; she used to love it so much, particularly the times she and her mom and dad would bring a picnic basket with lunch that they would enjoy while sailing around the lake. But those times were over.

She looked forward to showing Benjamin around the lake. There was so much to see that wasn't visible from any of the public roads around the rim.

Sunny mentioned she'd invited Benjamin over, but she didn't tell her mom the whole truth about her plans. Aleen was so excited over her first business trip that she was a bit distracted, so she didn't question Sunny's invitation to her boyfriend.

There were some big questions bothering Sunny, so she was hopeful Sandy could help her think everything through. She pulled her reliable little car, which was racking up tons of miles, into the parking space in front of Sandy's office. After she buzzed her in, Sunny grabbed some water and took her seat in the middle of the comfy couch.

"Well, Sunny, you said in your email that you had a few things you wanted to talk about today." Sandy wore gray slacks and a beautiful lime-green silk shirt. Her blond hair was pulled back into a neat ponytail, and she finished off her look with a gold necklace with small green stones in it. She was very pretty and had such a warm smile.

With her encouragement, Sunny had been able to open up about some of her deepest fears. Sandy hoped she could help her today.

"I'm trying to figure out some stuff." Sunny started out uneasily.

"What stuff?" Sandy observed her young client with interest.

"It's about Benjamin," she said very quickly to make sure she got the words out.

Sandy raised her eyebrow. "Is there a problem?"

"No, no, I don't think so. I just feel like I'm falling in love with him." Sunny got up and paced around the office, stopping at the heavy curtains. "Actually, I *am* in love with him, to be honest with you. It's just so scary."

"Why, Sunny? Why is it scary?" Sandy asked.

She moved back to the couch and took her seat, grabbing the bottom of the cushion. "The last time I loved someone, and made love with him, he died. He was killed that same night. I know it's crazy, but what if it's me? What if I make love with Benjamin and then something happens to him? I would blame myself forever!" Sunny looked at Sandy with wild eyes.

"Sunny, it's not you. You shouldn't think that. Now, it *can* be scary to love someone, though. Isn't it?"

The young woman on the couch nodded. "That's the other part of it. When I gave my love to Stu, I gave him everything. He was my life. And then when I lost him, I thought I would die. I *wanted* to die to be with him. There's no way I could go through that again. Just couldn't do it." Her anxiety was getting the better of her.

Sandy gazed at Sunny with concern. "It's okay, Sunny. It really is. I understand why you're upset. You loved Stu so much, but this is a different love, a different person. What happened to Stu was a tragic accident." Sandy stopped to look directly at her.

She fiddled with her hair but seemed to regain control. "It was hard to meet someone so wonderful like Benjamin so soon after Stu died. I wasn't ready, and we were just friends for the longest time. I could tell he wanted to get closer to me from the first time we met. But since we became such good friends first, it gave me the chance to see what a really great guy he was.

"I'm scared to lose him but scared to make love to him, too. And what if it doesn't work out? It's just so hard." Sunny put her face in her hands.

"Love is forever a risk because it doesn't always work out. But I think you will find love is a risk worth taking. Are you thinking about making love with him soon?" Sandy asked, watching as Sunny took her hands from her face and continued playing with her hair.

"I, um . . ." She hesitated. "Umm . . . I, well, I'm trying to decide if we should make love tonight."

"That's a very big decision, one you should think through carefully. You also must be prepared physically as well as mentally." Sandy wanted to be sure her young client understood all the implications.

"I know. Believe me; I know. I'm just not sure what to do."

Sunny folded her hands in her lap and looked straight at Sandy, hoping she could help her find the right answer.

After her session with Sandy, Sunny returned home. Soon, she received a text from Benjamin stating he was on the way but was starved. She made a quick salad, got out her mother's famous salad dressing, and began preparing a quick pasta dinner. Nothing fancy, just bottled sauce.

Sunny thought about what her mom would do to dress up this meal, and she grabbed some fresh basil from the garden and washed it to shred on top. She also found the wonderful aged Parmesan her mother always bought and grated it so they could sprinkle it on their pasta.

There, Sunny thought, *not so bad for spur of the moment.* They might even steal some of her mom's open pinot noir. She was almost twenty now, so she could sneak one glass.

It wasn't long until Benjamin arrived, looking so handsome. Sunny put her arms around his neck and gave him a wonderful welcome.

"Oh, I like that," Benjamin said, returning her kiss. As they pulled apart, he spotted the ingredients for their dinner on the kitchen counter. "Wow, this looks pretty good, and I'm so hungry."

Sunny turned on the burner to get the water boiling for the pasta. She poured a bit of wine for each of them.

"Well, what's the occasion?" Benjamin asked, a broad smile across his face.

"Just us getting together." She smiled back at him.

Benjamin walked over to her in front of the stove and put his arms around her. "We need to get together more often." The kiss he gave her was long and sweet and lingered on her lips until the sound of the boiling pasta water forced them apart.

"Well, let's get this dinner going so we can have our boat ride." Sunny dumped the pasta in the boiling water and took the lid off the simmering sauce to check it.

Benjamin nuzzled her from behind. "I'm really looking forward to it. I've never been on Lake Sherwood before."

"I guarantee you're going to love it. The lake is so beautiful, and there's so much wildlife. Though, at this rate, it may be dark by the time we get back." Sunny smiled to herself, envisioning the possibilities for the end of their ride.

After the pasta was done, Sunny dished it up in warmed bowls and added the sauce, slivered basil, and freshly grated Parmesan.

Benjamin practically inhaled it. "Wow! You weren't kidding about being hungry."

Sunny was amazed at how quickly he finished the pasta and offered him more salad, which he eagerly accepted. She was still eating but wasn't really very hungry and was picking at it. She offered it to Ben, and he finished her leftovers as well.

"That was awesome for a quick, thrown-together dinner. It appears you *are* your mother's daughter when it comes to cooking." His broad grin showed this was a real compliment.

"Living up to my mom's standards . . . that's a tough one. Believe me; I have a long way to go to be a good cook, but I'm so glad you liked it. Now, help me clean this up and we can head out on the boat."

It wasn't long until they climbed down the back stairs through the yard and to the sixteen-foot ElectraCraft. Because it ran on electricity, it silently glided through the water. The homeowners' association had strict rules about the kinds of boats that could be used on the lake.

As this boat's top speed was only five miles an hour, it didn't cause much of a wake. Lots of folks called them "martini cruisers," as there were seats for about ten people and a big table at the back with plenty of room for food and drinks.

When Sunny was a young girl, her dad got her an inner tube and tied it to the back of the boat so she could float behind as her dad navigated around the lake. Sunny always waved at everyone on the other boats and the shore. She loved to see the fishermen trying to catch the bigmouth bass that had been stocked in the lake. It was catch-and-release, so those fish grew really large.

Growing up on the lake was special, and Sunny wanted to share it with Benjamin. As she was more experienced with the boat, she had him untie the ropes and jump in, and then she reversed the craft out of their space and into the open water.

"Wow, cool," Benjamin said, enjoying the view on the lake. It was always relaxing to silently float around, enjoying the mountains and scenery, getting up close and personal with the ducks, geese, and swans, and, of course, checking out any home renovation or construction projects on the lake.

Sunny sailed back near the dam, where there were some beautiful houses and a fantastic mountain view.

"I had no idea the lake was so big and there were so many houses," Benjamin said, admiring some beautiful gardens as well. "It must be fantastic to live here, so much beauty."

"It is. I can't think of a better place to grow up, but I am biased," she said, steering the boat near the shore. "It's your turn to be captain now." She slid over as Benjamin took her place behind the steering wheel.

"This is so strange," he said as he moved the wheel only slightly and the boat responded.

"My dad used to say it was more like a shed than a boat. When the wind kicks up, it blows this thing all over the place. I remember one time, the three of us came out on the lake, and we didn't pay any attention to the electric charge. We must have forgotten to plug it in, and when we looked down at the gauge, it was in the red zone and we were way on the other side of the water." Sunny laughed at the memory.

"My dad and I were ready to jump in and pull the boat back to our house. It was late in the day, and the patrol had gone in for the night. Thank God we didn't have to do that. Somehow we managed to limp in, cutting the engine when we had to just make it back to our dock. We learned our lesson on that one!"

Benjamin glanced down at the dial. "We're in the green, so no problem now."

Sunny grabbed some drinks she'd brought aboard, and they watched the sunset, leaning into each other and chatting. They floated by the rocky shore, some beds of reeds and the swans floating effortlessly with the mountains in the background as the light began to fade.

There were two marinas filled with other boats, mostly electric like their sixteen-footer. It seemed to Benjamin and Sunny like all the other boats were parked, as they didn't spot another on the lake for as far as they could see.

Pointing across the water, Sunny explained that all the houses higher on the ridge looked similar because they'd been built more recently and conformed to the new homeowners' association rules. The older houses had personalities all their own.

"Gorgeous," Benjamin commented, snaking his arm around Sunny as the last light dimmed. "I can see how wonderful it would be to live here. It's like a little paradise, hidden away."

"Do you think we should head in? It's starting to get dark now," Benjamin asked, pretty sure she would answer in the affirmative.

"I haven't told you how dangerous it is on the lake at night. It gets pitch black. You really can't see a thing."

"Isn't that why we should go in?" Benjamin questioned, a bit confused.

"Not necessarily," Sunny said, reaching under the big table, "because I came prepared." She held up two large lanterns. "My dad and I would sneak out sometimes when it was dark, and my mom would be so mad. We'd have to navigate with these lights. We almost drove right into the reeds one time." Sunny laughed, remembering her dad steering clear just in time.

"It sure sounds like you had some wonderful times on this lake, particularly with your dad." Benjamin pulled her to him.

"We did. I guess I've tried to wipe all good memories of my dad from my brain, but they're still there. So many, really." She looked like she'd surprised herself with that last statement.

"Well, it's not a bad thing to remember the good times." Benjamin kissed her head.

Sunny pushed back from him to stare directly in his eyes. "You could be right. But I'm feeling so much happier lately. . . . It's you, Benjamin."

"I'm glad. Really happy you think so, and you know how I feel about you. . . ."

He gently grabbed the back of her hair and tipped her face to meet his. His kiss was so wonderful and sweet. Sunny felt warm all over. She reached over to turn the key, shutting off the engine. In the middle of the empty lake, they would just drift now.

Benjamin continued to kiss her tenderly, brushing her mouth, her eyes, her throat, her ears, and her cheeks with his lips. As she unbuttoned his shirt, he explored her mouth with his tongue, and she tasted him, too. He slid off his shirt, and Sunny kissed his neck, his chest, and his belly before feeling how hard he was through his jeans.

She tugged him down to the floor and helped him remove his jeans, and he pulled off her T-shirt, kissing through her bra before undoing it and releasing her breasts into his hands. He caressed them before bringing his lips to her nipples. Sunny felt like she was going to burst.

As the geese squawked in the background, Sunny ran her hands over the bulge in Benjamin's underwear and kissed him there. He gasped and pulled her on top of him so he could kiss her passionately. When they'd shed the rest of their clothes, Benjamin couldn't wait any longer. He felt how ready she was for him. He held Sunny above him, and she slowly lowered herself onto him. When she felt him inside her, they moved together on the deck of the boat until she was rocked with pleasure and Benjamin came inside her with a loud groan.

"Sunny, oh God, yes . . ."

"Shh . . ." Sunny whispered and laughed. "You can't believe how sound travels on this lake."

Benjamin pulled her down to him again so they could look each other in the eyes. "Sunny, do you have any idea . . . ?"

"I do, Benjamin. I do." Sunny put her arms around him, and they held each other with the moon shining down as their only light. They stayed that way for quite some time before they dressed and used the lanterns to find their way back to shore. Jumping onto the dock, the two lovers secured the boat and ran up the steps to the house, holding hands as they reached the balcony, turning to take a last look at the stunning view, lights twinkling across the lake in the distance.

chapter forty

Durk

Six Months Later . . .

Durk looked out the window of his spacious, high-tech office at the gorgeous view of the mountains.

Things seemed to be slightly better for his new family. The baby was sleeping longer at night, and Gerrie was trying to get back to being her old self. She'd returned to work, so maybe that would help her recover, as work had always been such a big part of her identity.

He was still concerned about the baby and her, as she had many difficult and sad moments and just didn't seem as comfortable with Michael as she should.

It did worry him that the baby spent so much time with the nanny. When Gerrie was home before returning to work, she almost always had Meg around to help her. It was really tough for the babysitter to get any time off. And the few times Gerrie did have the baby all to herself, she seemed nervous and edgy.

Now that Gerrie was back at work, Michael hardly saw his mother, and it worried Durk. He shouldn't complain. He didn't see the baby that much either, as he was working ungodly hours lately. He was crossing his fingers that he wouldn't have to cancel his important Asian trip next week, which had been planned over nine months ago because of the involvement of the CEO.

Durk would be visiting all the engineering teams in Asia and making important stops to see partners in Hong Kong, Singapore, and Tokyo, and Don, the CEO, would be in all three cities for part of the agenda.

Gerrie kept telling him it was fine, but he worried about her on the weekends, particularly if she had to be alone with the baby. Meg usually took time off on Saturdays and Sundays, and Durk did his best to pitch in with the baby, but he knew he was pretty inept. He fed him, rocked him, and burped him, but that was about all he could handle.

Durk was never good at diapers, and when he tried to do it, Meg or Gerrie always had to fix them. He had struggled when Sunny was a baby, too, relying heavily on Aleen, and, of course, she took up the slack willingly.

It was so different with Gerrie and Michael, which he guessed was predictable, as he and his wife were older parents and sorely out of practice. But there was something else with Gerrie. She just seemed so unhappy and tense at times, even though she always told him that wasn't true and she was loving this second chance at motherhood with her new little family. He just didn't believe her.

However, he was glad his relationship with Sunny and Aleen had taken a much more positive turn with the birth of the baby. His daughter came over every weekend to see Michael and actually had a few brief, civil conversations with Gerrie.

So often, Durk found himself thinking about Aleen. He was filled with wonderful memories he shared with his ex-wife. Shaking his head, he tried to stop, as he knew there was nothing he could do about his feelings. *No one to blame but yourself.*

He was disappointed he hadn't been able to totally mend

fences with Ted yet. Her ex-husband had stopped by to see Gerrie and the baby several times, and the two men were cordial, but nothing beyond that.

It was so funny that the baby seemed to love Ted. Michael went right to him and laughed and grabbed at his fingers.

Gerrie had told him how good Ted had been with Stu as a baby, and he could believe it, seeing him with Michael. He really seemed to enjoy being with the baby, too. Durk had to admit he was a good guy, as not too many men would have anything to do with another man's son, especially in this circumstance. He hoped someday they could bury the hatchet.

Ted was sure close with Aleen, and they both told Durk their friendship was important. He wondered if it was more than that.

He had to stop feeling so jealous. There was no evidence their friendship was anything more than that, and besides, he had no claim on his ex-wife. She didn't want to end their marriage; he did.

Durk was fooling himself, however, in thinking he didn't miss his life with Aleen and Sunny. If he were honest, he was much happier then than now. But why was that? He thought it was because everything seemed so much harder now, with challenges around every corner.

With Aleen, it had been so easy. The problem was he didn't realize how wonderful his life had been before he flushed it down the toilet. What an idiot. He certainly couldn't ever tell anyone that, but it was the truth.

Why did he have the affair with Gerrie in the first place? Yes, she was beautiful, brilliant, and captivating, but there must have been something that propelled them into each other's arms. Durk guessed their easy rapport about work fueled their romance, but he did feel like he experienced some kind of midlife crisis, and his sex life with Ali had slowed down.

He wondered what Gerrie had seen in him? Did Ted just become too predictable for her?

She told Durk he was so handsome and dangerous when they made love for the first time. While he appreciated the comment about his looks, he didn't fully understand the dangerous part back then. He sure did now. The danger was they could lose everything if they consummated their lurking passions. They did, and they'd lost more than they ever dreamed.

Well, he had a full slate of meetings today, so he'd better snap out of this mood. This was his life, and he needed to get on with it, reaching for any happiness when he could. That was the way it was now, whether he liked it or not.

chapter forty-one

Gerrie

It was good to be back at work, where Gerrie could put on her professional persona. She felt more in control at her job and, frankly, missed it once she'd gotten her energy back after the baby.

The baby. What a terrible mother she was. She didn't give Michael the time he deserved, but she couldn't. She just couldn't. Michael reminded her so much of Stu as a baby, her precious son. She'd killed him, and she was afraid she would do the same with Michael. She even had dark and awful thoughts sometimes about hurting herself and him. God, she'd never had these kinds of thoughts before.

The time Gerrie spent with Michael wasn't a joy to her as she'd expected; most often, she just felt so exhausted by it all. How she had loved those moments with Stu when he was a baby, so what was wrong with her now?

Stop it now! she snapped at herself. *You do have some wonderful moments with Michael Stuart, like when Ted visited.* Oh, Ted. She needed to push him out of her mind and get her thoughts focused back on her career.

She'd just had a fabulous first week back at work, and she

didn't want to spoil it with all the usual guilt, sadness, and anger. *Just get on with it.*

Gerrie was glad her last meeting this Friday was with Trish. She'd been very sweet while Gerrie was out, sending flowers to her home as well as wonderful presents for the baby. Trish also sent her texts to see how she was doing and a beautiful spa gift set. While Gerrie didn't answer all her texts, she did send grateful messages when she had the energy.

After the accident, it seemed she had so few friends left. But she wondered if she'd closed herself off to people a long time ago, as her focus had always been her job. She just felt so alone now.

When Trish arrived, Gerrie jumped up to greet her, giving her a hug that demonstrated the real affection she felt for her friend and colleague. "It's so wonderful to see you," she told Trish. "I can't thank you enough for the flowers, presents, and gifts for the baby. You've been so thoughtful."

Trish returned the hug. "So glad you liked them. I've been anxious to talk to you. How are you doing?"

"I'll be honest with you, much more than I've been with others. The truth is it's been very, very difficult. I was so exhausted the first few months. I hardly got out of bed. Maybe I am just too old, because I feel like I've been a terrible mother. I just don't feel like I'm giving Michael the time he needs."

Gerrie thought these were the first honest things she'd said to anyone about her personal life for months. She lied to Durk every day about how she was feeling, because she didn't want to worry him.

"Are you sure you aren't being too hard on yourself? You've had to endure so much in your life, and it is more difficult being an older mother, I'm sure." Trish looked at her friend with real concern, as she could see beneath her beautiful makeup, perfect hair, and designer suit that Gerrie seemed more frail.

"To be perfectly honest, Trish, no. I'm being brutally open, rather than trying to mask my true feelings, which I've been doing for a long time. I tamp down all my anxieties and fears, but they're right there, poking at me all the time. Michael deserves better than that. Frankly, my husband deserves a better wife."

"I need to speak plainly here, Gerrie. I believe you need to get help to work through all of this. You're holding way too much inside. I think it's tearing you to pieces."

Her face darkened a bit. "Thank you for being up front with me. I haven't had many honest conversations lately. Believe me; I know I need help, and I promise I will get it.

"Perhaps I can have a wonderful weekend with my son, as Durk is headed out on his big Asian trip. I'll try and relax and get to know Michael Stuart. And I'll look up options for counselors for me. I should have done that right after Stu died, but I just plunged into my new life. I really thought the baby would solve everything, but I was so wrong. . . ."

Trish squeezed her friend's arm. "That sounds like a plan. I think you need to deal with so much from the past before you can move forward with your life. Please let me know if there is *anything* I can do to help."

"You are helping me right now, just being a friend. God, I've needed that so much," Gerrie told Trish. "Can't thank you enough. But I guess we better move on to our business agenda."

Once their meeting was complete and Trish departed, Gerrie felt a bit lighter. It did help to tell the truth about how she was really feeling. Perhaps things would take a turn for the better.

chapter forty-two

Ted, Gerrie, Aleen, and Sunny

After taking Hope and Cash out for their second morning walk, Ted was busy getting ready to host Aleen, Sunny, Benjamin, Vincent, and Richard for the Packers game. Being from the Midwest, it still felt strange that the first football games on Sunday were on at 10:00 a.m. in California.

He planned to put out snacks and sandwiches for lunch during the game, keeping it simple. He didn't usually have many gatherings at his townhouse, as it wasn't that big and certainly wasn't grand. Somehow, the Packers parties were a perfect fit, though.

Aleen was the first to arrive, and even though he told her not to worry about food, she brought some homemade guacamole and salsa along with lime tortilla chips. Ted didn't scold her, as her guacamole and salsa were out of this world. She used the jalapeños, limes, tomatoes, and cilantro from her own garden, and both dips were better than anything from the store. The Packers crowd liked their food spicy, so Aleen turned up the heat for football Sunday.

Once they got everything ready, they sat down for the few minutes before the other guests arrived.

"So how is your new job going?" Ted asked after he put the cheesehead out next to the television.

"I just love it. I'm learning so much. While I had an idea of what the job entailed before I was promoted, I didn't know the details of all the responsibilities. It's been challenging but good. I've gotten some wonderful compliments from inside and outside the department, so I'm thrilled.

"I don't want to sound arrogant, but I feel like I could do my manager's job down the line, after I complete some additional in-house training courses and finish my degree. Can you believe that?"

"Fantastic, Aleen. I'm glad you're finally giving yourself the credit you deserve," he said.

"Maybe that is one positive from the divorce. When I was married to Durk, I was content to stay in my position, because I liked it and my husband had the big job. I always knew I was capable of more, but I didn't want to take any time away from the family. When Durk left me, I knew I had to do more with my career, for many reasons." Aleen went a bit quiet after her last statement.

"Well, you should be so proud of yourself and what you've achieved. There's no doubt in my mind you can advance further if you want." Ted smiled at his friend, and she seemed to gain a real ego boost from his encouraging comments.

"I'm enjoying school, too, really getting into my courses. I know I should have completed my degree a long time ago, so I'm happy to *finally* be doing it. While school and work don't leave me much free time, being busy is a blessing."

Their conversation was interrupted by the doorbell, as Vincent and Richard arrived wearing their new Packers T-shirts.

"Wow, impressive. It looks like I've turned you both into real Packers fans," Ted said, welcoming his friends into his home.

"I wasn't much of a football fan before watching the Green Bay games with this bunch, but now I'm all in," Richard said with a laugh. "*And* I heard Aleen made her fabulous guacamole and salsa—another reason to love football Sunday."

Benjamin and Sunny arrived just as the game was starting. It was a back-and-forth game with the Packers's division rival, but in the end, Green Bay was behind with just seconds to go. A face mask penalty gave the Packers one more play, and they needed a touchdown to win. Unbelievably, the Packers quarterback threw the longest and highest "Hail Mary" pass the group had ever seen, and, even more remarkably, the Green Bay tight end caught it in the end zone for the winning touchdown.

Everyone erupted, jumping up and down and cheering and screaming. The fans at Ted's house hugged each other, having a hard time calming down. Benjamin grabbed the cheesehead and put it on.

"Wow, what a game," Ted said, looking around at his friends. "I think my blood pressure spiked on that last play."

The group turned to the food table after the game, and Aleen's guacamole and salsa were gone in a flash, as well as most of the sandwiches.

Vincent grabbed Ted and pulled him aside. "Great game and so much fun to share it with this gang," he said, pausing for a minute before he continued. "It's like a miracle, Ted, but I actually feel happy again. It couldn't have happened without you."

"And you've been a wonderful friend to me, so we're even," Ted said, resting his hand on Vincent's shoulder.

"Talking with you and then Sandy helped me finalize the break with Derek. I feel so lucky to have met Richard. And from the start, I've been open and honest with him about my feelings. So I took your advice."

"It's all you, Vincent, not me," Ted told his friend.

"*But* . . . I never would have made it to this point without your forgiveness and kindness, which most people in your situation—"

"Well . . ." Ted felt himself getting a little choked up and looked down at the floor.

"I just needed to let you know how indebted I am to you. I feel like I'm part of your family as well. You've made me feel so welcome. Richard, too."

"You *are* family," Ted said, patting his friend on the back.

"Definitely," Sunny said, grabbing Vincent in a hug.

"Thanks for everything," he replied, releasing Sunny and shaking Ted's hand. "We have to get going now. We have a party at Richard's brother's house."

Richard came to join them and embraced Aleen and Sunny before departing.

"You guys have a great time." Ted waved as the two men left.

The house cleared quickly, and Ted finished all the cleanup to get things back to normal. After he took Hope and Cash for a short walk, he sat down to watch the late game, which was already underway. He was surprised when the doorbell rang. Did someone forget something?

He opened the door and was shocked to find Gerrie standing there with her hair in a mess, makeup running down her face, and the red-faced baby crying—no, screaming. She held a diaper bag that was overstuffed with what looked like diapers ready to fall out.

"Ted, Ted, I need help. I didn't know what to do . . ." Gerrie cried, frantic tears streaming down her face.

"Come in, come in," he said hurriedly. "He's not sick, is he, Gerrie?"

"No, I don't think so. He's just so agitated, and I can't get him to calm down. Stu, Stu, please stop crying." She was yelling now. Ted observed her with alarm when she called the baby Stu.

"Let me hold him," he said, taking the baby from her. "You sit down. Rest."

Ted walked around the room, bouncing the baby and speaking to him softly. "It's okay, Michael. Are you tired or hungry? What do you want? You don't need to cry now, do you? It's okay, little man. You're all right now, aren't you?" He walked the baby around the room several times, and his gentle manner seemed to help the baby settle down.

He grabbed the bag from Gerrie and pulled out a bottle and a bib. "Good, it's still warm," he said more to himself than to his ex-wife or the baby.

"I tried to give him the bottle, but I couldn't get him to settle down. It was terrible," Gerrie said, still so distraught.

"It's okay now, Gerrie. Everything will be fine." He tried to reassure her and keep his own anxiety in check while gently bouncing the baby in his arms.

He sat on the couch with the baby and fed him, keeping a close eye on Gerrie. Michael sucked on the bottle and reached for Ted's face, calming down. His ex-wife sat in the chair with her head in her hands, not saying a word he could hear, but whispering to herself.

Ted was panicked. He had to get this baby to sleep so he could deal with Gerrie. She was a mess, and he'd never seen her this way.

After the baby finished the bottle, Ted walked him around the room again, patting his back, so Michael burped up a bit of milk and seemed to be getting a bit sleepy. While he comforted the baby and continued to rock him gently, he kept an eye on Gerrie sitting in the chair, wiping her face with a tissue.

As Michael started to drop off, Ted got up and used his free hand to pick up pillows from the couch and walked into his bedroom to combine them with the ones on his bed to create a space for Michael to sleep, hemmed in by the pillows. Ted put him gently in the middle of his makeshift baby bed, made sure he was going to sleep, and then tiptoed out to check on Gerrie.

"Gerrie," he whispered, "he's asleep. He's fine. Tell me what's going on."

She took her head out of her hands. "See? You're so good with him, and he cries bloody murder with his own mother. I killed Stu, and now I'm going to kill this baby, too. I'm a terrible mother, a terrible person. Well, you know that better than anyone." She was sobbing now.

"Please, calm down and stop this talk," he pleaded, kneeling in front of her to gently lift her head out of her hands so he could look straight at her. "Please."

"Durk is in Asia on an important trip with the CEO, and Meg had to go to a christening today, so I've been on my own with the baby since last night. I can't do *anything* right.

"I want to die, Ted. I do. I deserve it. The baby is better off without me. You, too. I was a bad wife to you, and I'm an awful wife to Durk. He's not you, Ted. I want *you!* Why did I do what I did? Why?" Gerrie couldn't stop crying now. She was out of control.

Ted couldn't believe what his ex-wife had just said, but he needed to get her to calm down. "Gerrie, stop blaming yourself for everything. You're not a bad person. You are a wonderful mother, and you were a great wife to me until . . ."

"Until I betrayed you and killed our son? Until then?" Gerrie got to her feet with a mad look in her eyes, and she couldn't stop herself from continuing. "Sunny said I killed Stu; I did. I drove him from the house that night when I told him I was leaving you, and he was killed. It's no one's fault but mine.

"You were the most wonderful husband and father, and I took all of that away from you in one night! What kind of woman does that?" Gerrie paced back and forth now.

"Sit down, Gerrie, please." Ted followed her around and tried to guide her onto the couch.

"Look how you calmed down the baby. What, it took you five minutes? I tried for so long! I wanted to kill the baby and myself." She looked at him with wild eyes before collapsing on the couch.

He knelt on the floor in front of her and took her hands in his. "Gerrie, look at me. Look at me."

She wiped her tears on her sleeve and gazed into Ted's eyes.

"Now, I need you to calm down, because I must ask you some important questions. You need help. I believe you've bottled up all these feelings far too long. Please stay with me now." He tried to speak as calmly as he could, but his heart raced a mile a minute. He was so scared for Gerrie and Michael.

"Oh, Ted. You are my rock." Gerrie looked at her ex-husband with real affection. "You always kept everything running smoothly in our family, and then I let you and Stu down, and he's gone. I know I don't deserve you, but I need you, Ted. So much. I love you and am so, so sorry for everything. Can you ever forgive me?"

Ted looked at his ex-wife with tears in his eyes. "Gerrie, I am so worried about you right now. I'm scared for you, Michael, and for me. Life in this world without you . . ." Ted couldn't continue and stared down at the floor.

"I feel so tired. I'm exhausted all the time, with no hope of happiness again. I feel guilty about causing Stu's death, guilty about leaving a wonderful marriage and hurting you, guilty about being a terrible mother to Michael, guilty about marrying Durk and being a terrible wife to him . . .

"I know in my heart that I made the biggest mistake of my life by having the affair, and I have ruined two families. I can see Durk misses Aleen and Sunny so much, and I love you and miss Stu so much—"

Just then, the baby started to cry.

"Stu, Stu . . ." Gerrie called out.

"You stay right here. Don't move." Ted ran over to check on the baby. It looked like he needed to be changed, so he grabbed the diaper bag and quickly cleaned him up. Ted had never changed a diaper so fast. Thank God he remembered how.

He walked Michael around the bedroom, as he could see he was as exhausted as his mother. Once he was sleepy again, Ted put the baby back in his "pillow pen" and ran to Gerrie.

Ted sat down next to her on the couch, taking her hand in his. They remained very still for a minute, listening only to the sounds of cheering from the television. Ted had forgotten the television was on, much less that the late-afternoon game was still being played.

Gerrie was staring at the screen, not really seeing what was on.

"I need to ask you a favor, Gerrie." He talked calmly and directly, hoping she could answer him in the same manner.

She turned her head to look at him, eyes blank.

"I think it would be best if you were able to get some rest. Can you try and sleep in the other bedroom? I want to see if we can get some help for you while you and the baby rest. Does that sound okay?"

Gerrie nodded, seemingly ready to fall over from exhaustion. "Let's go to the bedroom." Ted took her arm and helped her walk to the spare room. After she slipped off her shoes and sweater, he eased her down on the bed and covered her with a throw. "You just sleep now. As long as you need." He quietly shut the door and then ran over to the phone.

"Aleen!" Ted said into the receiver, a bit more panicky than he wanted to sound. "I need your help. Gerrie came over with the baby, and she is in a terrible state. I just got them both calmed down, and they're asleep now. Do you have Sandy's cell phone number?"

Ted wrote down Sandy's number on a sheet of paper. "Got it. I'll call her. And can you please come help with the baby while I deal with Gerrie? As quickly as you can."

Ted was able to reach Sandy at a family event, and she said she would get to Ted's as soon as she could. Sandy knew an awful lot about Gerrie from the counseling sessions with him, Aleen, and Sunny, so she understood the difficulty she was in, blaming herself for everything that had happened to the two families.

It only took about five minutes for Aleen to arrive, and she knocked softly on the door, careful not to wake up Gerrie and Michael.

Ted hurried to the door to let her in. "I'm so glad you're here," he whispered with great relief. "We should try to be quiet and not wake them up. From what I saw, both Gerrie and the baby need rest."

"What's happening?" she whispered.

"Durk is on an international trip, and the nanny had a family event today, so Gerrie has been on her own. She couldn't get Michael to stop crying, and from the looks of her, she hasn't slept a wink. She is totally out of sorts, almost hallucinating.

"She blames herself for Stu's death and the breakup of our families. Gerrie feels she killed Stu, just as Sunny said."

"Did she say it that way?" Aleen looked horrified.

"Yes, she mentioned what Sunny said and then admitted she'd thought of killing herself . . . and the baby." Ted had a hard time getting those words out. "She also called Michael 'Stu.'"

"Oh my God, Ted, we would never want her to feel this way.

This is awful. She really needs help. She is sick." Aleen started pacing the room.

"It's the worst thing I've ever seen, other than the night our son died." Ted looked down at the floor, trying to control his emotions. "I would never wish this on her or anyone. I love Gerrie; I've never stopped caring for her." Ted sat on the couch, still staring down, as Aleen eased in right next to her friend.

"I know that, Ted." She patted his hand. "Just as I couldn't get over my feelings for Durk, as hard as I tried."

Ted turned to Aleen. "You should know something else. She made it clear she still loves me, and Gerrie said Durk misses you and Sunny so much. From what she said, I suspect he would be a lot happier back with you."

Aleen appeared shocked as she took in the full meaning of what Ted just told her. "Oh God, I knew I felt something between us when he stopped by and told us about the baby and had breakfast, but I wouldn't have dreamed . . ." She stopped talking, but the wheels in her head were turning.

"We're going to have to call Durk, but I'd like to have a professional opinion about Gerrie's state of health before we reach out to him. I'm sure he'll be worried, perhaps panicked being so far away, and I would prefer to have more facts beforehand.

"Hearing this news from across the world will be difficult enough in itself. You'll need to make that call," Ted said, matter-of-fact, and Aleen fully understood.

Her brow furrowed as she thought of just how to have this conversation with her ex-husband. "I think my head is going to burst. Gerrie was the strong one . . . we all thought. She always seemed so in control."

"Well, here's something else. She's not well enough to take care of the baby, especially when she's having thoughts of harming herself *and* Michael. I also think he's picking up on her anxiety, so we have to take care of him right now. Obviously, he has a nanny, but we're going to have to rearrange our schedules, particularly until Durk returns."

Aleen nodded her agreement.

"You, Sunny, and I have to spend as much time with Michael Stuart as we can. I don't believe Gerrie has properly bonded with him, and you've said Durk isn't very good with babies. I don't think Michael's had the parental attention he needs to be healthy. I suspect he thinks the nanny is his mother."

"God, this is terrible . . ."

"If I'm honest, I'm afraid Gerrie is going to need some inpatient care," he said, gazing at his friend with genuine sadness and concern for his ex-wife.

Aleen went into the kitchen to get a glass of water.

"Sorry, Aleen, I should have asked you if you wanted anything."

She walked back into the family room with a glass for Ted as well. "Not a problem. You've been busy." She sat in the chair across from him and took a long drink. Hearing this news had left her totally parched. "What's going to happen, Ted?"

"Not sure. We have to get the right care for Gerrie and look out for the baby. Whatever happens after that, I don't know."

He could hear someone walking up to the door and ran over to see it was Sandy. He quietly opened the door and invited her in, keeping his voice down.

"Ted, Aleen, it's good you're both here. Please, tell me what happened with Gerrie." Sandy got right to business and looked at Ted intently just as the baby started to cry.

Aleen went into the next room to pick him up, marveling at the pillows that surrounded and protected him. Ted did all this while he had a frantic woman in the other room. She shook her head at his resourcefulness.

"So how are you doing, Michael? Are you hungry? Let me check your diaper." Aleen could tell he needed to be changed and grabbed a towel from the bathroom to lay Michael on, retrieving a clean diaper from the overstuffed bag. He didn't fuss too much while she cleaned him off with the baby wipes. He smiled at her as she nuzzled his chest.

"You are such a good boy, aren't you?" Aleen whispered, tickling him. "We don't want you to cry now, 'cause your mommy needs her rest. You're going to be just fine, Michael Stuart, just fine now." Aleen spoke to the baby quietly but confidently. She wanted him to pick up on her calmness.

"Let's get you back into your jammies and see if you want a bit of milk." Aleen continued to try and entertain the baby. She peered into the diaper bag and was thrilled to find another bottle of formula. As soon as she could, Aleen would call Sunny and ask her to pick up some food for the baby and more formula. Michael was too young for regular milk, and this was the last bottle, so he would need more very soon.

"First, I need to heat up this bottle for you, my little man. You must not have had much to eat today, huh?"

Michael laughed when she touched him on the nose. When she came out of the bedroom to go to the kitchen, she could see Sandy and Ted were still deep in conversation.

Still holding the baby, Aleen took out a pan to boil water to heat up the formula. Thank God she knew her way around Ted's kitchen. The baby seemed to be enjoying looking around at the new environment, bouncing his little arms up and down.

She took him over to the window so he could see Hope and Cash chasing each other around the courtyard. *I'm sure they'd rather come inside, but they'll have to wait for now.*

When Hope and Cash saw her with the baby at the window, they jumped up on the glass, as they wanted to come in after being banished to the courtyard for so long. They were used to having the run of their home.

"So sorry, guys. I just can't let you in. Just be good dogs right now." Aleen hoped they would stay quiet. "Michael, see the doggies. Aren't they funny?"

Michael laughed, and he seemed to be following the dogs with this eyes.

"You'll have to wait to meet them in person. Right now, you need to have your bottle."

She took the baby back in Ted's bedroom to feed him. He lapped it up, and she walked him around the room until he became drowsy and seemed to want to sleep again. *This baby is really tired*, Aleen thought.

Once she put him down, she called Sunny. Aleen gave her a broad outline of what was going on, and Sunny was clearly concerned. Benjamin had already left, so she would go directly to the store and be right over.

Joining Sandy and Ted in the living room, Aleen sat next to him on the couch. "What happens next?" she inquired.

"I need to talk to Gerrie, so perhaps Ted should go in with me so she doesn't panic. I know a lot about her but have never met her," Sandy said. "I'd like to ask her a series of questions, but from what Ted has told me, I believe she'll need some inpatient care. I can't be sure until I spend some time with her."

Sandy and Ted got up and went in the spare bedroom.

It wasn't long before Ted came out and joined Aleen in the family room. "She woke up and didn't panic. She knows Sandy is here to help her. She asked about the baby, and I told her he was perfectly fine."

Ted ran over to let the dogs in, as they were starting to bark.

Hope and Cash bolted in and ran to greet Aleen. "Guys, no barking and behave now," she told them quietly.

The dogs soon turned their attention to Ted, and he stroked them until they calmed down and lazed about near his feet.

"Fingers crossed we can get her the help she needs," he told his friend. "Sandy thinks Gerrie may have serious postpartum depression, complicated by the grief of Stu's death, which she hasn't dealt with properly. She wants to get her the expert help she needs immediately." Ted ran his hands through his hair nervously.

"I can understand why she wasn't able to properly grieve for Stu. The person she most needed to do that with—you—was no longer in her life," Aleen said.

She got up to refill her glass of water. It seemed the serious conversations had left her so thirsty. Then she walked back into the family room and took her seat next to Ted.

"Gerrie puts up a front that she is the strongest among us, but it turns out she was holding all of this in, crumbling inside bit by bit," he explained. "I knew something was wrong, but I had no idea how bad it was."

Aleen agreed. "Gerrie has a way of seeming superhuman with a tough exterior that is hard to penetrate. I guess that's the way I always saw her."

Ted cleared his throat and dabbed at his eyes with his handkerchief. "I knew she could put up a front when we were married, but I could see through it. With the divorce and the bitterness, I hardly spent any time with her. And Durk probably didn't see all the signs."

He got up and saw through the window that Sunny was coming to the door with bags of groceries. He let her in, and she handed the bags to her mom, who took them into the kitchen.

"What's happening?" Sunny asked urgently. Hope and Cash were jumping on her legs and couldn't figure out why they weren't getting any attention.

"Honey, Gerrie had some sort of a breakdown. Sandy's in there with her, trying to plan the next steps. It's clear she needs professional help. It may not be the best for her to see you and your mom right now. I just don't know.

"Part of the issue is she feels she ruined all our lives and killed Stu. I don't know how to tell you this, but . . . your words to her about killing Stu have stuck with her. I know you were upset at the time, and, frankly, if I were Gerrie, I would blame myself for Stu's death, too." Ted was blunt with Sunny; she needed to understand the seriousness of the situation.

Sunny grabbed her head. "You know I was devastated when Stu was killed, but I would *never* want this to happen. I know she loved Stu, but I was so angry with her and broken up. I was out of my mind at the time."

Ted held out his arms, and she walked forward. "I am so, so sorry," she whispered, hugging him.

"Honey, you have nothing to be sorry for. You said something out of grief and anger at a terrible time in all our lives. Most people would have said the exact same thing. Now, calm down, please. We need to be totally in control, for Gerrie's sake."

Sunny nodded and took out a tissue to dry her eyes.

"I'm going to have to check on her and see what Sandy says about her condition." He gave Sunny another hug and headed back to the guest bedroom.

The baby started fussing, so Aleen darted into Ted's bedroom to pick him up, Sunny at her heels. "There, there, little man. You can't be hungry so soon, can you? I'm just not sure if your mommy gave you any solid food today. Let's go see what your sister got from the store, should we?" Aleen walked out with the baby to the kitchen to pick out some baby food.

Sunny reached out to take her brother from her mother. "Hey, little brother, what do you want? I got you all kinds of things, like strained bananas, chicken, carrots, beans, oatmeal. I didn't know what to get, so I grabbed all kinds of stuff for my baby brother." Sunny let Michael grab her hair, and he held on tight, giving her a smile. "What a beautiful smile you have, Michael Stuart. You are so special."

She walked into the family room with the dogs jumping on her legs. When she sat down, Hope and Cash quickly leapt onto the couch next to her and Michael. The baby seemed fascinated with them and reached out.

"Guys," Sunny said to the dogs, "be good around the baby. Understand?" She held the baby in one arm and petted the dogs with her other hand, keeping them at a safe distance from Michael. Hope and Cash almost seemed to smile, but they didn't jump around so much, and the baby was transfixed watching the corgis.

"Good, you're all quiet." Sunny looked at the baby and the dogs with affection.

Ted came out of the bedroom and went into the kitchen with Aleen, and Sunny quickly joined them with Michael.

"Gerrie is going to go to an inpatient facility. Sandy and I will take her. She wants to see the baby before she leaves."

"Should we get out of the way?" Aleen asked.

"No. Please stay. You can feed the baby after we leave. Gerrie knows you're both here and that you will take care of Michael while we get her situated. She's calmed down considerably. Just be gentle with her, and I think we'll be okay," he whispered to Sunny and Aleen.

Ted took the baby from Sunny and brought him into the bedroom with Gerrie.

"My beautiful boy." She gazed at him with pure love. "I am sorry I haven't been a very good momma. I promise I will try to be better."

Ted was glad to see Gerrie calmer and more like her old self. He sat on the bed with Michael. "Do you want to hold him?"

Gerrie shook her head. "Thanks, Ted, but I couldn't take it if he started crying—or should I say screaming—again. I'm trying my best right now, but I still feel a bit fragile. You've always been so good with babies . . . better than me."

She bent over to put her shoes back on. "Please direct me to the bathroom so I can try and clean myself up."

Sandy eyed her warily and stood very close to the door to make sure she was all right. Ted understood what she was doing; Sandy was afraid she might hurt herself, and it scared him. Gerrie came out after just a few minutes, and it was apparent she had tried to smooth her hair and wash the caked makeup and mascara from her face.

When Gerrie walked into the living room, Sunny and Aleen took a few steps toward her but kept their distance. "We just want the best for you, Gerrie. We'll help Ted take care of the baby. Just get well," Aleen said with tears in her eyes.

"And I'm sorry, Mrs. Hammand, for what I said. I know how much you loved Stu, and he loved you. Like Mom said, we just want you to be okay." Sunny quickly wiped away the tears on her cheeks. She was trying to be calm, as Ted had asked.

"Thank you, both of you, for helping Michael and being so understanding. I will try to earn your forgiveness someday." Gerrie seemed exhausted after saying those two short sentences. She headed out the door with Sandy, and Ted handed the baby to Aleen, quickly following after them.

When they were gone, Aleen and Sunny hugged each other with Michael between them and the dogs scampering around their feet.

chapter forty-three

Ted

Gerrie didn't say much on the ride over to the nearby treatment facility; she just seemed totally drained. Once they arrived, Ted and Sandy gave the doctors and staff at the facility all the background on the tragedy of Stu's death and the broken marriages.

After she settled in and was comfortable in her room, Ted drove Sandy back to his place to pick up her car. He agreed he would set up another appointment with her to talk about his own feelings, as it was clear he had been upended by the day's events. He couldn't stop thinking about what had happened that afternoon. What Gerrie said could change all of their lives. Did she mean it? He wasn't sure how to react.

It was dark now, as their saga took all afternoon and part of the evening.

Ted walked into the condo, and Hope and Cash came running to greet him. "Sorry, you guys, we just weren't paying enough attention to you two today. I'll do my best to make it up to you." He grabbed the dogs and hugged them.

"I took them for a walk, and Mom gave them some food, so I think they're fine," Sunny said, approaching Ted.

He felt like he could relax for the first time in hours. "I'm least worried about the dogs right now. They look perfectly happy and healthy. Thanks to both of you for taking such good care of them and the baby. How's Michael?"

"We fed him, and he ate so much!" Aleen told Ted, joining the conversation. "He's been just fine, a little fussy, as he probably hasn't been eating or sleeping properly over the last twenty-four hours. He went out like a light after his big meal and is sleeping soundly now."

"Good," Ted said, relief apparent on his face. "I was thinking about him while I was away."

"I'm making tea, so I'll get a cup for you as well, and you can tell us what's going on." Aleen poured Ted and Sunny tea and brought the steaming mugs over to them.

"Well, Gerrie seems to have settled in well, and she will receive a full evaluation in the morning when the key doctors are in. She's exhausted, so a good night's sleep will allow her to better articulate her concerns in the morning. Sandy was fairly sure they would put her on some medication right away to help with the depression.

"Having Sandy help navigate everything was beyond helpful. She really didn't need to come over and help us on a Sunday, but thank God she did. I had no idea how to handle the situation, and I didn't think calling 9-1-1 was a good idea. Seeing paramedics would likely remind Gerrie of the accident and upset her further. I'm so glad you had Sandy's cell number, Aleen."

Ted took a sip of his tea, piping hot and satisfying as it warmed his throat.

"Did you talk to her about contacting Durk?" The thought of talking to her ex-husband about his wife, the baby, and this situation made her very, very nervous.

"Yes. Consulting with the staff there this evening, it is clear Gerrie needs lots of rest, so it may not be a great idea for Durk to cut his trip short. I understand he's due back Wednesday, so if you can convince him, see if you can get him to stick to his schedule. That's only two days away with the time difference. I know he's going to be worried, but it's probably best for Gerrie to rest and gather herself before she has to confront any of us again. Today's events really took it out of her."

Aleen and Sunny were hanging on his every word.

"Aleen, Gerrie asked that you call Trish and explain the situation to her and request she deal with everyone at headquarters. With the time zone differences, she'll be better able than Durk to reach people here. Obviously, Durk will cover everything with the CEO, as they are traveling together.

"Surprisingly, Gerrie said she had confided in Trish about seeking help, so she'll understand. Perhaps Trish can frame it as exhaustion for those at work."

Aleen nodded. "That makes perfect sense."

"Let's just say she'll be out of work at least two weeks, as that won't sound too alarming. The truth is Gerrie probably needs a lot longer than that to recover, but we just don't know how long right now."

Sunny piped up. "Do you think she'll be at the hospital for weeks or maybe even months?"

"We just have no idea, honey. Gerrie was concerned about announcing a long absence from her job. The odds are she'll be away from work for some time, and she understands that. I'm just trying to carry out her wishes at this point. She can always extend her leave once she understands the treatment plan.

"From what I could gather, after she's released from the facility, she'll have an intensive period of outpatient treatment. What will happen in the future, I just don't know right now." Ted rubbed at his temples; he had developed a massive headache.

While he went to get some aspirin, Aleen carefully

composed an email to Durk and asked he call at his earliest convenience. "I think it must be well into the morning now in Tokyo, so Durk is probably in meetings until later in the day." Aleen put her phone back in her purse. "I told him there were some 'family matters' we needed to talk about, but I know he'll worry when he sees it."

Aleen grabbed her purse and headed to the spare bedroom. "I'll call Trish now before it gets much later. Give me a few minutes."

Sunny sipped her tea.

"It's a lot to take in, hon." Ted came over and sat down next to her on the couch.

"I'll do whatever I can to take care of Michael. He's my brother. I'm going to learn a lot about babies!" she said.

"Well, here's what I was thinking for our next steps. Gerrie gave me her house keys, so I'll stay over there tonight. That way the baby has all his things handy. The nanny usually comes by about seven o'clock on Monday, so I'll explain what's happened.

"I'll bring my computer so I can do some work from there. Maybe you can come by when you're done with school and your mom can take over when she's off work."

Sunny nodded in agreement.

"I have this feeling that Michael needs us right now. Gerrie hasn't been herself, and your dad has been working long hours. Michael spends so much time with the nanny; it isn't good. Gerrie knows that." Ted got up to open the French doors to let the dogs into the courtyard to do their business. *No dog walking tonight,* he thought.

"When your mom is done talking to Trish, I can head over to the house with the baby so we can get him to sleep in his own bed." Ted sat down again.

"I guess I'm going to have to take the dogs, too. They can't stay here on their own," he said, planning his next move out loud. "Let me put a bag together with their stuff. . . . Gosh, it's just like the baby—"

"We're going with you," Sunny said firmly. "I bet you haven't been in that house very much since Stu died, and we need to face it together."

Ted looked at Sunny and squeezed her hand. He knew the beautiful young woman sitting next to him was exactly right.

chapter forty-four

Sunny

While Ted and her mom packed up the baby's things and got him dressed and ready to go, Sunny sent a text to Benjamin. She had called him earlier, and, of course, he was concerned about everyone.

Can't wait to see u, she wrote.

Me 2, he answered.

Will call u later, Sunny texted back.

She put her phone back in her bag and tried to figure out what would happen next. It seemed like everything was breaking apart and changing again. She knew her mom still cared for her dad, but how could he really leave Gerrie in the state she was in? And what about the baby?

Sunny pushed these thoughts out of her mind. One step at a time, as Mr. Hammand had said. That's the only thing that made sense right now.

Ted drove Gerrie's car with the baby's car seat, and Sunny stayed in back with Michael. Her mom followed behind with the dogs in Ted's car. The baby's eyes fluttered open when they put him in the car seat, but he seemed fine. She found one of his stuffed toys, a cute chipmunk, and made it dance around in front of him.

"Oh, you like that," Sunny said to Michael as he laughed and reached out for the toy. "We didn't do a very good job at Mr. Hammand's, because we didn't have anything for you to play with, did we? I didn't even know this was in the bag, but I think you wanted to sleep a bit anyway, didn't you?"

Sunny kept up a steady stream of conversation with the baby until they arrived. Ted parked in the garage and left the door open so Aleen could follow them into the house with the dogs and the food they bought for Michael. He gently lifted the baby out, and Sunny took his diaper bag.

Turning the lights on in the hallway and kitchen, Ted led Sunny into the house. Walking around with the baby in his arms, he surveyed his old home. The baby gurgled and made all kinds of sounds as they moved about the house.

They could hear Aleen had gotten the dogs out of the car and was taking them into the yard.

Going up the stairs, Ted and Sunny didn't say a word, as they both knew what they were going to do. Walking down the hallway, they stopped in front of Stu's room.

Sunny said to Michael, "This is your brother's room. Stu was just the best."

Ted opened the closed door and walked through, flipping the light switch. Sunny gasped as she entered. The room looked exactly the same as the day Stu died.

She sat on the bed. "The last time I was in this room, it was the best afternoon of my life. It was wonderful, and I was so happy . . ." Sunny ran her hands over the bedspread, remembering every detail of making love with Stu there.

Ted sat next to her, and the baby reached out and grabbed at Sunny's face.

"I've only been in here a few times since Stu died," Ted said, looking around at all of his son's things. "Gerrie and I just couldn't face cleaning it out. Since we were hardly speaking, we didn't even begin to work through our grief. I think that's a big part of what has caused her to have this breakdown."

Sunny nodded. "I know. We've had each other. And Vincent. It took us a few months, but we did start to talk about everything and then see Sandy. Doesn't sound like she talked to anyone, and then she blamed herself for Stu's death."

Ted sighed, hearing his son's name. Sitting in the bedroom of his dead child, bouncing the baby who was both Stu and Sunny's new brother, felt unreal. He looked around, studying every detail of Stu's belongings, the things that were special to him. There were so many photos . . . of his friends, Sunny, Ted, and Gerrie. His eyes glistened as they settled on the photo of the family together, Gerrie grinning for the camera.

"Will you go see her tomorrow?" Sunny asked gently, understanding how difficult it was to be in this room.

"It's up to the doctors. She may just need to rest tomorrow. It's unusual they would speak to an ex-husband, but Sandy explained the situation and Gerrie told them to keep me updated.

"Of course, if she wants to see me, I'll go. When Durk gets back, he'll work with the doctors and Gerrie on her care, but I'm hopeful he'll allow all of us to continue to help."

Sunny was indignant. "He has to. We're family!"

"Technically, Sunny, you're family, as Durk is your father and Michael is your brother. Aleen and I are nothing to Gerrie and Michael."

"That's so not true," she said, a bit angry. "You're family to me, and technically, you're 'nothing' to me. Family's a lot more than blood."

He smiled. "You're pretty smart for a teenager."

"It won't be that long till I'm twenty," Sunny said cheekily. "Hey, and there is one other thing. Gerrie still loves you, and that counts for a lot."

"Yes, she did say that today, and I really think she meant it, but she has a lot to work through now. Gerrie needs to recover before she makes any big decisions about her life."

Ted rocked Michael while Sunny sat next to him on Stu's bed, both lost in their thoughts about the young man who was no longer with them, the baby who was just starting his life, and the mother of the two boys, who was struggling mightily.

chapter forty-five

Aleen

After Aleen and Sunny returned home, Durk had emailed to say he would call shortly. Sunny went to her room to have a long call with Benjamin, and her mother was glad, because she was nervous about her conversation with her ex-husband. Would it be short and to the point? Would he address his feelings honestly?

She paced back and forth in the kitchen, which wasn't helping her calm down. Even though it was late, she grabbed the open bottle of pinot noir and poured herself a generous glass. Maybe the wine would help her get through this conversation.

It was almost midnight when the phone rang. "Hello, Durk?"

"Aleen, it's me. Your email worried me. What's going on?" Durk sounded a bit frantic and breathless, like he'd been running.

"You sound a bit out of breath. Are you okay?" she asked, genuinely concerned.

"I literally ran to my hotel room so I could have some privacy. I'm fine. Just tell me what's wrong."

"Gerrie had a bit of a breakdown." Aleen spoke calmly but firmly. "She couldn't get the baby to calm down, and the nanny had the day off, so she went to Ted's. She was frantic for help, at wit's end, Durk, hysterical."

"I asked her again and again if I should go on this trip, and she told me over and over it would be fine." She could hear Durk's anguish and regret over the phone.

"Sandy, our counselor, came over to help Gerrie. She felt it best for her to have inpatient care, so she's at the facility Sandy recommended that is only ten minutes away. It has an excellent reputation."

Aleen held her breath for his response, but as she could only hear his breathing on the other end of the line, she continued recounting the events.

"Ted is at the house with the baby and will explain everything to the nanny in the morning. Sunny, Ted, and I are working to make sure the baby is with one of us as much as possible. There is a concern that Michael hasn't properly bonded with Gerrie. But please don't worry about his care; we've got it covered . . . Durk . . . Durk . . . are you there?" Aleen's apprehension was growing by the second.

"I blame myself for so much of this. I could see Gerrie was struggling, but I didn't know what to do. I really didn't, Aleen." Durk's emotions were clear; his voice, traveling halfway across the world, was faltering now.

"If there's one thing I've learned over this terrible period of time, it's that placing blame doesn't work, so please don't do it. We've just got to work our way forward now. Please, Durk."

It took him a few moments to reply.

"If I'm honest with myself, which is very hard to do, I can't say I'm totally shocked about this breakdown. She closed herself off, Ali, and wouldn't talk to me. We blame ourselves for Stu's death, and it must have been eating her alive." The words started pouring out of him now.

"So much so she couldn't spend time with Michael. The nanny has been taking care of him. Gerrie couldn't even get out of bed for so long after he was born. Then, when she seemed better, she went straight back to work, so she hardly saw Michael at all.

"I should have gotten her help a long time ago, but I didn't know what to do. She kept telling me she was fine, just fine . . ." He stopped, his emotions taking over.

"Durk, we don't have to cover everything on the phone right now. We can talk when you get back," Aleen said gently and hung on, holding her breath.

"No, Ali, no! You have to tell me what she said. I want to know; I need to know. I can't sit over here across the world without knowing *exactly* what's happening. I can talk to the doctors tomorrow, but I would much rather hear it from you.

"My life is falling apart, *again*. It's tearing me up, so please tell me everything." There was silence on the other end of the line as he waited for her to continue.

"Let me start with the baby. We believe you're right, and Gerrie admitted as much, that she hasn't been the mother she should be. She actually said she thought about harming herself and the baby."

"Oh my God, no . . ."

"Durk, she also called him 'Stu' when she was most distraught."

Her ex-husband just hung on the line.

"Gerrie's getting the care she needs now, and the baby is fine." Aleen tried to reassure him. "All three of us vow to spend lots of time with Michael until you get back, perhaps after, if you let us. The doctors feel she needs rest right now and are encouraging you to stick to your schedule. Honestly, I don't think she can face you or anyone right now." She paused to breathe.

"You know I would drop everything and get back there as soon as possible?" Durk asked, hoping for an affirmative reply.

"We all know that, and if it would help Gerrie for you to be back here right away, I would tell you that. I understand you're flying back on Wednesday with Don, on the company jet, and that saves a lot of travel time anyway.

"Gerrie needs to rest and recover. I know it will be hard, but with the time difference, it will be Wednesday before you know it." Aleen could tell by his silence that he agreed.

"What did she say about me?" Durk said it so quietly it was hard for her to hear. "Don't spare me; tell me everything."

"She said the two of you caused Stu's death and you stayed together because of your guilt about the tragedy. She also said she thought you would be happier back with me and Sunny."

Durk couldn't answer, so she continued. "Gerrie said she still loved Ted and needed him to help her take care of Michael. I'm sorry to be so blunt, but you asked to know exactly what she said."

"No, Ali, I need to know the truth." Durk was silent for a time before continuing, and Aleen had no idea what to say to fill the gap.

"I'm sorry. I am so sorry for hurting you and Sunny. If we could go back in time and bring Stu back, we would. We absolutely would."

"I know that, Durk," she whispered.

"Gerrie was right; we did feel bound together by Stu's death and the full realization of what we'd done. We both knew our union was a mistake early on, but we had to keep going. Our families were torn apart because of us. Then she got pregnant.

"The depth of despair we feel is so deep. . . . It's hurting everyone, including our baby, our beautiful son. I've got to step up now, Ali, and do what's right for him and all of us!"

The tears were flowing down her cheeks, and Aleen tried to get a word out but failed. She could tell Durk was crying, too. He never cried. . . .

"Can you do me a favor, Ali?"

"Yes," she whispered.

"Will you tell Sunny how sorry I am and how much I need her—and you—to forgive me? Please do that for me."

"I will," Aleen said, unable to utter anything else. The line was silent for a moment before Durk broke the silence.

"I'm assuming you handled everything for Gerrie at work?"

"Yes, I did. Trish will get the message to her staff that she's exhausted and plans to take two weeks off. No one needs to know anything else. We assume you'll cover everything with Don."

"I will. I need you to email me or call with any updates on Gerrie and the baby. If I don't hear from you or Ted several times a day, I'll worry. Just use my private email."

Aleen didn't realize she was clutching the phone so hard her knuckles had turned white. "Yes, yes, of course."

"And, Ali, thank you for all you've done. You didn't need to help Gerrie. How many women would . . . ?" He couldn't finish the question, and Aleen struggled with her emotions as well.

"Please, let Sunny know how proud I am of her for helping Gerrie and Michael." Durk sounded tired and defeated.

"I will. I promise. I'll also email you the doctor's contact info, and you can call for updates, which I know will be difficult with the time difference."

"Good, thanks," Durk replied. "When I'm able to reach them, I'll ask the doctors to share information with Ted as well. From what you've said, he's been a great help to Gerrie so far.

"Both of you amaze me, frankly. Your empathy, your forgiveness . . ." The phone went silent as Durk tried to gather himself. "And, Ali, when I get back, we need to talk," he said slowly and deliberately.

"I know, Durk. We do. We really do."

After saying goodbye to her ex-husband, Aleen gathered herself with a deep breath and took her wine to the window, taking in the night view of the lake. It was beautiful out there, like most nights, but this wasn't like most nights. No, not at all.

chapter forty-six

Ted

Dr. Martin, the physician working most closely with Gerrie, called on Monday to ask Ted to come by Tuesday afternoon. He told him she had a good day settling in Monday and was doing as well as could be expected.

Ted stayed over at the house Sunday and spent as much time as he could with the baby. Hope and Cash settled in beautifully; they made themselves at home as soon as they arrived. The nanny didn't fully understand everything, but she didn't ask many questions. He surmised she knew long ago that something was amiss with Gerrie and the baby.

Meg seemed to enjoy having the dogs around, as they were so funny and good-natured. She said she would be fine taking care of Michael and the dogs while Ted visited Gerrie.

He smiled when he thought of Michael, as he and Ted developed a wonderful relationship right away. Before he left to go to the hospital, he stopped in to stroke the sleeping baby's cheek.

Taking a detour on the way, Ted stopped by the tree to pin up some new flowers for Stu. He hadn't been there in a while, with the dramatic developments of the last few days. Once he had the red roses secured to the tree, he sat in the grass. He felt a strong need to talk to his son about everything that was happening in their family.

He spoke out loud, as no one was around. "Stu, I think your mom needs me. She actually said she loves me and wants me back. I'm not sure if she has her wits about her, but I guess I'll know soon. Not sure what to do.

"No matter what happens, I'll help her. She really needs all our support now so she can get better. I'll do my best for your brother, too. Boy, he reminds me of you. I know your mom was struggling with him, but Michael Stuart has been very good for me so far. I actually enjoy being with him, like I did with you. I must seem like such a strange man 'cause I love babies." Ted actually laughed aloud at himself.

"Helping you grow into such a fine young man was my greatest accomplishment in life. That and being a good husband to your mom . . ."

He had to pause as he tried to block the hurt and anger that started to well up; he promised himself he would be in control at this site, which was sacred to him.

"I loved every minute when you were growing up . . . when you were a baby, a toddler, when you and I played sports together when you were young . . . the Packers games . . . so many great times . . .

"Stu, do you remember that game we used to play when we driving on long car trips, guessing at answers to questions by looking to find things out the window? 'One for yes; two for no'—that's what we used to say.

"I'm not sure why I just thought of that. It was just a silly, made-up game because we could pretty much come up with the answers we wanted. I guess that was the fun part of it." Ted smiled at the memory of the driving vacations with his family.

"I wish you could help me decide what to do about your

mother. She hurt me so badly—and you. What you said to her when you left that night was in anger, and you didn't really mean it. I know you loved her.

"Other than losing you, the breakup with your mom was the worst thing to happen to me. Is it the right thing to think we could have another chance? Is that even possible after everything that has happened?"

Ted just sat silently as a gentle breeze kicked up, blowing a single petal off the roses tied to the tree. The petal fluttered about gracefully before falling to the ground in front of him.

"Well, I'm not a believer in these things at all, son, not at all, but it looks like you gave me your answer." He sat on the ground in amazement for a minute, reaching to pick up the single rose petal before standing and heading over to see Gerrie.

Ted was pleased Durk kept his promise and told Dr. Martin at the inpatient facility the staff needed to share all information about Gerrie with Ted, as he could help her far more than Durk right now. It seemed the doctors agreed once they heard the story of the affair, Stu's death, and the bitter breakup of the two couples.

Things could change when Durk returned, but Ted couldn't worry about that now. His focus was helping Gerrie recover and taking care of Michael Stuart as he'd promised.

When he entered her room, Dr. Martin was sitting next to the bed, talking to her. While she still looked tired, Gerrie seemed like a different woman than the one he encountered Sunday.

"You must be Ted. Please come in." The doctor stood to shake his hand. "Good to meet you in person after our conversations on the phone. Gerrie and I have had a number of good sessions, and she would like to talk to you." The physician nodded at her to be sure she was ready.

"Thanks, Dr. Martin," Gerrie said. "I'm so glad Ted is here. I certainly wasn't on my best behavior Sunday and need to apologize."

"There's nothing to apologize about. I just want you to get better," Ted said.

"Exactly right, Ted." Dr. Martin agreed. "Gerrie, if you need anything, just hit the call button." With that, her doctor left, and Ted sat in the chair next to her bed. The two took a long look at each other.

"The baby is doing great," Ted said in an animated fashion, trying to start out positively. "The nanny thinks I'm crazy, because I won't leave and let her do her job, but it seems to be working out. Oh, I had to bring the dogs over. I hope you're okay with that. I know you never wanted dogs in the house before."

"Of course the dogs had to stay with you. They can't take care of themselves. I'm perfectly fine with that. You're helping so much by watching the baby." Gerrie grabbed his hand and squeezed it.

"You should know Aleen and Sunny come by as much as they can. They love spending time with Michael Stuart."

Gerrie noticed how Ted's eyes warmed when he said the baby's name. "I'm glad, Ted. Durk and I haven't done right by the baby, I'm afraid, and we'll have to do better in the future. The three of you are showing us the way."

Gerrie took a big breath before continuing.

"Here's the thing. For me to get better, to recover, I've got to share my true feelings with Durk and you. After that, I need to be a better mother to Michael. It's also important for me to get along with Aleen and Sunny.

"But before I can do all of that, I have to pull out of this postpartum depression. I've started on medication, which should help. And then, the most difficult part . . . I need you to help me properly grieve for our son, which is at the core of everything that is wrong with me, I think."

Ted looked at his ex-wife and held her hand tightly now, as he could see how difficult this was for her.

"Gerrie, I know you can be yourself again. You're a strong, vibrant, and wonderful woman. You can do it, and I will do anything I can to help. You must know that." He touched her face gently.

"I pushed aside all my grief and tried to bury it in my new relationship, my job, and then the dream of having a new son. Unfortunately, the reality of a baby at my age, postpartum depression, my unresolved grief over Stu, and the realization I made a terrible mistake in leaving you . . . all of that came crashing down on me."

Ted moved out of the chair and sat on the bed next to Gerrie. Her words hit him like a ton of bricks, and he needed to be close to her.

"I wish I could have helped you," he said, trying to control his emotions.

"You did the only thing you could in turning away from me. I ruined everything you loved in this world. I literally couldn't live with myself." Gerrie stared down at the sheets for a moment. "And Durk and I clung to each other, as we had no other options. We both knew we wanted our old lives back, but we could never say it out loud."

Ted looked directly at her in amazement. "Oh, God, Gerrie, if Aleen and I would have known . . ." He dropped his head in his hands.

"We didn't even fully admit it to ourselves, much less each other. How could we with all the grief, anger, and hurt? It was an impossible situation. We were all trapped in it.

"The next step is for me to talk to Durk as soon as he arrives.

But I need your forgiveness before I move forward one inch. I'm stuck in place without it." Gerrie searched his eyes for his response.

"I forgive you, Gerrie. And Stu does, too. I stopped by the tree this morning, and he found a way to tell me. Don't ask how."

Tears welled up in Gerrie's eyes. "Thank you, Ted, thank you. You have no idea how much that means to me. I needed to hear that so, so much. I may seem a lot better to you now than I did Sunday, but please don't be fooled. I have a very long road ahead of me."

Ted moved closer and took her in his arms as she cried.

She grabbed a tissue to wipe at her eyes. "I have no right to ask you this, but when I'm better and we can all move forward, can you find it in your heart to give me another chance?" Gerrie put her hand over Ted's mouth. "Please don't answer me now. Just let me know if there is a chance."

"There's a very good chance." Ted pulled her to him again, and they held each other tightly, without saying anything. It had been such a long time since they reached out to each other; neither one of them wanted to let go.

chapter forty-seven

Aleen

Aleen sat at her desk at work, staring at her computer screen, when an email popped up from Durk's private account. She glared at it for a minute before opening it.

Dear Ali:

Sorry to have to say this to you in an email, but the time differences and staying up to date on Gerrie and the baby do not allow much time for us to talk. Plus, I'm not sure I could get through this on the phone.

How can I thank you for everything you've done for Gerrie and Michael? You are a rare woman. I guess I've always known it, but I lost sight of it for a while. Shame on me.

You're a wonderful mother and have been from the very second Sunny was born. I am so grateful, and our daughter adores you. Gerrie's struggles with Michael made all of that crystal clear to me. She will get better and be the mother the baby needs. I know it.

It turns out I have been lost without you, but that is a conversation we need to have in person. Being in Japan while my family is in crisis has given me a lot of time to think. As soon as I get back, family is the priority, and I will do everything I can to help Gerrie recover and devote the time to Michael he deserves. You and Sunny are my family, too, and the three of us need to figure out what that means in the future.

Can you ever forgive me for the damage I have done to our family? Is there a way we could start again, rethink what we mean to each other?

Can't wait to talk to you in person, Ali. Please stay up late and wait for me tonight. I'll see Gerrie, then Michael, and head over to see you. Sleep isn't a priority with my family suffering thousands of miles away. I can't rest until I see you.

Much Love,

Durk

Gazing out the window with tears in her eyes, Aleen couldn't get her mind off what her ex-husband had said about her and their relationship. *Will we get back together? How can we with everything Gerrie is going through . . . and the baby?* Her mind was reeling with all the possibilities.

There were so many work emails to handle, but Aleen just waved them off, as she was consumed by the family drama and what was going to happen next in her life. *There isn't much work getting done this week,* she thought, reaching for a tissue. What an intertwined mess there was for the two families to sort out!

Aleen recalled her conversation with Ted last evening, and it was good to know Gerrie was making progress. He cautioned she could still have a setback, but her recovery seemed to be off to an encouraging start.

Durk was heading directly from the airport to see Gerrie. He'd been communicating with Ted, Aleen, and the doctors, and he grabbed information from whomever he could reach, as communications were complicated by the time zone differences. She was glad Durk and Ted seemed to be able to get along for Gerrie's sake. *Interesting how a crisis can bring people together,* she thought, shaking her head.

It was wonderful that Durk had sent a long, heartfelt email to Sunny, too, describing what he hoped for in their relationship in the future. Sunny had printed it out and read it over and over with tears in her eyes each time. Her daughter shared the email with her mother, and Aleen got misty-eyed every time she read it, too. She pulled up the copy Sunny had forwarded to look at it again.

Dear Sunny:

Thank you for everything you've done to help Gerrie and Michael. As you know, I was asked not to cut my trip short to give Gerrie a chance to rest. This wouldn't have been possible without Ted, your Mom and you. I would have returned in a minute if the doctors thought I should. I have no doubt the three of you are taking excellent care of our boy and that Ted is doing everything he can for Gerrie.

Sunny, I have made mistakes—some big ones—that have gotten in the way of my relationship with you, and I am so sorry. Words can't express my love for you, my precious daughter, and I hope you can find it in your heart to forgive me. I can say with all honesty that it is very difficult for me to forgive myself for hurting you and your mother and for Stu's death. The sorrow will be with all of us for the rest of our lives, as you know all too well. To see you suffering, sweetheart, has broken my heart.

Right now, our focus must be on Gerrie and Michael Stuart. Their health and well-being is so important, and I'm proud that you have been able to put aside the pain from the past to come to their aid. You are a very special young woman. I hope when Gerrie is recovered, you and I can spend a lot of time together and try to rebuild the wonderful relationship we once had. Without you fully in my life, there is a hole that cannot be filled. Here's my promise—I will be a better father to Michael and you in the future.

When I go to sleep every night, I think of you and ask God to watch over my beautiful daughter. I tell him you have had to go through way too much grief and pain in your young life. If there was anything I could do to change the past, I would. I hope you know that. I also pray the future will be much brighter and happier for you and your mother than the past year has been. I will do everything in my power to make that happen.

Thanks again for everything you are doing for our family. I can't wait to give you a big hug in person. You make me so proud.

Much Love,

Your Dad

Placing her hands down on her desk, as if she were steadying herself, Aleen paused for a moment before grabbing another tissue from the ever-present box next to her phone. Her ex-husband's words tugged at her heart, and emotions surged inside her. *What will I say to Durk? What does he want to say to me?*

The fact that he was visiting Gerrie, stopping by the house to see the baby, and *then* coming over to talk to Aleen was making her very nervous. The conversation had to be of the utmost importance to him, as tired and jetlagged as he was going to feel.

The stress on him had been intense; it was probably worse for him, as he was so far away. Perhaps it was a good thing Sunny had a special study group tonight so she wouldn't get home until late. Aleen and her ex-husband did need some time alone.

While Ted was sharing a great deal about Gerrie's recovery, he seemed to be holding something back. Of course, there would be many things he and his ex-wife shared that were private and should remain that way.

Aleen gazed out the window again, lost in her thoughts. She tried in vain to focus on making progress on the presentation she was putting together.

Trish was returning today from a trip, and Aleen was anxious to talk to her in person about Gerrie. She was sure Trish would be pleased with the progress reports so far. The two women executives had become very close.

Just as she was turning her attention to the presentation, Allison, Trish's new assistant, poked her head in and asked that Aleen join Trish in her office.

She practically ran in and smiled at her former boss. "I'm *so* glad you're back," she told her.

"Me, too. I asked Allison to bring us some tea. I want to hear how Gerrie's doing. I'm hoping to be able to see her when she's ready." Trish moved some papers out of the way for Allison to put the tea down in front of the two women.

"I'm sure she would love to see you," Aleen said sincerely, taking a sip of the piping-hot brew. "They have limited her visitors at this point, only Ted and Durk. Durk returns late this afternoon. As soon as he lands, he'll head straight over to see her. I've done my best to keep him up to date via email and calls, and Ted has as well."

Trish took a sip of her tea and observed her former assistant closely. "So Gerrie's made a lot of progress from when we spoke earlier?"

"Oh, yes. She's started on medication and has worked to deal with her postpartum depression, which will help her be a better mother to Michael. The guilt she felt over Stu's death and hurting Ted has weighed her down.

"So . . ." Aleen continued. "In a big step forward, Gerrie has asked Ted for his forgiveness. I don't think she would mind me talking to you about all of this, as she made it clear to Ted that she wanted you to be updated."

Trish nodded. "Thanks. I'm glad. I've been so worried."

"Gerrie feels she must get better and then properly grieve for Stu, with Ted's help. She never had the chance to do that with the bitter breakup." Aleen stopped for a minute, as it hit her this story was about her life as well.

"It must be difficult for you to cover this ground again." Trish frowned at her.

"Revisiting the past has been painful, for sure. Right after the accident, all of us denied our true feelings. I know I was just numb when Durk said he was leaving me and then Stu was killed. It was only when Ted, Sunny, and I started having honest conversations about what happened that the three of us began to inch forward in dealing with our own pain and grief.

"It appears as if Gerrie and Durk just kept burying their feelings. At least that's what it sounds like from what they've both said. Once she's better, she can start working through all her emotions."

"And Durk?" Trish inquired with keen interest.

"We've agreed to talk, to have a real, honest conversation when he returns," Aleen replied, taking another drink of her tea to try to hide her emotions. "We covered some ground already, and believe me; it has shaken me to the core."

Trish eyed her employee and friend with admiration. "You know, not many people could handle the situation the way you have."

"If you would have seen the state Gerrie was in . . . I wouldn't wish that on anyone."

Trish fiddled with a pen on her desk. "When I talked to Gerrie the Friday afternoon before her breakdown, I asked her to get help. She said she would look for counselors but wanted to spend the weekend with her son, just the two of them, since Durk would be traveling. I saw a touch of panic in her eyes. I just wish . . ."

"Trish, you can't play the 'what-if' game; believe me. We've all done that far too long. I'm not sure what any of us could have done to prevent Gerrie's breakdown. No one knew the severity of her problems." Aleen ran her hands through her hair, remembering the desperation she saw in Gerrie. It had frightened her.

"I shouldn't say this to you, but I've not been my best this week at work. I have to get my attention back to that presentation for Don." She looked at the head of her department with chagrin.

"Don't give it another thought; the final draft isn't due until next week. Get out of here as soon as you can. You've had far more important things on your mind than work and some presentation that, frankly, is just like thousands of others. Promise me you will," Trish ordered as she stood to walk out of her office.

"I promise," Aleen said, stopping in the doorway. "And thanks for our chat."

She went back to her office, shut down her computer, and straightened up her desk so she could head out, marveling at the head of her department. Trish was not only a top executive; she was a good person. *Tough combination to find.* How lucky she was to work with her.

As she drove out of the parking structure, Aleen headed for Gerrie's house to see Ted and the baby. When she arrived, the nanny had already left, the baby was asleep, and Ted was cooking dinner. He'd set up two plates on the kitchen island, with beautiful, large wine glasses, and was busily preparing something that smelled delicious.

"What's all of this?" Aleen asked, clearly surprised he was cooking dinner for them.

"Well, I thought you could have a nice meal with me before you head home. Perhaps you can feed the baby when he wakes up." He was pouring chicken stock into a pan.

"Okay, what are you making?" She walked over to the stove to take a look.

"Champagne risotto with asparagus and crispy prosciutto," Ted answered matter-of-factly as he continued to stir in more chicken stock. "It will be ready in about fifteen minutes, and I insist you have a glass of wine with me." He had a pinot noir open and ready.

"Wow, what did I do to deserve all of this?" Aleen laughed and took a small sip of wine. "Oh, that's good."

"Glad you like it." He swirled his wine around in the glass and sniffed it before he gave it a taste. "To answer your other question, you deserve this because I suspect you haven't had a decent meal for a couple days because you've been worried about Gerrie, the baby, Sunny, me . . . and Durk."

"Hmm, you got me there. Food hasn't been high on the priority list lately. Work, either. I've found it really hard to concentrate on anything else."

"Me, too. I've done the absolute minimum I need to do just to keep up for key clients. Other things are much higher priority now."

As soon as the chicken stock was absorbed into the risotto, Ted poured in more to soften the Italian rice.

"I've been passing along information to Durk as soon as I

hear it from you. He's only been able to connect with the doctors once for a long conversation." Aleen took another sip of her wine; it sure tasted good after another stressful day.

Ted nodded. "The time zone differences are a real challenge. The two of us were able to connect today again, however."

"Well, then I suppose you know Durk is coming by to see me later this evening, after he visits with Gerrie and stops here to see the baby." Aleen looked right at Ted, as she was keenly interested in his response.

"I did know that. He wanted me to know his plans and about what time he would be here to see Michael." He poured in some more chicken stock and stirred the risotto.

"What are you going to do when you're both here in this house?" she asked as he continued to run around the kitchen, preparing dinner.

He put on an oven glove to remove a tray of asparagus when the timer went off.

"I'm not sure, but I hope he lets me stay here tonight. I don't think he's entirely comfortable with Michael at this age, and I think he's a bit afraid he might screw up. Plus, he'll be horribly jetlagged and doesn't need to be awakened by the baby, although Michael has slept really well the last two nights."

Ted put the freshly shredded Parmesan on the counter after measuring out what he needed to throw into the risotto.

"Gosh, I wish there was a hidden camera on the two of you!" Aleen laughed at the thought of Ted and Durk living in the same house.

"We'll manage," he said. "Our focus will be on Michael and Gerrie. We have a shared goal of their welfare and happiness."

"Well said." Aleen raised her glass to him. She had to say she was enjoying this impromptu get-together, but why did it feel like a mini celebration?

"I need to show Durk how to take care of Michael." Ted took a drink of his wine and looked at Aleen. "He admitted to me he hasn't spent enough time with him yet, and Gerrie hasn't either, which really bothered him."

She nodded. "I guess I didn't realize it at the time, but I believe Durk wasn't comfortable being alone with Sunny when she was a baby. All his anxiety disappeared when she started to talk and he could at least try to reason with her. As much as one can reason with a two-year-old."

Aleen grabbed two heated bowls out of the oven with the hot pads, as Ted was mixing all the final risotto ingredients together, including the asparagus spears cut in precise, angled pieces. When the bowls were filled, he crumbled the crispy prosciutto on top.

"That looks gorgeous and smells delicious." She sat on the stool and took her first bite after Ted sprinkled more Parmesan on top. "Wow. Who knew you were such a good cook?"

He smiled as he joined her to eat his dinner. "I guess I've fallen out of practice with no one to cook for."

The two friends chatted as they enjoyed the dinner and wine. Aleen thought this meal would be even more enjoyable if so many questions didn't surround the two families.

"Why do I feel you know something I don't?" Aleen looked at Ted, and he just shrugged.

Just then, they heard Michael crying on the baby monitor.

"I'll go get him. I assume he's ready for a bottle." Aleen went upstairs to Michael's room and got him out of his crib. She quickly changed his diaper and took him downstairs, jabbering to him the whole way.

Ted was heating up his bottle, so Aleen bounced Michael on her knee to keep him occupied. She noticed he looked much more rested than he did Sunday.

"He's doing better every day, isn't he?" she asked as Ted continued to clear dishes and check on the bottle.

"I really believe so. I'm trying to get him into a set routine, which will help him sleep. I hold him and play with him all the time, showering him with love and affection. It's clear he wasn't getting that kind of attention before. I know Meg was doing a very good job, but Michael isn't her baby."

Ted handed Aleen the baby's bottle, and Michael hungrily grabbed for it.

"It's good he's up now. I don't think it will be too long until Durk arrives. It really depends on how much time he spends with Gerrie. She's still trying to rest as much as she can, so I don't expect he'll stay much more than an hour or so." Ted talked over his shoulder to Aleen as he finished the cleanup and she fed the baby.

"I'll be on my way as soon as he finishes this. I don't want to be here when Durk arrives; Michael needs to be the focus." She walked the baby around after he ate and then handed him off to Ted with a kiss on his soft baby cheek.

"Goodbye, little man. I'll see you soon. You be good for your dad and Ted." Michael smiled and bounced around in Ted's arms.

"Thank you for a fantastic dinner. I'll have to get that recipe. And good luck tonight." Aleen took a final sip of her wine.

"You, too," Ted shouted to her as she walked out the door and headed home.

After the unexpected pleasure of dinner with Ted and spending some time with Michael, Aleen felt a bit lonely at home by herself. It was only a five-minute drive from the Hammands', and with time to waste, Aleen created all these different scenarios in her head about what would happen with Durk.

This was a man she was married to for more than twenty

years. She needed to calm down. But something was different tonight, and she knew it. Ted did, too.

Could she get over the hurt and devastation of the last year? Did she really want her husband back after he broke her heart? Could she trust him again? She couldn't be sure Durk wanted to reunite his family; that's what Gerrie said, but was that true? Was that her sickness talking or was it real? Durk implied he wanted to get back together, but did he?

Two glasses of wine were a risk for her, but Aleen felt it was one she needed to take. Maybe the wine would calm her down and act as a truth serum. She laughed, thinking she needed Durk to drink some, too, so he would tell her what he was really thinking. There could not be any pretense between them anymore.

Forgiveness was tricky. Would Aleen be weak to forgive him, or strong? Most people would totally understand if she never forgave Durk and chose not to see him again. That would be difficult, of course, as they shared a daughter, but a very high percentage of people would do exactly that, letting bitterness rule their lives.

She took a sip of wine as she tried to figure out whether to forgive him or not. Aleen grabbed her temples and massaged them for a few seconds. God, she wasn't sure what she wanted or what was best for her and Sunny.

There was one thing that had become clear to her over the last year—the more she focused on revealing her pain and fears and shared those feelings with others, the better she felt. The pain and hurt didn't go away, no, but it was lessened a bit. Maybe that's why Gerrie just cracked; she kept everything inside and pushed Durk and Michael away until it was just too much for her, as it would be for anyone.

Another key lesson for her was she couldn't as effectively

help others if she didn't first focus on herself. All the things Aleen had done to improve her health and fitness, her mental state, appearance, education, and career had built her confidence. She really felt good about herself.

When she listed the things she'd done this past year that she thought she would *never* do . . . well, she just shook her head. She truly was proud of herself and was a different person than before the breakup.

Aleen had learned long ago not to judge others. She couldn't hate Gerrie as she once did, not after seeing her fall apart under the weight of her grief, anxiety, and guilt. Gerrie had been through hell, and Aleen actually felt great sympathy for her now. Was that weird since this was the same woman who took her husband?

God, this is complicated, she thought, sipping her wine.

She got up and walked to the window with her glass. How many times over the last fifteen years had this view comforted her? She never tired of it, and it helped her now, calming her nerves just a bit. It was pitch black on the lake, but all kinds of lights twinkled on the other side, moving up the side of the mountain.

chapter forty-eight

Durk

Durk drove cautiously over to the hospital. He wanted to get there so fast, but he knew he had to slow everything down and be careful. There could be no more accidents disrupting this family.

He was apprehensive about talking to Gerrie and was sure she was nervous, too. They loved each other in a way, yes, but not enough.

Their marriage could never sustain the loss of Stu, the guilt they felt, and the feelings they still had for their former spouses. They both knew it early on, but there was nothing they could do. Nothing. They couldn't even form the words. Until now.

Would they be honest with each other about the future? What if their former spouses told them to go to hell? What would family gatherings be like if they reunited in their old pairings? *So many questions.*

Durk pulled into the hospital lot and parked near the building, as it was late and there were plenty of open spaces. He knew Gerrie's room number and headed directly there, the heels of his shoes clicking in rhythm on the linoleum floor. The hall smelled of antiseptic, like it had just been cleaned.

His heart was beating out of his chest when he opened the door to Gerrie's room and saw her sitting up, waiting for him. He went immediately to her, sitting on the bed, taking her in his arms.

"I'm sorry . . . I should have known you needed help. I should have been better with Michael . . ." Durk began, and Gerrie took his face in her hands.

"Shh," she said. "We've both made mistakes and suffered for it. We have to do what's right for our family now."

Durk sat up, taking her hand to kiss it. "If we could undo the past and bring Stu back . . ." Tears coursed down his cheeks.

"If we could have had our old lives back, we would have. You and I never said it, but we knew we both felt that way. The price we paid for our love was too high, much too high," she said. "And was it love or infatuation? I think we both knew after Stu's death that our union was a mistake. I longed for Ted and Stu just as you wanted your life with Aleen and Sunny."

Durk nodded. "I think we both built something special in our marriages and didn't realize until it was too late. And then the tragedy with Stu was too much, just too much . . ."

Gerrie was filled to the brim with sadness and regret, and it burst from her.

"Stu, my son, I am so, so sorry for driving you away that night. That horrible night!" she cried, shaking and sobbing, and Durk took her in his arms.

Her husband held her as she cried, as he knew she needed to let it out, to allow some of the grief to leave her, to give herself a chance at happiness once again.

chapter forty-nine

Aleen

When the doorbell rang, Aleen put her glass on the counter and rushed to greet Durk, her heart beating rapidly. When she opened the door and saw her ex-husband standing there, exhausted and pale, she did the only thing she could. She opened her arms, and he fell into her, holding her tight.

"Ali. Oh, Ali," he kept saying his pet name for her. "I am so sorry. So very sorry." Durk held on tightly before pulling back from their embrace to face her.

"It's okay now, Durk. Please come in and sit down." Aleen tried to lead him over to the couch, but he continued to talk and grabbed her arms so she would look directly at him.

"I've had days to think about what I wanted to say to you. I haven't been able to sleep. I'm exhausted and have no defenses left. I just need to finally tell you the truth about what I've been feeling." He looked directly into her eyes, and she nodded; she clearly wanted to hear what he had to say.

"I hurt you and Sunny so much when I left. And then, Stu . . . it was all my fault. I caused you and Sunny so much pain. The two people I loved the most in the world! I made a terrible, unforgivable mistake. I would totally understand if you never forgave me." He was frantic now, tears in his eyes.

"It's all right. Please. Calm down and come over here with me." She guided him over to the couch, and they both sat down.

"I made the greatest mistake of my life when I left. And then the accident and Stu's death sent us all into a tailspin. I guess the affair started because I wanted to feel young again and have someone think I was handsome and smart. Gerrie and I related so well over work that we became attracted to each other. It was all so stupid and so wrong."

Aleen didn't say anything, but nodded to encourage him to continue.

"All the time I was away on this trip, I was thinking about what Gerrie said about loving Ted and that she knew I wanted to be back with you and Sunny. It's the truth, Aleen. We just could never say it because we felt chained together in our grief and sadness, and the three of you hated us for what we'd done and blamed us for Stu's death." He paused and wiped his face with his handkerchief.

Aleen held her breath as he continued.

"We just didn't have any idea how to even start to make everything right, and Gerrie internalized everything, destroying herself."

Aleen took Durk's hand, frozen in place, unable to speak, hearing her ex-husband's true feelings for the first time since he'd left.

"That beautiful young man . . ." Durk couldn't say more as tears ran down his cheek, and he wiped his face with his sleeve.

"And Gerrie and I haven't been good with Michael, and I'm so worried about him. I'm afraid both his parents have let him down so far in his young life. Although, he seemed so much more content tonight with Ted watching over him." He stopped to look at his ex-wife.

"Durk, Michael is going to be fine. We're all committed to his well-being." Aleen stroked his face and hair to continue to calm him down.

"Will Sunny let me be her father again? To look into my daughter's eyes and see only anger and bitterness . . . it just hurt so much."

"I can't speak for Sunny, but she apologized to Gerrie after she saw the state she was in. Our daughter only wants the best for her family, which includes you and Michael.

"You would be so proud of how she immediately jumped in to do anything to help. We raised a wonderful daughter, and I believe she is emerging from her own grief now, which will allow her to rebuild her relationship with you.

"She read your email over and over. I'm sure Sunny wants the two of you to be father and daughter again."

"God, I hope so, Ali. I really hope so. I want my daughter back. . . . After Stu died, I wanted to hold her in my arms and comfort her, but she couldn't stand the sight of me. It killed me, Ali. It did." Durk ran his hands through his hair to try to get ahold of himself before taking both of Aleen's hands in his.

"And you, Ali. I never stopped thinking of you as my wife. Even though I don't deserve a second chance after everything I've done, I hope you will consider it. *But* first things first. I have to make it right with Gerrie and Michael."

Durk raised his head to look her directly in the eyes. "Can you ever forgive me? Can you?" He stared at Aleen with love and desperation in his eyes.

"I'm trying really hard. All I can say is I'll do my best. I know forgiveness is the first step for all of us."

They sat on the couch with their arms around each other

for a long time, in the beloved family home they had worked so many years to create together.

After more than an hour discussing their past and future, Aleen went to the kitchen to make coffee. While it was late, neither of them could think about sleep, and Durk wanted to see his daughter before going home to be with his son.

He stood when he heard the door open and shut, signaling Sunny was home. When their eyes met, she ran to him, shouting, "Dad!"

They fell into an embrace, and Sunny's tears rolled onto her father's shoulder. Durk touched his daughter's hair and tried to quiet her, even as his own tears stained his cheeks.

"It's okay now, honey. It's okay," he whispered, rubbing her back.

Sunny clung to her father as Aleen watched, sucking in her breath as she saw the two people she loved most in the world truly together again.

Sunny

Five Years Later . . .

"Sun-nay," Michael called out to his sister as she came into the house. "You have to come to my room and see my new digger." She loved how Michael said her name, with the emphasis on the last syllable. No one else pronounced her name like him, so it was a special thing she shared with her little brother.

He was such a doll and looked so much like Stu as a boy it was scary. Gerrie showed Michael photos of the young Stu and had put a few pictures of the boys side by side, and the resemblance was uncanny.

Sunny worshipped her brother, and the whole family did, too. Michael was at the center of everything.

"Okay, but you know we need to get going for our trip, so I'll just have a quick look." She took Michael's hand, and they climbed the stairs as her brother jabbered away about his new toy. Sunny had heard he loved to take it in the yard and dig up dirt. Her mom had told Michael maybe they could create an herb garden, using his digger to turn the soil.

She couldn't believe they were going on this crazy trip; it had seemed an unattainable dream for the longest time. Ted—he'd finally convinced Sunny to use his first name rather than "Mr.

Hammand"—had talked for years about going to the Midwest to see his family and then traveling to Lambeau Field, the home of the Green Bay Packers. They all talked about it, even when Stu was alive; Sunny just never thought it was really going to happen.

Both families were going, and Benjamin, too. Vincent and Richard would have made the trip as well, but Richard couldn't get off work. Dawn and Andrew made a serious attempt to join them as well, but just couldn't swing it with their jobs. Sunny vowed to bring them all back some really cool stuff from the Packers Pro Shop.

She was thrilled the family was making the trip; she knew it would be really special. Michael couldn't contain his excitement about going on the plane and then to Lambeau. He'd watched the games with his family from the time he was so young that the Green Bay Packers were imprinted on his brain. *Just like Ted and Stu.* Sunny smiled to herself.

The thought of Stu made her marvel at how far they had all come since he died. After Gerrie had her breakdown, everything changed. They all worked hard to help her get better, and it took a long time, but she did find her way back to herself.

The family traded off shifts to take care of Michael while Gerrie recovered. The nanny had helped, too, in those early years, but now that Michael was in "big boy" school, it was only the family who cared for him.

When Gerrie went back to work, she decided she wanted to do something different. After consulting with her boss, the CEO, she took a part-time job assisting him. Gerrie did special projects for Don and members of his team, and it seemed to work out well.

With fewer hours devoted to work, she spent much more time with Michael, and the bond between them grew over time.

Unless someone knew the sad story, no one would ever guess the trouble they had early in Michael's life.

Sunny spent as much time with her little brother as she could, and he loved his big sister. Benjamin saw him all the time, too, and he was an important member of the family in Michael's eyes.

Ted did forgive Gerrie and helped her recover. After she got out of the inpatient facility, she went through individual counseling and then joint counseling with Ted. They faced their grief over Stu head on and reunited.

With Ted and Gerrie back together, Michael spent more time with Ted than Durk. All of them understood the complexities of this, so Michael called Ted "Papa" and Durk "Daddy." It seemed to work, as Durk was diligent about seeing his son, and Michael often went on family outings with Sunny's parents.

Sunny's mom and dad got back together, too. It wasn't easy for her mother to get over the pain of their earlier split, but she worked on her own feelings and her dad dealt with his issues, painful inch by painful inch. It was clear they loved each other very much.

Dealing with their past actions had been a challenge for Durk and Gerrie, but they did it. Both of them knew it was a necessary step before moving forward with their lives. They admitted their union was a mistake, as they may have confused their sexual attraction and easy rapport about work as a kind of intimacy. They saw no way out after Stu died, as they felt isolated and branded as immoral people.

They both did everything they could to make it up to Sunny, Aleen, and Ted. For all, understanding and overcoming the pain of the past allowed them to form new relationships with each other that were different than the old ones. Durk and Gerrie also became much better parents to Michael. He was a happy and healthy little boy.

Sunny knew a lot of people thought the couples were crazy to get back together after the betrayal and Stu's death. *Sorry,* she thought, *it just doesn't matter what others think. My family is my family, and that's the way it is.*

When Michael ran into his room to show Sunny his digger, he was so excited he was literally jumping up and down. "Look, Sun-nay, it's big and works like this." He demonstrated how he turned the crank and the digger went down into the carpet. "Should we bring it with us to Lambeau?" he asked, eyes getting big.

"No, Michael, we're all packed and ready to go, and I don't think the digger would fit in your suitcase. We can play with it as soon as we get back. I promise!" Sunny took his hand to lead him away from the toy and back down the stairs. The van Ted ordered to take them all to the airport would be here in a minute, and Benjamin would meet them there.

After Sunny and Benjamin graduated from engineering school, they both decided to go on and study for their master's degrees. Sunny had just accepted an offer to join the same company as her mom, dad, and Gerrie, on a rotational engineering program.

She'd absolutely loved the internships she'd done at the company, prompting her to take the offer for full-time employment after she completed her master's. Sunny actually had multiple offers, but deciding on the rotational program at her mom and dad's company was an easy choice.

Durk was so proud of his daughter; he was always introducing colleagues to her when she ran into him during her internships or the interview process. It was kind of cute. The two of them had worked hard to overcome the issues of the past and tried to focus on the good times of their shared history, but they didn't hesitate to deal with the painful ones, too.

Benjamin was working on his PhD and was thinking of teaching or research. He was so smart and had many opportunities ahead of him. She was proud of him and loved him so much; Sunny knew how lucky she was to have had two fantastic guys in her life. Stu would always, always be in her heart, but Benjamin was so important to her now.

And her mom! She finished her business degree and was now studying for her MBA. She had been promoted again to manage a team in her department and loved her new job. Trish had turned out to be the best leader her mom had ever worked with, and she'd mentored her every step of the way.

As she walked down the stairs, holding Michael's hand, the adults below looked up at the little boy and the impressive young woman, and the love the parents had for their children was so strong it made Sunny feel warm all over. *My family.*

The trip to Milwaukee went smoothly; Michael spent most of the time playing games or watching movies on his tablet. The highlight was when the flight attendant brought him his own little wings to wear. He loved them and proudly wore his pin on his shirt the rest of the day.

When the group arrived, two rental cars had been arranged. Ted told his family they were too big of group to try to transport, so they divided up: Michael, Gerrie, and Ted in one car and Aleen, Durk, Sunny, and Benjamin in the other.

After they checked into their hotel, the whole crew headed over to Ted's brother's house where the entire family was gathered to welcome the California contingent. As it was July and the weather was glorious, they had a family barbecue—with a Packers theme, of course—to welcome the Californians and get them in the right frame of mind for their trip north to Green Bay and the hallowed ground of Lambeau Field.

The barbecue was lots of fun, and Michael had a blast with the other kids his age, running around the backyard, bouncing on the trampoline, and generally causing havoc. By the time they all headed back to the hotel, the crew was ready for some rest, with the exception of Michael, who chattered on about his new family friends. Once his head hit the pillow, however, he was out like a light.

The next morning was gorgeous as they took off to drive two hours north in their small convoy. The only person in their group who had been to Lambeau Field was Ted, and he hadn't visited for years. He was a shareholder, too, and booked a special experience for them.

He'd told them for months everything they would see: the recreation of Vince Lombardi's office, the Packers Hall of Fame, the statues of Lombardi and Curly Lambeau, the best pro shop in the NFL, Brett Favre's locker, the Lambeau Leap statue. . . . It was heaven for the Packers faithful. Gerrie wasn't that much of a fan, but she played along to humor the rest of them.

When they finally got there, the travelers were so surprised that the stadium just sort of appeared out of nowhere in the middle of a neighborhood. Sunny was sure there was no other stadium in the National Football League like Lambeau Field.

After they saw all the sites Ted had described, the highlight of the tour was before them. They were going to walk out through the tunnel and onto the field just like the players did on game day.

It was so fantastic to see the field they watched on television live and up close. As they walked out of the tunnel, Sunny literally shivered in excitement.

The tour guide was going through his spiel, but the group wasn't paying a lot of attention, as they all were drinking in the environment.

Gerrie pulled a football out of her purse and threw it to Michael. He ran around with it before throwing it to Ted. The tour guide was not very pleased, but this was a once-in-a-lifetime opportunity to throw a football on the field at Lambeau.

Benjamin came over to Sunny and took her hand. "Isn't this fantastic?" He gazed at her with so much love in his eyes.

"It just couldn't be better to be with the family, seeing them so happy." She saw Durk tackle Michael, and they rolled on the ground, giggling.

"I was hoping it might get better." Benjamin grabbed her hand and got down on one knee, taking a small box out of his pocket. "I just couldn't think of a more perfect place to formally ask this. Sunny, would you marry me?"

"Oh my God, Benjamin, yes, yes!" Sunny shouted, pulling him up into her embrace.

Benjamin kissed her tenderly and then opened the small case to show her the ring. It was the most unusual engagement ring she'd ever seen in that it had small green emeralds and yellow gemstones surrounding the diamond.

"Well, I know you don't like traditional rings, so a friend's mom, who designs jewelry, made this especially for you. In case you haven't figured it out, the green and gold are Packers colors, which I thought would be totally appropriate since we are at Lambeau Field." Benjamin smiled at Sunny, who had been the love of his life from just about the moment they met. They both knew they would be married someday, as their love was so strong and true.

"It's perfect, Benjamin. I absolutely love it!" Sunny slid on the ring and then kissed Benjamin as the adults and Michael gathered around to applaud and cheer. Michael did his version of a cartwheel, which he'd been practicing for weeks.

"Well, it looks like I'm the only one who didn't know about

this." Sunny laughed and hugged her mom and dad and then Ted and Gerrie.

"What a day!" she said. "But there is one more thing we have to do." She kissed Benjamin and embraced him again before taking Michael's hand and asking Ted and Gerrie to come with them. The four walked out to the fifty yard line, the exact center of the field.

Sunny dropped her purse on the side and pulled out Stu's favorite Packers T-shirt, the one she always wore when they watched the games.

"Michael, you take Papa's hand, and, Ted, you take Gerrie's." They all complied as Sunny took her brother's hand. "Now, we're going to sit down and lie back on the field. You remember what we're going to do, don't you, Michael?"

"I do, Sun-nay. I do." The four of them were on their backs, looking up at the sky from the exact middle of the field. "Papa, this grass is so scratchy."

"Michael, this is half grass and half artificial turf; that's why it feels so rough." He looked over at the boy who was like his son, reclining in the grass next to him.

"Wow, I didn't know that. I've learned so much today," Sunny said, glancing at Ted and then her little brother. "Michael, now why are we here?"

The four of them looked straight up at the beautiful blue sky with the puffy clouds lazing above them.

"We had to come to Lambeau 'cause we needed to. And my brother Stu would've come with us, but he's up in heaven in the clouds. Don't you think he's up there, Papa? Can he see us?"

Ted squeezed Gerrie's hand and then Michael's. He was in the grass at Lambeau Field, looking up at the sky with the three people who meant the most to him in the world. Ted couldn't love Michael or Sunny more if they were his own flesh and blood. And Gerrie, well, he knew life without her wasn't much of a life at all for him.

Before looking back at the sky to answer Michael's question, Ted turned to gaze at Gerrie as the tears flowed down her cheeks.

"Yes, honey, I do think Stu is up there and is looking down on us. He's smiling because his family is so happy. Just look up at the clouds, and you can feel he is with us." Ted turned his attention upward as tears streamed down his cheeks, too.

"Your little brother is so much like you . . ." Gerrie whispered. "We all love you so much, Stu, my precious son."

The four of them remained in the grass for some time, gazing up into the sky and basking in the strength of the love that surrounded them.

Acknowledgments

I was inspired to write this book by the many displays of flowers and items of remembrance placed next to roads to mark the passing of loved ones in vehicle accidents. I have seen these symbols all over the United States and around the world.

One day, I saw a bunch of red roses tied to a tree with the petals falling like tears, and I knew I must write this book.

As this particular display was near our home, I glanced at the spot every time I drove by, seeing fresh flowers and candles early on. I could tell the person who was killed at this spot was deeply loved and missed.

The flowers inspired me to write a story of love, betrayal, grief, family, and forgiveness. While none of the characters are real people, they became very real to me. These fictional characters aren't perfect and all did things they would come to regret. Some of their mistakes led to a chain of events ending in tragedy.

As grief and pain consumed the characters and relationships shattered, I wondered if they could find happiness again. I did think it was possible, but only through honest soul-searching and forgiveness.

I am indebted to my friend, Cindy Morrison, who had the real corgis, Hope and Cash, who inspired the fictional dogs by the same names. They were wonderful dogs and lived with her in

California and Switzerland. When they visited our home, Hope and Cash immediately took over, exploring every corner of the house inside and outside. Sadly, they are both gone now, but Cindy has two new corgis: mother, Cricket, and son, Ted. They are just as wonderful as Hope and Cash and make me smile every time I see them.

Sandy Abel, a family counselor, helped me understand counseling and bring realism to the scenes about family counseling and mental health treatment. Thanks, Sandy, for taking the time to help me portray this as accurately as possible.

I would also like to thank my talented editor, Cassie McCown, who makes my writing better. I learned of Cassie from best-selling author and college friend Kris Radish, who continues to inspire me and encourages me to keep writing. Thanks, Cassie and Kris.

And thanks to all of those at SparkPress: Kelly Bowen, Lauren Wise, Brooke Warner, Crystal Patriarche, Julie Metz, and Maggie Ruf.

I need to admit that I am a Green Bay Packers fan and shareholder. I was born and raised in Wisconsin, so being a Packers fan is in the blood, just as it was for Ted in the book. I started watching the games with my father when I was four years old, so it is deeply ingrained. I had the idea to incorporate the Packers and football into the book when my friend, Bill Shelton (a rabid Washington Redskins fan) told me after a tough Packers playoff loss that true fans are optimists and see every upcoming season as a time filled with hope and new possibilities. Thanks to Bill and Tammy Shelton for being such wonderful friends.

When my best friend, Barb Fleming, read my first book, *Hostile Takeover: A Love Story*, and said she couldn't put it down, I think I walked on air for days. Her husband, Tim, has been a great support to me as well. Even my husband, Roy Jones, lifts up an eyebrow of interest from time to time as I describe a character or plot point.

Life would not be complete without our family and friends in my hometown of Milwaukee and my husband's birthplace, Liverpool, England. Their support and encouragement, and that of friends from all over the world, continues to inspire me. I know I will forget someone, but there are so many other people to thank, including: Chris Piano, Sarah Mueller, Theresa D'Alessio, Sue Margis, Deb Cmelak, Sally Jacob, Erika Johnson, Henry and Joanne Piano, Angel and Mark Hessel, Nick and Jackie Piano, Maggie and Jon Manning, Joe Kern, Jackie Ashurst, James and Mary Halley, James Ball, Stephanie Ayres, Mark Gaterell, Barrie Bain, Vivian Bright, Debbie Countiss, Debbie and Chuck Nenninger, Allen and Laurie Taylor, Mary Klem, Kim Hunter, Paulo Lima, Margery Kraus, Brent Crane, Nick Ashooh, Dan and Meg Burnham, Sarah Reines, Sonia Fiorenza, April Kaplinski, Sandy and Chris Funcich, Carol Ramsey, Pat Jones, Karen and Bob Boult, Karen and Ian Jones, Ellis Jones, Carl Nimmo, Carla Jones, Anthony Murray, Lola Murray, Leanne, Paul and Sam Ratcliffe, Nicola, Paul and Archie Simmons, Ste, Claire and Holly Boult, Joey and Hannah Jones, Pam Hughes, Leslie Allsopp, Jim Nolan, Thomas Nolan, Monica Wakefield, Dan Wakefield, Barbara Leedale, David Polk, Judy and David Driscoll, Betty Hudson, Charlotte Otto, George Jamison, Catherine Blades, Steve Johnson, Jon Iwata, AnnaMaria DeSalva, Diane Dixon, Mike Paul, Andy and Helen Irving, Steve and Jenny Harris, Dan Ullrich, Dave Gess, Mario Ziino, Paul Henning, Don Williams, Kathleen Kosnar, Carol Herbstreit Kalinyen, Neil Morgan, Stuart Grimston, Faye Jones, Helen Mills, Gerrie Donlon, Julie Griffith, Cynthia Schwalm, Deborah Hibbett, Joel Cencius, Anne Panter, Jackie and Patrick Cummings, Ruth and Ken Vonderberg, Edie Winski, Sarah Guerrero,

Christine Cassiano, Andrea Rothschild, Kirsten Detrick, Ann and Dennis Wilm, Mary Unland, Kathy Johnson, Rena Glorioso, Carol Vollmer Pope, Jane Olig, Ann Emmers, Rochelle Kanoff, Hillary West, Nobuko Schlough, Leah Palmer and Jim Zondlo, John, Barb and Lauryn Burkhalter, Ray Day, Jane Randel, Clay McConnell, Jeff Winton, Jim Modica, Trish Hawkins Rowland, Cynthia Wands, Katie Capozzoli Borman, Tina and Rob Schoewe, Jan Kloeffler, Gene Medford, Leon Jansen, Carol Pawlak, Monique McLaughlin, Terry Mackay, Kathy Eckhardt, Monica Leon, Carol Harding Hahn, Laraine O'Brien, Paula Purcell, Joyce Finberg, Joan Goessl, Colleen Niccum, Neil and Bernadette Fair, Kathy Johnson, Madelyn Boumbulian Dunmire, Patty and Jennifer Haehn, Sharon Gibson, Kerry Beth Daly, Deb Bartlein Schmidt, and Carol Mucha.

An email, a word of support, attending an event, a share or "like" on Facebook . . . all of this has meant a lot.

This kind of encouragement keeps me writing and hoping my books tell stories that readers will enjoy and remember.

About the Author

 Phyllis J. Piano spent more than 30 years as an award-winning corporate communications expert for some of the world's largest companies. A world traveler, Piano has left the corporate world and has fallen back into the arms of her own first love: writing. Her first novel, *Hostile Takeover: A Love Story*, was published in October 2016, and received the Gold Medal at the 2017 Independent Book Publishers Association Ben Franklin Awards and first place in Fiction: Romance at the 2017 Independent Press Awards. When she is not packing a bag, making artisan sourdough bread, or cooking with lots of garlic, Piano is working on her next novel.

SELECTED TITLES FROM SPARKPRESS

SparkPress is an independent boutique publisher delivering high-quality, entertaining, and engaging content that enhances readers' lives, with a special focus on female-driven work.

Visit us at www.gosparkpress.com

Learning to Fall, by Anne Clermont. $16.95, 978-1940716787. Raised amidst the chaos and financial insecurity of her father's California horse training business, Brynn Seymour wants little more than to leave the world of competitive riding behind. But when her father is trampled in a tragic accident, she struggles to save the business—and her family—and is forced to reckon with the possibility that only the competitive riding world she's tried to turn away from can heal the broken places inside of her.

So Close, by Emma McLaughlin and Nicola Kraus. $17, 978-1-940716-76-3. A story about a girl from the trailer parks of Florida and the two powerful men who shape her life—one of whom will raise her up to places she never imagined, the other who will threaten to destroy her. Can a girl like her make it to the White House? When her loyalty is tested will she save the only family member she's ever known—even if it means keeping a terrible secret from the American people?

Hostile Takeover, by Phyllis Piano, $16.95, 978-1940716824. Long-lost love, a hostile corporate takeover, and the death of her beloved husband turn attorney Molly Parr's life into a tailspin that threatens to ruin everything she has worked for. Molly's all-consuming job is to take over other companies, but when her first love, a man who she feels betrayed her, appears out of nowhere to try and acquire her business, long-hidden passions and secrets are exposed.

Found, by Emily Brett, $16.95, 978-1940716800. ICU nurse Natalie Ulster has a desire to see the world and a need to heal, which is compensation for her own damaged heart. Natalie grabs life by the globe and accepts successive assignments in Belize, Australia, and Arizona. When Natalie meets Dr. Joel Lansfield she's not sure she's ready to make room in her heart for love. However, too many near-death coincidences force her to ask herself a frightening question: Is someone trying to kill her?

ABOUT SPARKPRESS

SparkPress is an independent, hybrid imprint focused on merging the best of the traditional publishing model with new and innovative strategies. We deliver high-quality, entertaining, and engaging content that enhances readers' lives. We are proud to bring to market a list of *New York Times* best-selling, award-winning, and debut authors who represent a wide array of genres, as well as our established, industry-wide reputation for creative, results-driven success in working with authors. SparkPress, a BookSparks imprint, is a division of SparkPoint Studio LLC.

Learn more at **GoSparkPress.com**